TALES FROM THE SINISTER CITY

THE LUNATIC'S CURSE

Prodigious praise for the writing of F. E. Higgins:

'Atmospheric, suspenseful and cleverly written with a love of unusual words ("gibbous", "crepitate"), it is not for the faint-hearted' *Sunday Times*

'Young readers with a taste for the macabre will find it deliciously scary' *Observer*

'Writing so atmospheric that the fumes from the noxious River Foedus seem to seep off the page and swirl round the reader' *Telegraph*

'If you can imagine Terry Pratchett's *Discworld* rewritten by a junior James Joyce you might get an impression of the playfulness, drama and disgust of Higgins's created world' *The Times*

'A deliciously rich mix of Gothic nastiness . . . and black humour . . . Higgins's prose has terrific verve, with glittering descriptive flashes' *Guardian*

'Gruesome, assured storytelling' *Evening Standard*

'[A] deliciously dark and satisfying experience' *Stirling Observer*

More twisted tales by F. E Higgins

The Black Book of Secrets

The Bone Magician

The Eyeball Collector

Delve further into the dark underworld of
The Sinister City . . .

www.fehiggins.com

TALES FROM THE SINISTER CITY

THE LUNATIC'S CURSE

F. E. HIGGINS

MACMILLAN CHILDREN'S BOOKS

This edition published 2010 by Macmillan Children's Books
a division of Macmillan Publishers Limited
20 New Wharf Road, London N1 9RR
Basingstoke and Oxford
Associated companies throughout the world
www.panmacmillan.com

ISBN 978-0-230-53232-8 (HB)
ISBN 978-0-230-75225-2 (TPB)

1 3 5 7 9 8 6 4 2

A CIP catalogue record for this book is available from
the British Library.

Typeset by Nigel Hazle
Printed and bound in the UK by CPI Mackays, Chatham ME5 8TD

To Patricia *et* Gulielmus
A posse ad esse

Excerpt from
ON MADNESS

Look well behind and to your front
Look always to the side
For madness creeps on soft-soled shoes
Dark-suited and wild-eyed
With hairy palms and pigeon-toes
And fingers splayed so wide
Beware, I say! Beware! Beware!
Or reader, woe betide!

Beag Hickory

CONTENTS

A NOTE FROM F. E. HIGGINS

It is late evening and I have finally laid down my pen. The curtains are drawn and I sit now by the fire in my study. Outside the snow has spread a blanket of white across the fields. And still more falls.

As some of you know, I have in my possession many objects of mysterious origin – too many now to mention. So tonight from the mantel I pick only two: the first, a polished disc of dark magnetite on a silver chain; the second, what we shall call for now an egg.

These simple objects are at the very heart of a dark tale of treachery and tragedy, deception and wickedness. I have looked back through time and uncovered a story that will cause your heart to beat faster and your breath to catch in your throat. Steel yourself, dear Reader, for at times you will be mystified and, I warn you now, at times you will be repelled.

But at all times you will want to know what lies ahead . . .

F. E. Higgins

PROLOGUE

An Eventful Supper

In nightshirt and robe, slippers and nightcap, Rex Grammaticus quietly entered the large dark-panelled dining room. On the far side of the room, lit in candle glow, he could see his stepmother, Acantha, and his father, Ambrose, at the table eating their evening meal. Rex had eaten earlier, at his stepmother's request, in the kitchen. One more change that she had made since marrying his father; one more way to push him out of the picture. It had only been eight weeks since the marriage but Acantha moved about the house as if she had lived there all her life. It was Rex who felt like the newcomer.

Silently Rex crossed the luxurious carpet towards the table. The two diners did not hear his soft-slippered approach. He stopped just beyond the reach of the candles' light to stand motionless by a shining suit of armour positioned against the wall. He watched for a few seconds as Acantha daintily dissected her fish into flakes and pushed it

1

about her plate. She held her knife like a pen and her right little finger stuck out at an angle. Ambrose, sitting opposite, was almost finished.

'Eat it up, my love,' said Acantha in that sickly sweet voice of hers that made Rex want to spit. 'It's bream, fresh today. I read recently in the *Hebdomadal* that fish is very good for the brain.'

'Always concerned for my health,' said Ambrose (and looked at her in that way of his that made Rex feel slightly nauseous), 'but I see you haven't finished your own,' he chided.

'I am not so hungry tonight,' said Acantha, and she smiled, showing her little pointy teeth. Rex shuddered. Acantha was just so . . . false. How could his father not see through her? He opened his mouth to announce his presence but hesitated to speak. Was it his imagination or was his father beginning to look a little odd? He was shifting around restlessly in his chair, twitching and jerking, and he was squinting as if the light hurt his eyes. Rex moved slightly and Acantha saw his reflection in the armour. Rex thought he caught a glimmer of something deadly in her eye. 'Come to say goodnight?' she asked sweetly.

Ambrose looked up from his plate. 'Ah, Rex, my boy,' he said, beckoning him over. 'Your tutor tells me you worked well today. Even on your Latin!'

Rex smiled and came forward. Acantha stiffened.

'I am not so sure about that tutor,' she said. 'I still think a good boarding school would suit Rex so much better. He spends too much time in the house. A boy of twelve needs to be out with others of his own age.'

2

Rex looked immediately to his father, who shook his head. 'No,' he said firmly. 'Much as I hate to disagree with you, I think Rex should remain at home for the time being. Rex is a talented boy and he wants to follow me in my profession. I am happy to teach him all I know and for that I need him with me. The tutor can provide the rest.'

Acantha changed the subject. 'Did I tell you, dearest, that I am having dinner with Mr Chapelizod tomorrow night? It's about the beggars again. I've been asked to join the committee. There are just so many now, on every step and corner; people find them offensive. Mr Chapelizod thinks—'

'Now, now, my dear,' said Ambrose, a note of gravity entering his voice. 'I hope you haven't forgotten what I said about your friend Mr Chapelizod today.'

'You mean that rumour?' said Acantha coolly. 'The one you won't tell me.'

Ambrose inhaled deeply and drummed his fingers on the table.

'Acantha, please do not think that I am questioning your judgement, but I have recently heard some very strange things about that man. Until I can verify whether or not they are true I must be cautious. So, for all of our sakes, Cadmus Chapelizod is not welcome in this house.'

'I did not think you were the sort of man to listen to rumours,' said Acantha evenly. 'You have enjoyed his company over dinner many times, just as I have. Besides, you shall not tell me what to do. If I wish to see Mr Chapelizod I will. You cannot stop me.'

3

Rex's jaw dropped at Acantha's cool defiance and Ambrose looked quite distressed. After all, in this day and age a wife was still thought of as a husband's property. A husband's word was law. Rex shrank back behind his father's chair, sensing an acute change in the atmosphere.

Ambrose whitened further. Now his right eye was twitching furiously. 'Wife,' he said between gritted teeth, 'it has been suggested to me that Mr Chapelizod has undesirable habits. I cannot stress enough just how undesirable. Matters too delicate for a lady. But, believe me, they are *very* offensive; practices that are quite against nature. You must cease your alliance with him immediately.'

Rex tried to imagine what habits the superintendent of the local lunatic asylum could have that would make him unacceptable in polite society. He resolved to ask his father in the morning.

'You have taken against him because of his position,' said Acantha. 'You think because Cadmus works with lunatics that he has no place in your sophisticated circles. But I enjoy his company. Besides, we have the same . . . how shall I put it . . . tastes.'

Ambrose stared at Acantha with a puzzled look. 'Tastes?' he repeated. Then his brow became smooth and his eyes widened as if he had just resolved something that had been troubling him. His face blanched completely and sweat poured down his forehead. Without warning, he leaped up, knocking his chair over in the process, thumped his fists on the table and shouted, 'No! No!'

Rex let out a little cry of alarm. What was happening

to his father? His broad shoulders were heaving, his face was contorted into a nightmarish mask. Then a terrible wailing sound, at first low but rising rapidly in pitch, came from somewhere and Rex realized that it was Ambrose. He watched in horror as his father put up his arms and started to wrestle with the air as if in combat with an invisible enemy.

'Oh Lord,' he cried, and his voice sounded strangled. 'What have you done to me? It's coming for me!'

'Father!' cried Rex. 'What's wrong?'

Ambrose turned and stared down at his son. To Rex he suddenly seemed ten feet tall. His eyes were bloodshot, veins pulsated in his temple, perspiration poured down his face. His skin was blotchy and, as Rex watched, great red pustules formed on his face and throat: huge lumps swelling up and distorting his features beyond recognition. Now Ambrose looked like nothing that existed on earth. He looked like a creature from hell.

In a panic Rex looked over at Acantha. 'What's happening? Can't you help him?'

But Acantha remained at the table stony-faced and cold-eyed. Waiting. Without warning Ambrose grabbed Rex by the arms, lifted him and threw him on to the table. Plates smashed and cutlery scattered. Ambrose held him down with a knee across his chest.

'Help,' yelled Rex. His father's face was within an inch of his own. Saliva spilt over his lip and ran down his chin to drip on to Rex's cheeks. And for years afterwards Rex would always recall vividly the overwhelming smell of his fishy breath. Now the pressure on his chest was so great he felt as if his eyes were about to burst. Ambrose pulled Rex's arm up to his frothing mouth, clamped his jaw around his wrist and bit down so hard he actually reached the bone. Rex screamed in agony and Ambrose seemed to hear the scream and looked down at his son. For a split second there was a glimmer of recognition in his eyes. But as quickly as it appeared it was gone. Then the door was flung open and the housekeeper, the butler and the bootboy came running in. Acantha simultaneously leaped from her seat and put her hands to her face in horror.

'He has gone mad! Mr Grammaticus has gone completely mad! Call for the constable! For Mr Stradigund! For Mr Chapelizod!'

Upon hearing Chapelizod's name Ambrose arched his back and howled like a wolf to the full moon. He dropped Rex's arm, ran to the suit of armour and pulled the sword from the hollow knight's hand. He raised the weapon above his head and sliced through the air to bring the glittering blade down on the table, severing his own hand. There was the most dreadful sound, a sound that Rex would never forget, and blood spurted everywhere. Ambrose turned around and his eyes were on fire.

'Is this what you want, Acantha, is it?'

Rex couldn't bear to look any longer.

Fearlessly the butler and the bootboy wrestled Ambrose to the ground. He lay there clutching his maimed arm, panting heavily, his dark red blood spreading across the rug. Acantha took hold of the water jug, stood over her husband of fifty-six days and smashed it over his head.

Ambrose lay motionless, for all appearances dead, his dented skull framed by the jagged pieces of the shattered jug. Rex, holding his own bloodied wrist, looked at Acantha in shock, incapable of speech. And he thought that she smiled.

1

A Room with a View

With a heavy heart Rex made his way up to the schoolroom at the top of the house. As he passed along the narrow corridors and climbed the stairs, his steps falling in time with the ten chimes of the clock, he paused on the half-landings of the maze-like house. He was reminded at every turn of his absent father. Ambrose had built the house from the ground up and his character and talent were to be found in every nook and cranny and arch and window. Framed scrolls and certificates on the walls testified to the genius of Ambrose Grammaticus, to his imagination, his skills and his creativity. Rex's father had won almost every prize in the field of engineering. He was hailed as a hero here in Opum Oppidulum, his home town, and far beyond. And beside the scrolls were sketches and paintings and ink drawings of the buildings he had designed, and articles from the *Hebdomadal* celebrating years of his success.

Rex entered the schoolroom deep in thought. Much as

he loved this house this was his least favourite room. He was good with numbers but he was not a natural language scholar. His father insisted that to be truly creative he needed a rounded education, not just technical skills, so he had engaged the tutor. But Rex struggled with the Classics; it had taken him a whole week to translate a simple story of a slave into Latin.

To make the schoolroom more palatable Rex had filled it with his own creations; delicate models of every shape and size and manifestation. Birds and creatures and vehicles. Many of them only existed within these walls; it would be decades, centuries even, before they would be seen on city streets. They hung on thin threads from the ceiling and rested on the mantel over the fireplace and balanced precariously on the edges of the bookshelves, taking up every available surface. Rex had designed and built them all, with his father's guidance, and they reminded him that there had once been better times.

The tutor had not yet arrived and, from habit, Rex went to the window and looked out. From up here, the fourth floor, he could see the snow on the mountain peaks that surrounded the Devil's Porridge Bowl, a huge natural dip in the Moiraean Mountains, the centre of which was filled by the dark waters of Lake Beluarum. Rex liked to say its name, to roll it around his tongue: 'Bel-warr-oom.' It was Latin in origin; he thought it meant 'the lake of beastly creatures' but he could not be certain.

The town of Opum Oppidulum, where Rex had lived his whole life, sat tightly packed on the upper edge of the steep pebbled shore of Lake Beluarum. No one knew for certain how deep the lake was, but around the time of the full moon there was a noticeable rise in the water level – Madman's Tide they called it – and in winter it could be quite stormy, almost like a sea. None swam in its waters either; they were too cold and, of course, every local child was warned of the monster that lurked beneath the glassy surface, just waiting to swallow up anyone who might be fool enough to enter the lake.

Rex reached up to open the window and his cuff slipped down to reveal the crescent-shaped scar on his wrist. It was fading but he could feel it. In the cold it would tighten and ache and remind him again of that dreadful night . . .

Things seemed to happen very quickly after Acantha struck his father with the water jug. Mr Cadmus Chapelizod turned up as if from nowhere, with two red-badged grey-uniformed men. Only moments behind him was Mr Alvar Stradigund, the family solicitor. Chapelizod immediately took control of the situation. With the help of his assistants he quickly and expertly strapped Ambrose into some sort of medical shirt which prevented his using his arms. Then the burly helpers lifted him on to a stretcher and secured him with more straps.

Mr Stradigund led Rex from the room and they sat in the hall. 'Let's have a look at that wrist,' he said gently, and took a clean handkerchief from his pocket and began to wrap it around the wound. 'Don't worry, Rex,' he said as he tied the corners. 'Chapelizod will take care of your father. He's an expert in these matters.'

'What matters?' asked Rex. He knew Mr Stradigund well; the old man was often at the house, even more so since the marriage.

Stradigund looked at him with sad, knowing eyes. 'Madness,' he said. Before Rex could reply the door opened and Chapelizod and his men marched past with Ambrose, still unconscious, out to the waiting carriage on the street. Rex tried to stand but he felt odd; his heart was racing and his head was spinning. Mr Stradigund supported him by his good hand.

'You know what to do, men,' called Mr Chapelizod from the top of the steps and seconds later the carriage took off. The sound of galloping hoofs faded quickly in the night. Chapelizod shut the door and nodded to Stradigund who stood up.

'Where are they taking him?' asked Rex in a panic.

'Somewhere he'll be safe,' said Mr Stradigund. 'I'll let you know as soon as I find anything out, I promise.' Then he left Rex with Acantha and he and Chapelizod went off to Ambrose's study.

Acantha looked at Rex. 'You should be in bed,' was all she said, and followed the men. In a daze, too confused to argue, Rex turned towards the stairs. As he passed the study he glanced in to see Mr Stradigund seated behind his father's desk with a quill in hand. Mr Chapelizod handed him a document of some sort. Stradigund looked up and saw Rex and smiled, oddly, but then Acantha, with a face like stone, closed the door and he heard the key in the lock.

As if in a dream Rex went up to his room. He lay on the

bed but he didn't sleep until the early hours. He couldn't understand what had happened but he was certain Mr Stradigund would sort it out. He had promised, hadn't he? A solicitor didn't break promises. Eventually weariness got the better of him and his heavy lids closed. But the face that haunted him that night wasn't that of his tortured father; it was Acantha's. He had seen the look on her face as Ambrose lost his mind, a look that he was never able to put into words. But he knew.

She had wanted this to happen.

Alvar Stradigund had come to the house almost every day at first. He and Mr Chapelizod and Acantha met in Ambrose's study and spoke in low voices.

Rex hung around anxiously waiting for Stradigund to emerge. 'Any news of my father?' he would ask.

And Stradigund patted him on the shoulder and smiled in a distant way, his worn face creasing up like soft paper, and said, 'He is doing well, Rex. Soon he will be home.'

Rex still believed him; and as long as he did he could endure Acantha, for he was certain that when his father returned she would have to go. She treated him with open contempt now, as if he were a noisome irritant, a fly ripe for swatting. But the Madman's Tide had come and gone three times since that bloody supper and a fourth was rising. Stradigund came less and less often and if Rex tried to talk to Mr Chapelizod he would not answer his questions. Rex's hope was turning to suspicion and fear.

Close to tears, Rex gazed out across the lake. The mist

had lifted and he could see straight across to Droprock Island. Legend had it that it was just that: a large boulder carelessly dropped by a passing giant. The island was small and steep. It had no beaches and there was nowhere to land a boat except one small natural rocky pier on this side. The rest of the island was unassailable, being sheer cliff. On its highest point, exposed to the ravages of the weather, Rex could see Cadmus Chapelizod's grim domain: the Opum Oppidulum Asylum for the Peculiar and Bizarre.

The sombre grey edifice had been there for centuries, but recently for Rex it had taken on a whole new significance. Day and night it was a constant reminder to him of his father; for since his moment of madness at the supper table Ambrose Oswald Grammaticus had been confined within the cheerless walls *of that very same asylum.*

So near and yet so far, thought Rex. He liked to think that the light he could see flickering high up in the asylum at night might be his father's light. He put his hand up to shade his eyes from the low sun. Was there something in the water? Perhaps it was his imagination, but a huge dark shape seemed to be moving slowly across the lake, just under the surface. His heart jumped. There *was* something! He was sure of it now. A shadow, a giant shadow . . .

'Good morning, Rex.'

Rex started at the sound of his tutor's voice and he turned to see the young man of no more than five and twenty years enter the room.

'Good morning, Robert,' he replied. Acantha had

13

insisted that Rex call him 'Sir' and that in turn the tutor address Rex as 'Master Rex', but in the privacy of the schoolroom each dropped the formalities and used first names.

Robert held a pile of books under one arm and paper and quills under the other. 'How are you today?' he asked and then shook his head slightly. 'Still looking out of the window, I see.' He came over to join him. 'Droprock Asylum,' he said, 'built over three hundred years ago for the poor and confused of Opum Oppidulum. Did you know, because the island is so small and rocky there's nowhere to bury the dead so they constructed a maze of tunnels beneath the asylum, the famous labyrinthine catacombs where all the bodies are laid? Apparently there's an underground lake too.'

Rex smiled wryly. The shadow was gone – if it had ever been there; perhaps it was just a cloud – and the asylum stared back at him, its dark windows like soulless eyes. His heart burned to think that his father was over there, unable to leave, but there was nothing he could do.

'Any news?'

'Mr Stradigund only says that Father is doing well, but he will not say when he is to return.'

'Rex,' said Robert, and there was hesitation in his voice. 'You know that I have the greatest respect for your father . . .'

'But?'

'But I fear that he will not be back for some time yet.'

Robert closed the window. The autumn air was chilling. He looked at Rex with worried eyes. 'I know nothing for certain, but there is talk among the servants that your father is very ill, much worse than anyone thought, and that Mr Chapelizod has no plans to release him.'

Rex turned sharply and went to sit down at his desk. He brought his fist down on the wooden surface. 'It's just not fair,' he muttered. 'It's not right. You weren't there, Robert. You didn't see what happened. You didn't see how Acantha did nothing! It's all her fault, I know it. But with Father in the asylum how can I prove it?'

Robert looked worried. 'Rex,' he cautioned, 'I know you are not on the best terms with Acantha, but as long as your father is on Droprock Island you must play a careful game. Acantha holds all the cards. And, with Stradigund and Chapelizod working for her, she is very powerful.'

Rex clenched and unclenched his jaw. Rex and Robert spoke freely. There was a friendship between them that went deeper than teacher and pupil, and in these uncertain times Rex considered him the only person in the house he could talk to frankly. Rex suspected now that Robert shared his concerns about Acantha. 'What do you mean, working for her?'

Robert lowered his voice. 'I only know what I hear, both in the house and beyond its confines. Recently I have heard talk of an old law, *Lex Dierum Centarum*—'

'Huh,' snorted Rex, 'more Latin!'

Robert laughed softly. 'It means "the Law of a Hundred Days" and, although I am not familiar with it, it seems that it might have some bearing on your father's illness. If you like, I can find out more about it.'

Rex grabbed Robert by the sleeve and for a moment he looked almost as mad as his father had on that fateful night. 'Oh, please do,' he urged. 'I am becoming desperate. Acantha hates me and wants to get rid of me. As for Stradigund . . . I thought he was a loyal friend to us all . . . but I am no longer sure of him either.'

'Rex, you must be *very* careful in whom you place your trust,' said Robert, and then his face froze and he stood up quickly. 'Now,' he said with authority, 'tell me the meaning of the term *boustrophedon*.'

'What?' Rex was confused at the rapid change of subject.

'Now,' said Robert meaningfully. 'Right now!'

Rex stood and began. 'Er, well, it's something to do with ploughing. The word *bous* in Greek means cow and . . .'

A sound behind him caused Rex to stop and look over his shoulder. Acantha was standing at the door. Rex looked at her solid figure and red face. She rarely came up here; the stairs were becoming too much for her.

'Robert,' she snapped. 'I wish to see you after.'

Robert smiled obsequiously. 'Of course,' he said.

With a contemptuous snort Acantha turned on her flattened heel and left.

2

Memories

Rex stood glumly behind his father's desk in his study. He liked to come here when he was feeling down. The blotter was cleared — Acantha used it now — but pushed to one side, surrounded by rolled-up sketches and diagrams, stood a precise model in miniature of the bridge for the city of Urbs Umida: Ambrose's last project, the one he had been working on before . . . well, just before. Rex had helped to construct it. He took a moment to fix a piece that had broken off and his finger came away covered in dust.

Gloomily Rex crossed the room to a large table whereupon lay a jumble of metal pieces: cogs and wheels, nuts and bolts and springs and fine wires. This was where he and his father had worked together, not on buildings, but on the smaller moving models they both delighted in: clockwork vehicles on wheels; delicate metal creatures that could walk stiffly on four or six or more legs; upright marching figures only a few inches high. 'Toys,' Acantha called them with a dismissive wave of her hand. She had not dared to call them that when Ambrose was in the house. Rex sighed heavily. He realized now that if he wanted things to change he was going to have to do something himself. But what?

The study door opened and Acantha entered the room, visibly grinding her jaw with irritation. Rex's face instantly became a blank slate. He had quickly learned not to show any emotion in front of his stepmother.

'Did you not hear me calling?'

'No,' said Rex in the neutral tone he had taken to using when he had occasion to speak to her.

Acantha narrowed her green eyes. She was undoubtedly pretty, with clear skin and a small nose, but Rex suspected she was older than she said and there was certainly more flesh on her since Ambrose had been taken away. She was living well in his father's absence. But her lips were thin and mean, and always would be, even though she painted them to fill them out. It was all part of the deception.

Was it really only last year that Ambrose had first brought Acantha home? It seemed like an age now since he had been happy. He recalled how she had entered the house, even then with an air of entitlement, and had stood at his father's side. Her face smiled all the time, and she complimented Ambrose on his taste and talent and his son, but from the sidelines Rex saw what his infatuated father hadn't. Acantha was wearing a mask beneath which she was false and insincere, and aroused in him only suspicion. She even smelt odd. But in his father's eyes Acantha could do no wrong. Rex sorely resented the time Ambrose spent with her, time he used to spend with him.

'I hardly see you any more,' Rex had complained rather sulkily one day.

'I'll admit that I am working long hours at the moment,' said his father. 'You know I have an important project that I must finish, the bridge in Urbs Umida. And, of course, I must spend time with dear Acantha.' At the mention of her name his eyes sparkled. 'Please try to understand, Rex, Acantha has brought me great happiness after years of being alone. Do not spoil it for me.'

Rex was silenced, realizing that he was being selfish. But he was not ready for what his father said next.

'Soon enough we will all have more time together, for Acantha has accepted my proposal of marriage.'

And so Acantha took her place in the house that Rex and his father had shared for twelve years. One evening, shortly after the marriage, she had come up to Rex's room. She stood in the doorway with her chamber candle.

'I do hope we can be friends, Rex,' she said. 'I realize that this is a great change for you. But be reassured – I will never try to take the place of your mother.'

And, true to her word, she made no effort to be a mother to him. In fact, when Ambrose was out of the house, she made no effort with him at all. She was not openly hostile but it was clear to Rex that he was of no interest to her. And then she had suggested boarding school. Ambrose had resisted but now that he was gone Rex feared for his future.

Rex had not known his own mother; she had died when

he was only a few weeks old. Ambrose always said that he looked like her, with his narrow eyes and his thick wavy hair, and Rex could certainly see the resemblance when he looked at the portrait over the fire in the dining room. But in her heartfelt absence he had been brought up by his father. When Rex showed his talent for design Ambrose did not hesitate to encourage him. He was proud to say his son had inherited his gift from him. He looked forward to the day when Rex could take over the business, AmGram Design, Engineering and Construction. He showed Rex how to measure carefully, to draw with accuracy, to scale up and scale down, and finally how to bring to life in wood and metal the complex sketches on the paper.

But none of this was of any interest to Acantha. She looked pointedly at the model on the desk and laughed spitefully. 'He's not coming back, you know. He's a lunatic, completely mad. Droprock Island is far and away the best place for him.'

'But why can't I go to see him?'

'You know Mr Chapelizod's rules. No visitors are allowed for at least a year after an incarceration, especially in a case as bad as your father's. Anyway, you might want to be careful, boy. If you ever set foot on the island they'll take you in too!'

'My father is not mad,' stated Rex firmly, and held her gaze with his unblinking hazel eyes. 'And he won't be there for a year.'

Acantha snorted. 'Have you forgotten? He attacked you; he is a dangerous maniac. He could have killed you.'

Rex shook his head. 'He was delirious – he didn't know what he was saying or what he was doing. He must have been ill,' he protested vainly. 'A proper doctor would have seen that.'

Acantha dismissed his objections with a quick nod of the head. She spoke sharply. 'I have no time for this. I'm expecting visitors shortly. I want you to keep out of the way. Stay in your room until you hear otherwise.'

Rex suppressed the urge to snarl at her. She looked over at the table and its jumble of pieces, and tutted. 'It's time this was all tidied away,' she said. 'I will tell the maid. It won't be for much longer anyhow.' Then both heard the jangling doorbell and Acantha's face brightened. 'They are here,' she said. 'Remember, do not disturb me.'

Rex stood motionless, staring at the back of the door for some moments after she had gone, the knot in his stomach slowly unwinding. He returned to the table and gathered up some of the pieces. 'It won't be for much longer,' she had said. It could only mean one thing – *school*.

Rex didn't trust Acantha any further than he could spit. And who exactly were these visitors she was expecting? Suddenly he was gripped by a strong feeling of unease. He knew where she would meet them: in the library. Quickly he left the study. He could hear voices in the parlour and he took the opportunity to slip into the library and hide between the shelves.

3

A Meeting of Minds

Rex eased a slim volume from the shelf – a manual on gases and their nature – and peered through the narrow gap. He now had a clear view of his father's reading desk. There was no natural light in the library – the heavy curtains were kept closely drawn – and it was always cool. His father had a fine collection of books and protected them from sunlight. Acantha, if nothing else, seemed to appreciate this fact and generally left the room undisturbed. Rex suspected she sold the odd volume or two when she fancied. She might not care for him or his father but she knew enough to look after something that might make her money.

The door opened and Rex watched three people enter; Acantha came first, her wide skirts brushing the parquet floor, then Cadmus Chapelizod (easily recognizable by his rotund silhouette) and Alvar Stradigund, taller than the other two though slightly stooped. All three sat at the reading table and in the shadows cast by the orange light of the gas lamps Rex thought they resembled a trio of conspiring devils. Acantha looked oddly excited. It was not an expression Rex saw too often on her face. She was tapping her fingers impatiently on the table. Rex wasn't sure whom he detested more, Acantha or Chapelizod. As for Stradigund, he was almost surprised to find that faint hope still flickered in his heart.

'Well,' said Chapelizod, 'shall we begin?'

'Where's the boy?' asked Stradigund.

'Don't worry about him,' said Acantha dismissively. 'I have a plan for him. Have you the information?'

'I have indeed,' replied Chapelizod and he slid a sheet of paper across the table to her. Acantha snatched it up and read it aloud.

OFFICIAL DECLARATION OF INCURABLE INSANITY
This document is the sworn testimony of
Mr Cadmus Chapelizod.

I, **Mr Cadmus Chapelizod**, as Superintendent of the Opum Oppidulum Asylum for the Peculiar and Bizarre on Droprock Island, do testify on my life in this Official Declaration of Incurable Insanity, that Ambrose Oswald Grammaticus, once resident of the town of Opum Oppidulum, has on this date the fifteenth day of October been pronounced *Insane* **and** *Wholly* **beyond recovery**. It is my professional assessment that he has been in this way for One Hundred Days thus bringing into force the *Lex Dierum Centarum* otherwise known as the '**Law of a Hundred Days**'

C Chapelizod

Rex frowned. The Law of a Hundred Days? So Robert was right.

'As you are aware, Acantha,' explained Stradigund, 'this law states that where a person is in an asylum for that duration with no improvement then it is fully within the rights of the immediate family, in this case the wife, to take control of all that person's wealth and worldly goods.'

Chapelizod then handed Acantha another document. 'This is the official medical report from the asylum.'

'Excellent, excellent,' murmured Acantha. She read it to herself, with a little laugh here and a 'very true' there, running her outstretched little finger rapidly back and forth under each line. Then she put the two documents to one side and turned to Stradigund.

'And what about the will?'

Stradigund handed over a wad of twice-folded yellow paper, secured with the bright blue seal of Grammaticus. 'With the invocation of the *Lex Dierum Centarum* neither this will, nor any other that might be in existence, is enforceable. Now that your husband has been officially classified as an incurable lunatic, in the eyes of the law of this land, everything that he owns, the house, his money, the horses and carriages, and of course his company, AmGram Design, Engineering and Construction, is now yours to do with as you please.'

Acantha stood up and went to the fire. 'I have waited a long time . . .'

'One hundred days to be exact,' sniggered Chapelizod.

'. . . to do this,' she said, and she tossed the will on to the flames. The three of them watched it burn with undisguised glee.

Rex was also watching but hardly with glee. You grinning demons, he thought bitterly. He fought the urge to leap out at the conniving threesome before him and . . . and what?

I have no power here, he thought. He could have kicked himself. He should have done something sooner. But he just thought – no, *wanted* to think – that his father would come home. His mistake had been to trust Stradigund. All those times he had patted him on the shoulder and told him not to worry, that he was doing his best, when in fact the duplicitous snake was in on it too! Acantha's plan was obvious now – to have Ambrose declared insane and then to take control of all of his wealth. But you could not leave insanity to chance, *so she must have driven him to madness.*

But how? And what vile secret bound these three so that Chapelizod and Stradigund would betray their professions and their oldest friends? So many unanswered questions! With an effort of some magnitude Rex calmed himself and listened again to the continuing conversation.

'Well,' said Stradigund as the charred remnants of the will floated up the chimney, 'that will put an end to his credibility. You recall, Cadmus, that Ambrose came to me with that dangerous rumour – a writer for the *Hebdomadal* had told him of some beggar who had a wild story about you.'

'Pah!' spat Acantha. 'You know what I think of beggars, nothing but pests they are.'

'Perhaps we should suggest the committee employ the

services of a pest controller,' said Chapelizod and laughed longer than was necessary at his own joke.

'So, Acantha, what of your plan for the boy?' asked Stradigund. 'He could cause trouble. He asks questions and is suspicious of you. Is it wise to have him in the house?'

Acantha pursed her painted lips. 'For the time being I think he is better off where I can keep an eye on him,' she said. 'He's a cunning little beast. I just want to make sure he doesn't know anything he shouldn't. It would look suspicious to send him off straight away. They say to keep your enemies close after all. As for the future, I have decided to send him away to the Reform School in Urbs Umida. He has acquired a certain look of defiance. That place will knock it out of him!'

Rex stifled a gasp. No! he thought. The Reform School in Urbs Umida, the most godforsaken city in the land! How then could he possibly free his father? And what of his own future? The Reform School offered no education, merely a curriculum of violence and fear. This was much, much worse than he had thought.

'I think we should celebrate with a hearty supper,' said Acantha. 'Early next week perhaps, after our committee meeting?'

Stradigund raised his eyebrows. 'Hearty?'

'At the very least meaty,' she replied. 'What do you think, Cadmus?'

Chapelizod looked surprised. 'Can you organize it that quickly?'

'Oh, I believe so,' said Acantha confidently. 'My butcher

is particularly good. He'll go out of his way to help me. I'll have the kitchen girl send him a message to bring round a nice joint. Something special.'

Stradigund shot a glance at Chapelizod who nodded enthusiastically. Rex, still reeling from Stradigund's betrayal, was now revolted. It seemed his father's life was no more important to this carnivorous trio than their next meal. Was there no limit to their wickedness?

'Very well. The usual time?'

Acantha nodded.

''Tis a pity Ambrose will not be able to make it,' sniggered Chapelizod.

'He will be missed,' chipped in Stradigund.

'And he *so* liked my cooking,' smiled Acantha. 'Let's have a drink to celebrate? Today has been a long time coming.'

'Patience is a virtue,' said Chapelizod with a broad grin. There was a little flash of light and Rex saw that he had acquired a large gold tooth. Acantha rang for the maid who arrived promptly (she dared not do otherwise), then scuttled away to return with a silver tray upon which sat three glasses and a bottle of red wine.

'From Fitzbaudly's,' smirked Acantha. 'A '59 no less.'

Straight from Father's cellar, thought Rex bitterly. Oh yes, Acantha, you certainly know how to enjoy yourself.

Stradigund did the honours, pouring the ruby liquid into the deep-cut crystal glasses. Acantha held hers up to the light.

'To us,' she said, and her eyes sparkled with the crystal. 'And to the Society of Andrew Faye.'

The others repeated the toast then flung their heads back and took a long draught of the liquid.

'Now, I must away to catch the boat,' said Mr Chapelizod, and all three stood to go.

Rex raged silently behind the shelf. He realized that the odd feeling creeping through his veins all the time he watched this vile trine was one of impending doom.

Andrew Faye? he thought. Who on earth could that be?

4

A Disagreement

Rex watched as Acantha led Stradigund and Chapelizod from the library. They had nearly finished the bottle and all three were in a merry mood. All his suspicions had finally been confirmed: Acantha was in league against his father with Stradigund and Chapelizod. Stradigund's betrayal hurt the most. Rex had trusted him, he had even confided his fears about Acantha to him, and all the time the lawyer had been plotting against him. Robert had been right: Stradigund and Chapelizod were strong allies. No doubt Acantha will pay them handsomely for helping her, thought Rex, recalling Chapelizod's gold tooth with distaste. Maybe I should be grateful that she didn't just kill Father. He didn't like to think that perhaps being in the lunatic asylum might be worse than death.

But that begged the question, why *not* kill him? Firstly, it was not so easy. There was always the small matter of the body, usually the reason murderers didn't get away with it.

Far easier to imprison his father in such a way that no one would hear his protestations. And who would believe the ravings of a lunatic? With Stradigund to advise on legalities, no doubt Acantha was well aware the law stated that when a man died his wife did not inherit a husband's wealth; it went first to blood relatives.

And that would be me! thought Rex. So by declaring Ambrose insane she had bypassed the laws of inheritance.

But how could she possibly have known that he was to lose his mind like that?

He kept coming back to the same answer: Acantha had a hand in his father's breakdown. And, if so, then it was no wonder that Chapelizod and Stradigund had arrived so swiftly that night. They must have been lying in wait. Chapelizod had declared Ambrose insane within minutes of his arrival, despite barely examining him. As for the Law of a Hundred Days, Stradigund must have dug deep to find that one.

The whole ghastly scene began to replay itself in Rex's mind. He hated to think of it; it made him feel physically ill. In an effort to block out the full horror of what he had seen he had taken to reciting a poem, a piece of doggerel, something he had heard in the town from a travelling bard.

Oh, how I love to wander, wander, wander
Wander, wander along.
And as I go, a-ho-ho-ho,
I always sing this song.

The clock struck the seventh chime of nine as Rex emerged from his hiding place. Too late, he heard Acantha's elephantine footsteps outside in the hall and before he could do anything the door opened. He stood frozen on the spot. Acantha was framed in the doorway, her feet planted apart, her face flushed, and she was swaying ever so slightly.

'Rex,' she said unusually calmly. 'I thought I told you to stay in your room.'

'I know,' said Rex evenly. 'But I needed something to read.' Thinking quickly he held up the book of gases.

Acantha blinked slowly. 'How long have you been in here?'

'Oh, not long. I saw you and Mr Stradigund and Mr Chapelizod come out.'

Acantha arched an eyebrow. She looked as if she was about to say something but changed her mind. A self-satisfied expression washed over her hot-cheeked face. 'Well, perhaps you should take advantage of the library; there is plenty to learn in here.'

'Robert teaches me well enough.'

'Robert? Oh, I have let him go.'

Suddenly Rex knew he could stand it no longer. Her knowing, fleshy, complacent face, her barbed remarks, the way she spoke about his father. Something inside him exploded.

'You . . . you cruel, foul-smelling witch!' he shouted and lunged violently at her. 'I know you sent him there because you wanted him out of the way. I know it!' He raised his fists to beat upon her but she grabbed him by the wrists.

She was strong, far stronger than he could have anticipated, and her eyes were wild. And there was that smell from her, a smell that she couldn't disguise with all her expensive perfumes and waters. And suddenly he knew what it was.

She smelt like an animal.

'Look at you,' she hissed, and spit came out of the corners of her mouth. 'Look what your father did to you.' She thrust his arm upwards to reveal the scar. It was red and pulsating from the pressure. 'You ungrateful wretch. *I* saved you from him. I wonder if I should have bothered. If you're not careful, lad, you'll end up with your father. I'm warning you now. The sooner you're gone from here, the better.'

Rex pulled away and pushed past her. He tore up the stairs, three at a time, and ran to his room, slamming the door. He threw himself on to the velvet counterpane. He wanted to cry, but he wouldn't let himself. He wouldn't give her the satisfaction. As he turned, a crackling noise came from under his pillow so he reached in and pulled out a small square of folded paper. He opened it and recognized immediately Robert's handwriting. With a sinking heart he read:

My dear Rex,
This is a note written in haste and I apologize for my penmanship – all those times I complained about yours! Acantha has dismissed me. I can only suppose she wants to hire a tutor of her own choosing. I will not be staying in Opum Oppidulum – Acantha will

not give me a reference – so it is doubtful that I will see you again.

I wanted to wish you luck, Rex. I fear you will need it. And I wanted to tell you not to give up hope. I know that your circumstances are not easy but you are resourceful and you know the value of perseverance. *Disce pati*, as the saying goes. You are your father's son, Rex, and I am certain that you can find a way out of your difficulties. I intend to travel to Urbs Umida, not the most pleasant of places I know, but I should be able to find another position there. You can write to me at the Nimble Finger Inn until I get settled.

With very best wishes,

Robert

Postscript: I couldn't leave without saying how good your translation was, about the slave. The verb you were looking for was *compungere*, to 'prick' or 'sting'.

Rex folded the letter and put it in his waistcoat pocket. He knew there was not to be a new tutor. Tears stung his eyes. *Compungere*. He wouldn't have known that.

5

Article from

The Opum Oppidulum Hebdomadal
A QUESTION OF BEGGARS
by
Cecil Notwithstanding

Although there is little doubt that Opum Oppidulum is a lovely place to live, like most towns it is not without its problems. For some months now there has been growing unrest about the rather large number of beggars on the streets. Although there is a certain amount of sympathy for these unfortunates, this does not take away from the fact that they are a nuisance and an eyesore.

I am pleased to be able to report that the mayor has put together a committee to solve this problem. Cadmus Chapelizod, the superintendent of Droprock Asylum, is to head the committee. Among the other esteemed members is Mrs Acantha Grammaticus, the wife of the renowned engineer Ambrose Grammaticus (unfortunately in the asylum at present owing to mental illness). Mrs Grammaticus is quoted as saying:

'Both Mr Chapelizod and I are committed to achieving a satisfactory resolution to this problem. We have much sympathy with both parties involved, beggar and citizen alike. Mr Chapelizod and I fully intend to find a solution to ease their respective misery and if possible to put them out of it completely.'

6

The Great Escape Plan

Ambrose Oswald Grammaticus turned over slowly in his incredibly uncomfortable bed — if a pile of straw on the rocky floor of a cell not big enough to jump in could be called a bed. He groaned as his bones creaked. On the wall beside him was a tally, sets of four parallel lines crossed with a diagonal; over a hundred days crossed off.

'Here, Ambrose, have a bit of this,' said a voice close to him. 'You've got to eat, for when we get out, you'll need energy.'

'Get out?' Ambrose managed a laugh. 'Tell me, Hooper, how are we to do that? Are we not locked in all day and all night?' He looked over at the cell door. Yes, as he expected, the rusty iron-barred door was firmly closed as ever.

'Don't be like that,' said the cheerful voice.

Ambrose had grown used to his companion's unrelentingly sunny nature, but he still marvelled at the fellow's ability to see the silver lining not just on some clouds, but on *every* cloud, no matter how black it might be. If it had been a century or so later the fellow would have been diagnosed with Felix Semper syndrome, a disease characterized by the sufferer being in a permanent state of happiness, gullible and trusting to the extreme, and completely incapable of relating to the real world. But, ironically enough, being permanently happy, Hooper was able to take his imprisonment in his stride.

'And is that really such a bad thing?' Ambrose often asked himself as he watched Hooper smiling day and night (not that he could tell the difference between the two in here). He could not deny that this blithe fellow had kept him from giving up for a long time. But these last few days he had felt a change. He was ill. His whole body ached, his head throbbed and he was growing weaker, racked with terrible cravings. He felt as if he had reached the end of his powers of endurance. He looked at Hooper. He was hardly any better off, not a pick of meat on his bones. He laughed to himself. They truly were a revolting pair.

'Ah, don't be like that, Ambrose,' cajoled Hooper softly. 'Never say never! Eh? What would young Rex think if he knew that his father was about to give up?'

At the mention of his son's name Ambrose made an effort and sat up. Hooper, a short, red-elbowed man with bushy eyebrows, was proffering a bowl of what could only be described as mud soup.

'What's in it?' he asked.

'Who knows?' laughed Hooper. 'No meat, I'll wager, but it don't taste that bad.'

Meat! The very thought of it caused Ambrose to quiver violently. He cradled the bowl awkwardly with his left arm and took a spoonful, and resisted the urge to spit it out. Then he took another. Revolting as it was, his starved body craved nourishment and he ate without stopping. A mouse crept out from the corner and looked at him but he kicked it away. Hooper grabbed it. 'Something for later,' he said, and broke its neck.

Hooper then pulled from his pocket a piece of ragged paper-thin cloth, upon which was sketched a blurred but complicated diagram. 'What about the escape plan?' he said. 'You know, your Perambulating Submersible?'

My Perambulating Submersible, thought Ambrose with a smile. Hooper actually believed it was viable. Ah, well, he wasn't going to disabuse him of the notion. The 'idea' was a boat that walked underwater. Hooper, having been a competent draughtsman prior to being declared insane, had very carefully drawn it (guided every step of the way by Ambrose) using a fingernail he had bitten to a point. Ambrose didn't ask what Hooper had used for ink: he knew. His sensitive nose could smell the blood, old and dried as it was. To take his mind off it he scooped up another large spoonful of the soup.

The underwater boat might be real but the escape was merely a fantasy — at least to Ambrose — to while away the hours. Hooper, however, had taken to it with such fervour that now he really did believe it was possible and he pored over the design for hours every day suggesting changes and refinements. Ambrose secretly was really very pleased with it. In truth it was an idea he and Rex had been working on long before his present misfortunes. But they had not pursued it — Acantha had put paid to that.

'Ah, Rex,' murmured Ambrose, 'what a great invention it would have been! And you, you held the key!'

'We'll build it,' said Hooper excitedly, 'and cross the lake floor, like a giant crab, and then we will be free.'

'Yes, of course,' said Ambrose encouragingly; he didn't have the heart to point out the many, many flaws in the great escape plan.

Ambrose finished his soup and lay back down. Hooper's optimism was in direct contrast to his own crushing feelings of sadness and despair. He had only survived this long by eking out his hope, but hope was not a limitless resource. Now he was resigned to never seeing Rex again. He thought of Acantha, although he didn't want to, and spat with disgust on the floor. He lifted his crippled left arm, looked at it with regret then let it fall. His heart became as rock. What a fool he had been, blinded by love, to trust her. He could see it now, her shy smiles and her fluttering eyelashes, and all the while she was conniving against him, with that evil monster Cadmus Chapelizod. Ugh, the whole business made him feel sick. And the irony of it all was that at that moment he really *was* mad — from love and, he suspected, something much more sinister.

Rex had been left in her care! Ambrose hardly dared to think what suffering the poor boy had endured since he had been sent to the island. His mind went wild with possibilities, each worse than the last. He could only hope and pray that Stradigund might be able to help. But he had not even visited. In fact it was Alvar Stradigund who had introduced him to Acantha in the first place and not for the first time Ambrose's fevered brain wondered if that was significant. I am becoming paranoid, he berated himself. I suspect even those closest to me. The truth of it is I have failed and Rex suffers on account of my failure.

As for Cadmus Chapelizod, he wasn't fit to run a dog-house let alone an asylum. Was not an asylum supposed to be a place where troubled minds could be at ease, could even hope to heal? 'Chapelizod' and 'healing' were as words from two different languages. The residents of Droprock Island all suffered in filthy cells, subjected to the cruelty and whims of the warders, wondering if they were to be fed or not. And they all heard the screams from the cell down the end wherein the warders, and Chapelizod, performed their 'cures'. Chapelizod had taken great pleasure in taunting him about his misfortune, telling him that he would never be released and how he now kept Acantha company.

Ambrose closed his eyes. He wanted nothing more than to never wake up again. When he did wake some hours later he wished immediately that he hadn't. He wrinkled his nose and opened his eyes, only to be confronted by Hooper's grinning toothless face. He was so close he could smell his foul breath but he could hardly complain; his own was no better. He looked around and became aware that something was different: there was noise, unfamiliar noise, coming from outside the cell. And he could smell burning. But unusually it wasn't flesh.

'Look,' said Hooper.

Ambrose turned his head to where Hooper pointed. It was a second or two before his dulled brain could take in what he was seeing. The cell door was open. He sat up quickly, a little too quickly, and his head spun.

'How did you do that?' he asked in amazement, suspecting a trick or, even worse, merely a dream.

'I didn't. Someone came along and opened it a while back.'

'Why didn't you wake me?'

'You looked like you needed the rest,' said Hooper simply. 'I've been up there – it's mayhem I tell you. Fires and everything. I found this, though. I thought it might be interesting. You like to read.' He handed Ambrose a book.

Ambrose took it and tucked it into his trousers. He would have a look at it later. Then he staggered up awkwardly from the straw on stiff legs, regretting that he hadn't eaten more. If they really were to escape, and now it looked a distinct possibility, then he would need all his strength. In fact, if it wasn't for Hooper, he would probably be dead already. Hooper had forced him to eat even though the thought of food made him feel ill.

'Come on,' said Hooper, 'we've got work to do.' Waving the ragged diagram he hobbled out of the cell.

Ambrose peered cautiously out into the rocky underground corridor. He too had been taken down it on more than one occasion for his 'cure', and always in the presence of Cadmus Chapelizod. 'My special patient', he had called him.

41

Hooper was already some distance ahead. 'Wait,' called Ambrose, limping after him.

And off they went, a shambolic pair hardly alive, down the dark tunnel. All around echoed the sounds of shouting and whooping, high-pitched laughter, some cheering even, and running footsteps from above. As they went towards the stairs up into the asylum proper, they met a tall thin man going against the tide.

'Come with me,' said the man, 'if you wish to stay alive.'

'Why? What's going on?' asked Hooper.

'It's simple,' replied the pale stranger. 'The lunatics have taken over the asylum.'

7

A Not So Great Escape

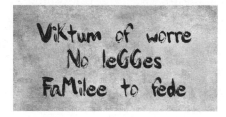

Viktum of worre
No leGGes
FaMilee to fede

'Spare a cripple some coins,' cried Simon, brandishing the worn board whereupon were scrawled his mendacious claims. 'Spare us a penny, a shilling. Whatever yer have, I'll take it.'

He sat not in a doorway but right in the middle of the pavement so people couldn't help but see him. Despite the most inconvenient nature of his position, it was a constant surprise to him how many people did *not* see him. They must be walking along with their head in the clouds, he thought. What was it they said – none so blind as those who can see? He didn't quite understand it but he sort of knew what it meant. These fellows could see all right but they just couldn't see *him*.

43

Simon might not always have been a beggar but he had always been a lazy good-for-nothing. He had no family and could honestly say that he was truly alone in the world. What he could not state with such veracity was that he was a cripple. The four-wheeled platform beneath his legs was a deceptive piece of work. Under the tatty blanket his legs dropped into a hollow. He had been scooting around on it for so long now that it was second nature to him to do so. When he reached the end of the day and went back to his lodgings he sometimes didn't even get out of the trolley. His legs were happier in that position than any other and it actually hurt to try to straighten them out. To stand up was a near impossibility. His calves and thighs had withered from lack of use and the reality was that he could probably have exposed them to the passers-by and they would have been equally generous with their donations. It would not be hard to be equally generous; their donations on the whole were few and far between. Beggars were not looked upon kindly in Opum Oppidulum. He and his beggar friends had all heard there was a committee now to get rid of them. It was in the *Hebdomadal* (a few sheets of which lined the seat of his trousers).

Night fell and Simon was heading home. He was wheeling himself away down the dark cobbled streets (ooh, the dreadful bumping!) when he became aware that he was being followed. He trundled along a little faster. The footsteps quickened. He slowed, so too did they. Unnerved and alert to imminent danger he pushed down hard with his bandaged hands and travelled remarkably quickly along the littered streets. The debris of the day's market was strewn on the ground, making his journey all the harder. Fruit skins and vegetable peelings caused him to career from side to side, but on he went rounding corners, whizzing between a strolling gentleman's legs and skidding over a lady's skirts. There was much screaming and abuse in his wake and at one stage he was struck a glancing blow by a rolled-up copy of the *Hebdomadal*.

Eventually he allowed himself to slow, hopeful that he had shaken off the follower, doubtless a fellow after his takings. Catching his breath he turned down the alley that led to his lodging house and saw that he had not evaded his pursuer at all. At the end of the alley stood the shadowy figure of a man. He had one hand on his hip and the other behind his back. He was not especially tall but he was sturdy.

'What do you want?' asked Simon. 'I have nothing to give.'

But the man didn't speak. He stepped forward and brought round his arm from behind his back. Simon thought it seemed abnormally long and it was only when he felt the stunning blow that he realized the man was holding a club.

8

A Delivery

Dear Robert,

I hope my letter finds you in better spirits than I. It's barely sunrise but once again I am awake. I am greatly worried. I have not seen a light in the asylum for days.

After what I overheard in the library I know that I am my father's last hope. As far as Acantha is concerned, he will never get out. I cannot help but wonder about this fellow she mentioned, Andrew Faye. What part might he have played in this sorry affair?

Rex lifted his pen and shivered. Time was not on his side. In the absence of Robert he felt very alone. A sound from the street caught his attention and he went to the window. He saw a horse and cart drawing up outside the house. A rotund man jumped down from the driver's seat. He was carrying a parcel under his arm wrapped in paper and tied with string; a length of it was trailing behind him. The man had the gait and bearing of a tradesman and, instead of going to the front door, he opened the gate in the railings and descended the steps to the basement kitchen.

Shortly afterwards the man returned to his cart without the package. 'Ho, Blackbird,' he called to his horse, cracked his whip and they were away.

Perhaps that is the mysterious Andrew Faye, mused Rex as the cart disappeared down the street. But, regardless of the man's identity, if he was any sort of friend of his stepmother's then he was no friend of Rex's. With a sigh he returned to his letter.

Since you left I spend most of my days in my room, keeping out of Acantha's way. The front door is locked, as is the kitchen door, and the ground-floor windows. I am not unduly worried, I can get out if I really want to, but right now I am undecided on the best course of action. I have considered going to the constables to tell them of my suspicions, but what exactly do I suspect? That Acantha somehow drove my father mad? It sounds ridiculous. And with Chapelizod and Stradigund on Acantha's side, how can I possibly persuade anyone that a crime has been committed. In truth, Robert, I don't know if one actually has! I could try to get over to the island. But, even then, what can I do? I have no money and certainly

Chapelizod will not allow me to see my father.

All I know for certain is that time is running out. To help Father and straighten out this terrible mess I need proof that Acantha is behind it all. But where would that proof be? I can think of only two places: here in the house or on Droprock Island.

Rex laid down his pen and rested his head in his hands. He was utterly exhausted.

He woke when the housekeeper rattled at the bedroom door a couple of hours later. 'Yes, yes,' he called out, then waited until she had gone away before going out to the landing. He could hear her below complaining to Acantha.

'Don't mind him,' said Acantha. 'He will be going away soon enough. I plan to enrol him in a boarding school where he will be with boys his own age.'

'An excellent idea,' said the housekeeper. 'He has been nothing but miserable since all that business with his father. I don't suppose there is any hope for poor Mr Grammaticus?'

'None at all. He is utterly beyond help. I doubt he will ever be allowed out.'

'Such a shame,' said the housekeeper. 'But, I must say, I still have nightmares about it. I can't bring myself to look at that sword.'

'Yes, yes,' said Acantha briskly. 'Now, tell me, was there a delivery this morning?'

'Yes, madam. Cook took it in. She was wondering what you would like her to do with it.'

'Tell Cook not to worry. I will prepare the meal to-night.'

'Dinner for Mr Stradigund and Mr Chapelizod again?'

'Indeed,' said Acantha. 'As before, you and the rest of the staff may take the evening off.'

The housekeeper was happy to oblige and said as much. At least once a fortnight since Ambrose had been incarcerated, her mistress had relieved the servants of their duties to entertain the solicitor and the asylum superintendent and sometimes a third party. No questions were asked. The servants were always happy to have some free time.

At midday Rex emerged from his room to fetch some food from the kitchen. Acantha had gone out – he had seen her leave – and Cook was busy at the table preparing vegetables and making pastry for the evening's meal. She looked up when he came in and gave him a sympathetic smile. She felt sorry for him. Before Mr Grammaticus went mad he and Rex had spent hours together building those funny little toys, some of them even moved! Such clever fellows!

'Another letter for Robert?' she asked, taking it from Rex's hand. 'I'll see it's sent, and I won't tell Acantha, don't you worry.'

Rex smiled gratefully.

Poor boy, thought Cook. She knew Rex hadn't been happy about his father remarrying. But no man is an island, she thought philosophically (if not ironically). And who was she to comment on it anyway? Cook knew her place, below stairs in the kitchen.

'Take what you want,' she said, nodding to the larder,

and Rex helped himself to bread and cold meats and a big bottle of ginger beer. Cook watched as he examined the tied package on the counter, delivered that morning by Acantha's preferred butcher, some fellow she used when she cooked for her friends.

'Don't you touch that, young man,' she warned. 'It's for tonight. Special cut. The mistress is to prepare it herself. Some sort of fancy beef dish, I believe.'

'I'm sure I won't be invited to supper,' said Rex.

'I hear you're off to school soon,' said Cook. 'Shame that. There's a travelling show on the way with a two-headed man and a set of whip-cracking quadruplets. Maybe you'll still be here to see it.'

'Who knows,' said Rex. 'Who knows!'

The afternoon passed, night fell and Rex finally went to bed. He was well-fed but no nearer a solution to his problems. Again it was a long time before he fell asleep. He could hear the sounds of laughter and singing and the clatter of knives and forks from below where Acantha was entertaining her cronies. There was no sign of the mysterious Andrew Faye, but they weren't letting his absence curb their celebrations and as the night wore on they became louder and more raucous.

They carouse at my father's expense, thought Rex resentfully.

When he did sleep he dreamed that he was sitting in the kitchen with Acantha and Chapelizod and Stradigund feasting on a huge pig. He didn't want any but Acantha kept waving a forkful of meat in front of his nose. It smelt the way she smelt in the library. They were all laughing, with blood dripping from their mouths and running down their chins. 'Here's to Mr Faye,' they kept saying, and every time they toasted him they raised their glasses with such abandon that they showered each other with viscous scarlet wine. Finally a faceless figure appeared in the doorway. 'I am Andrew Faye,' he said mournfully, and then he turned to Rex and said his name.

'Rex.'

Rex turned over in bed and continued to dream.

'Rex. Wake up.'

Rex opened his eyes. A skeleton in rags stood over him with wild eyes and no teeth and in place of a left hand there was a rusty hook. He opened his mouth to scream but a dirt-encrusted, odoriferous and very real hand clamped down over his mouth. He could feel that the hand was trembling.

'Rex, please,' pleaded the voice. 'Don't scream.'

Rex, trying to breathe through the hand, twisted wildly. Who was this intruder? Was he here at Acantha's instruction? Then a terrible thought struck him. He stopped struggling and peered into the dark, but still he could not see properly this shadowy, crooked figure bending over him. He felt the hand move away from his mouth and heard the rasp of a match. Then the candle beside his bed flared up.

'Do you know me now?' asked the man, holding the light up to his tangle-bearded face.

'Yes,' mumbled Rex in shock. 'But, Father, how did you get here?

9

A Nocturnal Adventure

The ragged man sat down on the bed breathing heavily. He smelt very bad, like rotting meat, and in the light of the candle Rex thought he had aged decades.

'You look terrible. What has happened to you? What have they done to you?'

Ambrose shook his head slowly. 'Rex, don't worry about me. I am here now and our time is short.'

'I have seen the lights in the windows of the asylum, on the island.' Rex was babbling, with excitement and fear and relief. Was this not his dream come true? To see his father again? 'Was one of them yours? I was sure it was.'

Ambrose looked a little confused. 'The light?' Then he smiled. 'Yes, it has been a great comfort to me to know that you could see me.'

'How did you get here? Did Mr Chapelizod let you out? Surely not! So you must have escaped!'

'I may be mad,' said Ambrose drily, 'but I'm not stupid.

52

There's always a way. My er . . . room-mate, Hooper, he helped me, and a chap called Walter Freakley.'

'You're not mad,' began Rex, but Ambrose shook his head.

'No time for that debate,' he said. 'Get up. Dress yourself; we're going out.'

'But how did you get in?'

Ambrose held up a piece of bent wire. 'A lock is hardly an obstacle for a Grammaticus,' he said with a knowing smile.

Rex sneaked a look at his father as he pulled on his clothes and boots. He felt slightly revolted. He was so thin and his exposed skin was covered in scabs. The wound to his head had not healed properly. When he coughed it was a long wet cough. And the smell . . . it was overpowering.

Ambrose noticed his staring. 'I'm not so well,' he explained, 'but I had to see you.' He stopped talking and took a deep breath, as if trying to inhale all the air around him.

'You're exhausted,' said Rex. 'Lie down, on the bed.'

'Maybe I will,' he murmured, 'just for a moment.' Rex noticed that his frail body hardly made a depression in the covers he was so light.

'Acantha has taken control of everything – the house, your money, the company,' said Rex quickly. 'And she plans to send me away. Robert has been dismissed. She has declared you legally insane. Stradigund discovered a law, the law of a hundred days—'

'Stradigund?' repeated Ambrose, and he shook his head.

'I knew that Chapelizod was involved but I had hoped I was wrong about Stradigund.' A note of bitterness had crept into his voice.

'They've been downstairs for hours,' said Rex excitedly. 'You could confront them.'

Ambrose sat up. 'They're in the house? The three of them?'

'Well, certainly Stradigund,' said Rex. 'I saw his carriage. It's one of Acantha's supper nights. I know Chapelizod was invited too and possibly Andrew Faye. Do you know him?'

'Andrew Faye?' spat Ambrose with surprising venom. 'Then we must go. Hurry up,' he said, suddenly impatient. 'We have to leave. They must not find me here.' He looked closely at his son and Rex thought he saw something in his father's red-rimmed eyes, a searching look. 'What do you know of Andrew Faye?' he asked.

'Never even seen him,' said Rex. 'Why?'

Ambrose shook his head. 'It doesn't matter. What matters is that you are safe.'

'Safe? From what?' But his father's face didn't invite further query.

'Ready?' asked Ambrose. 'Then let's go.'

Shortly after, in the creamy light of the waxing moon, Rex and his father made painful progress through the shadowy streets of Opum Oppidulum. Rex held on tightly to his father's hand, his right hand. He couldn't bear to look at the hook on the left. He was in the grip of an uncontrollable torrent of emotions: fear, excitement, hope, dismay, sadness. He wanted to ask so many questions but he didn't want to know the answers.

Over one hundred days looking out across the lake every night at the dreary asylum. Watching for a shadow across the lighted window, always hoping for this very moment. And now that the moment was here it was tainted with dread and uncertaintly. It was not how Rex imagined it would be. It was supposed to feel very different.

They walked for a half-hour or so, leaving the broad familiar streets near their house and heading east through the marketplace to the poorer side of town where the streets narrowed and the gas-lights were spaced further and further apart.

'Was . . . is it very bad?' asked Rex finally.

'Let us not dwell on such things,' said Ambrose quietly. It seemed all his energy was being put into the simple act of placing one foot in front of the other.

'They wouldn't let me visit.'

'Chapelizod allows no visitors,' said Ambrose. 'It suits him that way.'

Rex was unable to hold back any longer. 'Are you going back?'

'Never,' said Ambrose.

Rex's heart lifted immediately and then plummeted. There was something in his father's tone that told him to read between the lines. 'Never' could mean many things.

'Rex, I came to see because you are my son and I love you,' said Ambrose matter-of-factly. 'And to give you something for when I am gone.'

'You're going?' Rex phrased it as a question but he knew that it was a statement of fact. 'But you said—'

'I cannot come home. Too many things have changed. I have changed, more than you know. Now it is your future that matters.'

Rex took a moment to consider this answer. 'Well, let us both go somewhere together,' he said determinedly.

Ambrose took a deep breath. 'I cannot go with you,' he said, and there was a profound sadness in his eyes. 'It is dangerous for me to even spend time with you.'

Rex wrinkled his brow. 'I don't understand. Surely as soon as you can prove that you aren't mad then you can come back to Opum Oppidulum, take the house back and Acantha will have no more claim on you.'

'You want me to prove that I am not mad?' Ambrose laughed harshly. He held up his hook. 'How can I when the evidence is right before me?' Instinctively, Rex shrank from the rusty hook. Ambrose saw his reaction and was immediately remorseful. 'I'm not the man I was,' he said softly. 'I trusted Acantha and I was duped. Now I cannot trust myself.'

'What are you saying?' asked Rex. 'You were not mad — you were sick; you must have been. It's the only explanation. It's not a crime to be tricked. Acantha is a monster. If you don't come back I'll . . . I'll kill her!'

Ambrose grabbed him by the shoulder and hissed. 'Monster? What do you mean? What has she done to you?'

Suddenly Rex was frightened. 'She hasn't done anything to me, exactly,' he said nervously. 'But she is going to send me to the Reform School.' Then he couldn't control himself any longer and he broke down in tears. 'Oh, why can't you come home and we'll be the way we used to be, before Acantha?'

Ambrose hugged Rex tightly. Rex buried his face in his rags and could feel that there was almost nothing left of his father's once sturdy frame. He felt his warm breath on his hair and his nose digging into his scalp. He heard him sniff deeply and then he was pushed away again.

'I can't go back, Rex, it's too dangerous, for both of us. Acantha will just have me arrested. I am officially insane. I have lost all my rights. How does a madman prove his sanity?'

Separated, they began to walk again, in silence. Rex could see that his father had changed in body, yes – but surely his mind was still intact? Could his illness not be cured? What was this danger he talked about? More confused than ever, he was beginning to understand that his life was far more complicated than he had thought possible. But he didn't have much time to contemplate this realization before Ambrose came to an abrupt halt.

'I hope you've been keeping up with your Classical studies,' he said suddenly.

'As well as I can without Robert.'

'Very important,' he said, 'to know your Latin and Greek.'

Rex shook his head. His father was behaving very oddly.

They stood on Cuttlesack Lane outside what appeared to be an old shop. Rex noted that there were no goods in the window and the frosted glass was fly-spotted on the inside. Thick cobwebs stretched from one corner to the other. Above his head a sign swung gently to and fro. Some of the letters were missing and all he could read was:

Ant n Sarpalius
Bo y Com difi tions

Rex flinched as Ambrose knocked sharply and deliberately on the door with his raw-boned knuckles. A panel in the door slid across and a pair of eyes appeared in the slit.

'Ambrose Grammaticus,' said his father softly. 'I wish to see Mr Sarpalius.'

The panel closed and the door opened. Ambrose pulled Rex through into a tiny low-lit room. There was a counter in front of them behind which was a heavy black curtain that hung from ceiling to floor. A cheap tallow candle burned smokily in a holder and a strange odour, not wholly unpleasant, thought Rex, hung on the air.

The door closed behind them and the man who let them in pulled aside the curtain. 'Room at the end,' he said with a nod.

The corridor beyond the curtain was narrow, only wide enough for one person to pass through at a time, and there were more curtains at intervals along its sides. Rex jumped as he felt a spatter of hot wax on his cheek from a gut-tering candle on the wall. The smell from the shop was even stronger back here. One of the drapes was not fully drawn and in the brief second Rex had to look behind it, he saw a man lying face down on a table. Another man was leaning over him and in his hand he had some sort of tool. It was sharp, and the tip was covered in a red liquid.

Blood? thought Rex in horror. What else could it be? Was this man a surgeon? He caught the fellow's eye and he raised his head from his work and smiled, displaying a mouthful of large black teeth. Then he leaned over again and Rex saw that his patient clenched a stick between his teeth.

And its purpose was to prevent his crying out.

'Father, what are we doing in this place?' whispered Rex. But Ambrose didn't answer. For the first time ever Rex's faith wavered. He wondered if he was wrong; could everyone else be right? Was his father really insane?

They reached the final curtain. Ambrose held it back and pushed Rex forward into darkness. Rex stood there shivering. Fear overwhelmed his senses. There was someone else in the room. He could hear steady breathing, neither his nor his father's. Then there was the sound of a flint being struck against steel and the room lit up. Rex screamed. Out of the yellow light emerged the face of a grinning monster with black eyes surrounded by scales, and from his mouth there emerged the forked tongue of a serpent.

10

The Painted Man

Rex's scream was stifled as for the second time that night a hand clamped firmly over his mouth to silence him. He felt the sharpness and weight of iron on his shoulder and he was spun round.

'Nothing to fear, son,' said Ambrose. 'It's pictures, merely pictures.'

Rex steadied his breathing and steeled himself, and opened his eyes, for he had screwed them tightly shut. The monster was still there, grinning, but he could see now that his father was right. This was no beast, just a man with pictures on his face and down his neck and up his forearms and across the backs of his hands. He seemed to be painted with colourful scales, like some sort of reptile, and glinting in the candlelight Rex could see huge golden hoops in his ears. But he was not imagining the man's tongue; it really was forked and he seemed to enjoy Rex's discomfort as he repeatedly flicked it in and out of his mouth.

'Arrh!' growled the man suddenly, his head darting forward like the snake he resembled.

Rex jumped back and the man laughed.

'Anton Sarpalius?' asked Ambrose.

The painted man nodded.

'Walter Freakley gave me your name. I'm pleased to meet you.'

He held out his hand and Rex recoiled at the thought of touching the scaly skin; he anticipated it would be as slimy as he imagined a snake might be. The man smelt strongly of sweat and tobacco, but Rex noticed that he had long fingers, artist's fingers.

'I haven't much time,' said Ambrose.

'I can work fast,' replied the reptilian fellow. 'What is it you wish me to do?'

Ambrose directed Rex to sit while he and Anton engaged in a whispered conversation. Rex took the opportunity to look around the room. Windowless and bare, apart from a couple of chairs and a low table, it was small and hardly welcoming. There was a cupboard in the corner, the doors of which were half open, and Rex could see within an array of brown glass bottles, further convincing him that this unlikely-looking man was a surgeon. Perhaps he was going to cure his father. He certainly looked ill. A noise caused him to glance over at Anton and he was shocked to see that he had taken out a cut-throat and was sharpening it on a leather strap. Ambrose seemed to think that it was unnecessary and Rex was pleased to see Anton lay it down again.

Finally they shook hands and Rex knew that a deal had been made. Anton pulled the servant's bell at the wall and a few minutes later the fellow from the front of the shop arrived with a tray of drinks, one for each of them. While Rex enjoyed his sweet-tasting liquid, Ambrose and Anton watched him closely and sipped from their own wooden mugs in silence. The clock struck one and he began to feel sleepy. Presently his eyes were so heavy he felt as if he needed pitchforks to lift them. He put down his tumbler. His head was swimming.

'Father,' he began to say, but Ambrose only looked at him and smiled sadly. After that everything seemed confused. Rex remembered being taken to the table to lie down and the last thing he saw was the face of the monster looming over him. And the last thing he felt was fingers running through his tangled hair.

The next sensation Rex had was the coldness of the night air on his cheeks. He was still lying on his back but now something was digging into him. Where has the ceiling gone? he wondered, for he could see the incomplete moon and the stars. He felt sick and his head was throbbing. He was vaguely aware that someone was nearby. He began to think that he was in the middle of a nightmare, that his father had not come back at all, but then he caught a strong whiff of decay and he knew that it was all very real.

Then his father was standing over him. His eyes were shining in the light of his lantern.

'Where are we? Where's Mr Sarpalius?'

'Are you all right?' asked Ambrose softly. 'How do you feel?'

'My head hurts,' said Rex. He touched his scalp and when he took his fingers away they were sticky with blood.

'You fell on the shingle,' said Ambrose, staring hard at Rex's bloody hand. His voice was strangely muted. 'It will heal.'

Rex tried to focus on his surroundings. He sat up slowly, his head spinning and his ears ringing, and he could hear an odd crunching sound. He realized with a shock that he was on the stony shore of the lake. 'What are we doing here?'

Ambrose sighed and knelt down with difficulty. He put his hand on Rex's shoulder and it felt very heavy. 'Rex, there's so much you don't know, and I don't want to tell you, but believe this: I love you and I want the very best for you. You must promise me that you will not go back to Acantha. You were right about her – she is not to be trusted. I found that out too late. I can only pray that she has shown a little humanity towards you and not . . .' He didn't finish his sentence, but coughed long and hard.

'Humanity?' said Rex sarcastically. 'Oh, there's plenty of that, if you consider humanity treating me as if I don't exist! I won't go back. I'm going to stay with you.'

Ambrose shook his head slowly. 'You cannot.'

'Then what is to become of me?' Rex was tired, his head ached badly and he was frightened. He didn't want puzzles, he wanted answers. 'Just what is going on?'

'Listen, Rex,' said his father. He paused for a long time, searching for the right words. 'I have a . . . disease. It's like a curse. I cannot trust myself to do what's right. It's too late for me; I'm not strong enough any more. But Acantha must be stopped. I found information on the island, all the proof you need to expose her, but I couldn't bring it with me – it was too dangerous. Maybe it is the disease that makes me so untrusting, but I was afraid, afraid that it might fall into the wrong hands. Oh, Rex, if you can face it, you must go to Droprock Island, find the proof and take it to someone you trust . . . my friend on the *Hebdomadal*, Cecil, he will know what to do with it.'

'But how will I find it?' asked Rex in exasperation.

'Just use your head.'

Suddenly there were shouts and the sound of running feet on the stones. Ambrose spoke quickly. 'Rex, I wish I could tell you more but the less I tell you, the less you can tell others. It's safer this way. If Acantha gets her hands on you I know she will try to find out what I have told you.'

'But you haven't told me anything!' protested Rex.

'Take this,' he said, and he pressed something into Rex's hand and closed his fingers around it. 'You must get to the island. The asylum is safe now; Chapelizod is gone. The answers you're looking for are there.' His voice was no more than a hoarse whisper. 'And remember: don't fly too close to the sun.'

'What?' Now his father really was talking nonsense.

'Just do as I say, Rex,' he urged desperately. '*On your head be it.*'

Ambrose started to walk away, still facing Rex. Rex struggled to his feet, but he was woozy and having trouble standing. 'Just take me with you,' he pleaded, reaching out to his retreating father, but he fell to his knees, his legs unable to carry him.

'I can't.' Rex knew in his heart that this was the final goodbye. He didn't understand why and he didn't think he could bear it.

'Remember the good times, Rex,' called Ambrose, and his voice was breaking. 'Before all of this. Remember me as someone who loved you. Not as . . . as a monster.'

A monster? Rex felt as if he had sustained a crippling blow. This was all so terribly wrong. Then there was a shout and three burly cloaked figures came running down the shore.

'There he is,' shouted one of them. 'The escaped madman. Catch him, boys! Catch him.'

Ambrose tried to run but he was too weak, and the yielding shingle made it even more difficult get away. The constables were upon him in a matter of seconds. Rex watched as his father fell to the ground with a terrible crunch and lay there unmoving. And through blurred and swollen eyes, Rex saw them chain him and drag him away.

He never saw him alive again.

11

Out of the Frying Pan...

Cadmus Chapelizod stumbled out of the freezing shallows and fell heavily to the shingle. He was cold and wet and he knew that he smelt very bad indeed. 'Oh Lord,' he kept saying over and over. 'I made it. I can't believe I made it.'

After the lunatics had escaped and gone on the rampage, he had wasted no time trying to contain them but had immediately hidden where they were least likely to look for him – in one of their own abandoned cells. After a couple of days under a pile of stinking straw he judged that the noise from above had quietened and dared to emerge. It seemed that everyone was gone, but, just in case, he disguised himself as one of his former charges and ran down to the jetty, hoping against all hope that the ferryman might still be there. His relief was immeasurable when he saw the cloaked figure in the boat. Without further ado he leaped in and barked at him to take him across the lake to the town. He spoke not another word during the crossing, merely stared straight ahead at the lights of Opum Oppidulum and prayed earnestly for his safe delivery.

And now he was here. He could have wept with joy! He looked around him. They had landed quite far down the shore; in the fog the ferryman must have missed the jetty, and now the boat was nowhere to be seen. Cadmus didn't care. He suspected that the ferryman was in cahoots with the escapees; after all, hadn't he just rowed him to town even though he must have thought he was a lunatic? He would arrange for the man to be arrested along with anyone else who had escaped and could be found.

Cadmus still couldn't believe what had happened. And it was made all the worse by events from the past. For ten years he had been in charge of the asylum with no complaints from anyone. Well, no one who mattered. He had taken the job when the previous superintendent had gone soft and allowed a dangerous murderer to escape. Ten years without a hitch and now this! At least he had been spared his life; the other murderous escapee, apparently unreformed, had killed his foolhardy predecessor.

Cadmus gritted his teeth. As for those treacherous cowards, the warders! If he ever got his hands on them they would pay, each and every one, for subjecting him to this humiliation. It was the head warder who was responsible for the whole mess! As far as he could work out, the escape was all his fault. Somehow one of the lunatics had got hold of his keys.

Cadmus tried to gather his thoughts. He knew what to do: he would go to Acantha's. She would help him. And she would have food. He needed to get his strength back. She must be wondering what had happened to him; he had missed the last meal and had been unable to send an explanation.

Cadmus stood up and shuddered. He could still feel their hands on him, grabbing him, trying to kill him! He had shaken them off; after all they were half starved and hardly strong enough to stand up, let alone hold him down. But the smell and the feel of their scabious hands and the sight of their weeping sores and the look of their running eyes . . . Ugh! It was too much to bear.

His clothes were torn and his face was scratched, and in this state of disarray he began to make his slow, painful way up the shingle until he reached the road. The lights of the town were beacons of hope and he began to feel as if he could actually be back to normal before too long. As he stumbled along he heard the sound of hoofs from behind.

'Oh, thank the Lord,' he rejoiced. His ordeal was almost over. He turned to see a small cart and horse approaching. The driver drew up beside him.

'I need a ride into town, my good man,' said Chapelizod in his usual authoritative tone. 'I have had some bad luck.'

The driver looked doubtful. 'That's what they all say. You look like a beggar to me. We don't like beggars in Opum Oppidulum.'

Cadmus sighed. 'I will pay you as soon as we get back to my house.'

'Where is your house?'

'Er, well, actually I come from the asylum on the island.'

Chapelizod realized his mistake as soon as the words left his mouth.

The driver smiled. 'So you are a lunatic *and* a beggar?'

'No, no,' said Chapelizod. This wasn't going at all the way he had hoped.

The man jumped down from the cart and Chapelizod took a step back. A feeling of unease replaced his relief. There was something odd about this fellow's demeanour. Chapelizod had been around enough madmen to know the signs.

'I'll help you,' said the driver in a low voice now laced with menace. 'I'll put you out of your misery.' In an instant he swung his unnaturally long arm round and hit Chapelizod over the head. He fell to the ground and he looked up to see a haze of glittering stars. He put his hand up to his mouth and felt his gold tooth. It has come loose, he thought angrily. 'Hey,' he protested but then the stars went out.

12

Article from

The Opum Oppidulum Hebdomadal

A TRIBUTE TO AMBROSE OSWALD GRAMMATICUS

by

Cecil Notwithstanding

It is with great regret that I announce the premature death of Mr Ambrose Oswald Grammaticus last week. He was a friend of mine and a gifted man.

A native of Opum Oppidulum, Mr Grammaticus was considered by many to be one of the finest engineers and designers of the century. In his lifetime he designed and constructed many breathtaking buildings and structures, all of which serve only to enhance and improve the lives and environment of those who live in them or near them. He founded his company, AmGram Design, Engineering and Construction, when only barely out of his teens and through dint of sheer hard work turned it into one of the most successful businesses in the country.

Before his untimely death Mr Grammaticus was working on a project to construct a much needed second bridge over the river Foedus in the city of Urbs Umida. It is now unlikely to be completed. In recent years he proposed to build a bridge across Lake Beluarum to Droprock Island. And there were rumours that he had plans to improve the east side of Opum Oppidulum which is suffering from ne-glect and is home to hordes of troublesome beggars.

Tragically Mr Grammaticus was struck down earlier this year by a violent and incurable disease of the brain which rendered him incapable of leading a normal life. He had only recently remarried, his first wife having died twelve years ago. Mr Grammaticus spent his last months in the asylum on Droprock Island under the professional care of Mr Cadmus Chapelizod. His death comes shortly after the recent revolt at the asylum.

Mr Grammaticus leaves behind a son from his first marriage, Rex, who is reported to be as talented as his father.

13

An Invitation from the Mayor

In a city some days distant from Opum Oppidulum, Dr
Tibor Velhildegildus (a doctor of the mind rather than of
medicine) was contemplating a letter that had recently
been brought to his consulting rooms by fast messenger
and – for Dr Velhildegildus insisted that things were done in
the proper manner – handed to him on a silver platter. He
read with his lips moving, softly enunciating the words:

Dear Dr Velhildegildus,
Allow me to introduce myself. I am the chief councillor
of Opum Oppidulum, a small, thriving town beside
the world famous Lake Beluarum. I wish to draw
to your attention the most pleasant nature of the
town; centuries old and of great historical interest to
scholars of the past, today the town is populated by
friendly and welcoming people. We are very proud to
say that Mr Ambrose Grammaticus (recently deceased),

72

the celebrated engineer and designer, was a native of the town.

We are also known for our mental institution, the Opum Oppidulum Asylum for the Peculiar and Bizarre, situated on Droprock Island, where we provide a safe haven for those who are feeble in the mind, discombobulated or eccentric in their habits.

Unfortunately a rather disturbing occurrence came to pass in the asylum recently. The blame lies squarely at the feet of the ex-superintendent, Mr Cadmus Chapelizod. It has come to light that as a result of Mr Chapelizod's wanton neglect conditions in the asylum deteriorated badly. The inmates expressed their displeasure by breaking out, vandalizing parts of the building and then all fleeing. We wish to put this to rights with urgent immediacy.

Dr Velhildegildus, it is my understanding that you, as a doctor of the mind, enjoy a great reputation in Urbs Umida; your practice on the north side is highly regarded and your reputation for satisfaction is unrivalled.

With this in mind I have a proposition for you: would you do us humble citizens of Opum Oppidulum the honour of coming to our town (you are now aware of its wonderful nature and situation) and taking over as superintendent of Droprock Asylum? You will be well rewarded; the patients' families are most anxious for cures or long-term care (diseases of the mind present such inconveniences to a family) and pay handsomely.

As an added incentive we, the councillors, have voted to increase the salary that goes with the post to what we are sure you will agree is a generous sum.

At present the asylum is empty apart from a cook and a caretaker. The warders, unfortunately, deserted their posts in the revolt and the lunatics drowned in Lake Beluarum.

If you are unsure, please come to visit us before you make up your mind. I suggest that you take a carriage at our expense and reply in person.

Yours etc.,

Dr Velhildegildus looked at the letter and chewed the inside of his lip thoughtfully. Hmm, he mused. Opum Oppidulum. He had vague memories of the place, for he had spent some time there once with a rather lovely lady friend.

Dear Meredith, he thought, I wonder where you are now.

She certainly had some novel ideas.

But in truth at the time he could hardly wait to leave! And, having left, he had built a very good life for himself in Urbs Umida. Certainly Urbs Umida had its faults, but Opum Oppidulum? Over four days' travel away, if he recalled correctly, and right beside a freezing lake. Exactly who was the lunatic here? He looked around his plush and comfortable rooms and laughed. Not even the hounds of Hades could drag him back! So he put the letter away in the drawer of his desk and sat back to contemplate in comfort his good fortune.

Tibor Velhildegildus considered himself a man of learning, style and good taste, and made great efforts to present himself in this way. Understandably therefore, he lived on the north bank of the river Foedus among the wealthy and successful. He only ventured south of the river, where the city was of an entirely different nature, when necessary and avoided if he could its crooked pavements (for it was his preference when travelling about to use a sedan chair).

Practically, he saw little reason to venture over the bridge. His business, after all, was to fix heads and there was no doubt in his mind that the mental well-being of the rich elite was vital to the survival of a city. He also believed that a good day's work deserved a good day's pay. And every day was a good day for Dr Velhildegildus. There was great demand among the well-off for his 'services to the mind'. A man of many talents, Tibor had soon tapped into that aspect of a rich man's psyche that believes quality of service comes only with a high price; his services must have been top quality for certainly his prices were very steep.

Dr Velhildegildus lived in a spacious set of rooms, consisting of not one but two floors, in one of the most fashionable parts of the north side. The largest room on the ground floor, wherein he now sat, was given over to his consulting salon, complete with an outrageously expensive leather couch, matching chair and a valuable, finely crafted desk at which he wrote his patients' notes. When in the middle of a consultation, he sat in the chair at the head of the couch so he could not be seen. He said that he did not wish to influence his patients with his countenance. The truth of the matter was that often times he was yawning.

As for the mental health of those paupers and gin-addicts on the south side? Well, what time had they for problems of the mind! They were too busy trying to scratch a living. Besides, Tibor had observed that over the river the behaviour of the mad southerners (and there were many) varied only marginally from those who behaved in a way that was considered normal. It begged the question: what was normal and what was mad? But he felt disinclined to answer it. It had little bearing on his practice.

Tibor sighed and drummed his fingers on the desk. Then he took the letter out and read it again. If truth be told, he was bored, intensely so, and was looking for a change. Could this be it? No, he thought, and replaced the letter in the drawer. The money was insufficient. He was well-off here. If he were to return to Opum Oppidulum he wanted more. Much more.

The clock struck midday and his next patient was announced, a Mrs Cynthia Ecclestope. She had been suffering badly with her nerves. Tibor suspected she might benefit from his most successful technique, one he had employed with great success before leaving Opum Oppidulum and had been refining and using ever since. He took a small box from the desk and unlocked it. Nestled in the folds of green baize lay a large smooth disc of black rock on a long silver chain: his precious Lodestone.

He took it out and held it up to the light. It swung gently to and fro and he followed it with his eyes. Tibor used this polished stone in what he termed the 'Lodestone Procedure', a technique by which he could realign the humours in the body and cure all manner of mental ills. At least that is how he presented it to his patients. In fact he employed his indubitable powers of persuasion and this magnetic rock to send his customers into a sort of trance. In the trance they were in a very suggestible state and volunteered all sorts of information (generally about their wealth) that could be used afterwards without their even realizing they had divulged it. Mrs Ecclestope, with her simple intellect and her nervous disposition (not forgetting her rich husband), was a perfect candidate . . .

Some time later a very satisfied Mrs Ecclestope, relieved of the burdens of her mind (and a substantial burden of silver from her purse), thanked Dr Velhildegildus and tripped lightly away.

'Same time next week,' called Tibor after her.

The day's work over – professionals did not work afternoons – Tibor was looking forward to a light lunch at his club. He had just put on his new hat (on account of the unusual shape of his head all his hats were made to measure) and taken his cane from the elephant's foot umbrella stand (all the rage these days) when the servant called to him.

'What is it, man?' he asked with irritation

'Melvyn Halibutte has sent for you, down at Irongate Jail.'

Tibor raised his eyebrows. 'How interesting,' he murmured.

Now, you could be forgiven for thinking that the governor of Irongate Jail would be an unlikely friend of Dr Velhildegildus, but birds of a feather flock together and although Tibor and Melvyn were on different sides of the river they flew in very much the same direction. Tibor knew Melvyn Halibutte would not call upon him for any trifle. Besides, Melvyn kept a well-stocked drinks cabinet.

So he called for a carriage and ventured south.

14

The Merry Inmate

For those of you unfamiliar with the legendary city of Urbs Umida, and the notorious south side of said conurbation, to acquaint yourself with it you need only picture a place so foul and mephitic that merely to think on it brings tears to the eyes and a stinging to the nose. If that is not enough for you then use your imagination further to people the revolting streets with evil-eyed incorrigible swindlers, nimble-fingered pickpockets, heavy-browed thugs and gin-soaked layabouts in blood-streaked rags; a kind of multifarious pigswill of turpitudinous humanity all fighting to survive, for certainly it could not be called living.

Those of you who *do* know of Urbs Umida, doubtless you can tell that little has changed in this hellhole 'tween times.

On account of the large crowds still lingering after a public hanging, the carriage driver had insisted that Tibor get down and make his own way to the jail gates. To add to his displeasure Tibor could see quite clearly the dark silhouette of the fresh body on the gallows already being pecked at by the crows. A passer-by threw an apple core at the unfortunate, whose only crime had been to pinch a gentleman's peruke.

Urbs Umida was indeed a harsh and cruel place.

It might only have been a matter of a few dozen steps but Tibor was feeling distinctly out of sorts by the time he presented himself to be waved through by the gate-keeper. He was escorted to the governor's office and only felt safe once he stepped inside the spacious, warm and very tastefully decorated and furnished room. It could not have been in greater contrast to the prisoners' quarters below. Truly, it did not do to get on the wrong side of the law in Urbs Umida.

Governor Halibutte was waiting for Tibor, and the two men greeted each other – not necessarily as old friends, more as two people who knew that their relationship was always beneficial, each in his own way to the other. It worked like this. Tibor declared the prisoners insane and Melvyn seized their assets – as he was legally allowed to do to pay for their treatment, an insane prisoner being considered far more expensive than a sane one and incapable of managing their own finances – and they split the money. As for the prisoner, mad or not, he was left to his own devices in the cells below. A simple yet very rewarding plan.

'My dear Dr Velhildegildus, how are you?' asked Melvyn enthusiastically. As usual the conversation went no further without first a brandy and light refreshment: today honeyed figs with cream, in sharp contrast to the meagre slabs of cold porridge being served down below.

'So,' asked Tibor, 'what news, my friend?'

'Ah, well, something very exciting,' replied Halibutte, rubbing his fat hands together.

'I should hope so too,' murmured Tibor, and he couldn't help but glance down at his muddy shoes. They had been gleaming when he left the house. Not any longer.

'Well, it concerns a fellow, a filthy vagrant, who was picked up last night. He is, needless to say, completely mad. Despite this, he is perfectly happy but most insistent that he has something of great interest to impart. He says that he heard about you in the taverns and has refused to discuss the matter with anyone else.'

Tibor was vaguely flattered that his reputation was abroad but this was countered by the fact that this particular admirer appeared to be a genuine southside lunatic.

'I fail yet to see how this was worth my journey,' said Tibor with a smile.

'I do understand what hardship it is for you,' laughed Melvyn, and he looked down at Tibor's shoes. 'But in this life everything has its compensations.'

Tibor was growing impatient. 'But if this fellow would not say anything then how did you know he was worth listening to?'

In answer Melvyn went to his desk and unlocked a drawer. He took out a red velvet drawstring pouch and opened the neck. He held it out to Tibor who leaned over to look inside. Instantly a broad smile crossed his face.

'Oh my,' he said softly. 'Oh my.'

'He says there are more,' whispered Melvyn, and he tittered excitedly.

'This man is definitely worth talking to,' said Tibor.

For in the pouch were two delicate, glittering diamonds.

By the time Tibor and Melvyn Halibutte reached the new prisoner's cell door Tibor was in a state of great discomfort and regret. He had covered his face with his handkerchief as soon as they had descended to the cells. The smell was indescribable. Literally. Try as he might, Tibor could not think of a single word that adequately expressed the aroma of the place. It was nothing less than a physical assault. Melvyn also had a handkerchief over his face but he seemed rather less affected. It was not that he was immune to the smell, just more used to it. He beckoned to Tibor to come over.

Tibor, adjusting his handkerchief, croaked, 'Could we not have brought him up to see us?'

Halibutte frowned. 'Now, Tibor,' he said, 'do you really think I would allow one of these fellows in my office? Think of the fleas!'

Tibor examined his dire surroundings and realized immediately the stupidity of his question. The prison cells were as Mars is to Earth when compared to Halibutte's refined quarters; where one had a thick plush carpet upon which to tread, the other had only a layer of straw, dead mice and foul-smelling mould. Where one was light and airy and pleasing to the spirit, the other was dark and claus-trophobic and soul-destroying.

As he followed the governor into the bowels of the pris-on, Tibor also had to endure the taunts and shouts and, once or twice, the saliva of a multitude of prisoners who had nothing left to lose. Most were on their way to the gallows and none was likely ever to be released. To see such a finely dressed fellow as Tibor pass by the bars of their cells was an opportunity too good to miss. Tibor had already decided to discard his shoes when he returned home, but by the time he reached Hooper's cell he was resigned to burning his entire outfit, even the brand new mauve foulard he had tied so jauntily around his neck before leaving.

Some things were just beyond salvation.

Under different circumstances he might have said the same about the ragged fellow who occupied the cell on the other side of the door. But this chap, he was worth a lot more than appearances might suggest. He sat on a small bench against the far wall. He was in a wretch-ed state, bruised and cut, without a tooth in his head. Tibor could tell this because the man was smiling and laughing.

'So, you say he was picked up last night?'

'Yes,' said Melvyn. 'He was in the Nimble Finger Inn and apparently wouldn't stop laughing. So a fight began and eventually there was such a ruckus that the constables had to step in.'

'Must have been quite bad, then,' remarked Tibor. Usually the constables preferred to let the fights in that particular establishment reach a natural conclusion: death or flight. 'Is it safe to go in?'

'Oh, I believe so,' said Melvyn. 'After all, he was the victim. He has shown no violent tendencies at all.'

Melvyn unlocked the door and Tibor stepped in. The man gave a great big smile. It was not a pleasant sight.

'Would you be Dr Tibor Velhildegildus?' he asked, and stood up and thrust out his hand.

Tibor immediately put his own hands behind his back. 'I am. And who might you be?'

'My name is Hooper. Hooper Hopcroft.'

15

A Deadly Diagnosis

'I hear you can cure madness,' said Hooper.

'Well, I do not wish to appear boastful,' said Tibor, 'but, yes, it is true that I have a very successful record in that department.'

'Then I wish you to cure me. Or at least to declare me sane so I do not have to stay in prison or go to an asylum.'

'An interesting proposition,' said Tibor, 'and one to which I will give my full consideration. But you must understand a cure does not come cheap. What means have you to pay for this? Might I suggest this?' Tibor held up the velvet pouch. The diamonds were not in it but Hooper wasn't to know.

'You're welcome to it,' said Hooper. 'There's plenty more where that came from. I can guarantee it.'

Tibor could actually hear Melvyn rubbing his hands together behind him.

'Excellent. Well, my good fellow, if you can direct me to these diamonds I am sure it will cover all costs. I will certify you sane and you will be free to wander the world as you wish. You will have money and good clothes, which, as any man knows, are the true mark of sanity.'

This instant diagnosis seemed to please Hooper immensely, though of course his expression rarely exhibited any other emotion. 'You have a deal,' said Hooper.

'Excellent. And where are these diamonds to be found?'

'I will draw you a map,' said Hooper obligingly. 'I have some cloth here.' He pulled a piece of cloth from his pocket but in his haste he dropped it and Tibor, spotting that it seemed to be a diagram of sorts, stooped to pick it up.

'And what might this be?' he asked, holding it up between the tips of his white-gloved (he was resigned to their burning too) finger and thumb.

'Oh,' said Hooper, 'it's a plan for a vessel, a Perambulating Submersible. My friend Ambrose Grammaticus designed it; I merely drew it. We were to make it so we could escape.'

Tibor's ears pricked up. Grammaticus? The famous engineer? Wasn't he the fellow planning to build a second bridge across the Foedus here in Urbs Umida? Not one of his better ideas, thought Tibor. Why give the southsiders another way over?

'I see,' said Tibor slowly, and examined the diagram more carefully. For many years people had been trying to find a way to explore properly the mysteries of the deep. There were plenty of failures but if a fellow such as Ambrose Grammaticus put his mind to it then it was highly likely to be successful. Tibor immediately saw an opportunity to increase his wealth dramatically. For, have no doubt about it, Dr Tibor Velhildegildus worshipped first and foremost at the altar of Mammon.

'You could use it to walk along the bottom of the lake to look for diamonds,' suggested Hooper helpfully. 'That's where they are. But wait until the full moon. The water level rises and it'll stir up the diamonds.'

'You mean Lake Beluarum, in the Devil's Porridge Bowl, by the town of Opum Oppidulum?' Tibor liked to be precise in these matters.

Hooper nodded. 'You know it, then?'

'I know of it,' replied Tibor thoughtfully. His mind was working fast. Suddenly the post of superintendent of Droprock Asylum was looking like a far more interesting proposition. Fate, in the form of a vagrant lunatic, was presenting him with an idea that could make him the huge fortune he sought: a vessel that travelled underwater designed by a renowned engineer. And, as if that wasn't enough, a hoard of diamonds to boot. Ambrose Grammaticus might have been mad, but wasn't genius part madness?

Suddenly it wasn't going to take the hounds of Hades to get Dr Tibor Velhildegildus back to Opum Oppidulum – merely a rather less supernatural horse and carriage.

He turned to Melvyn. 'No need to worry,' he said. 'You can leave us. The guard can keep an eye on things until I'm finished.'

Melvyn needed no encouragement and left. Tibor reached into his waistcoat pocket and took out his Lodestone. He turned back to Hooper. 'Tell me more, Mr Hopcroft,' he crooned mellifluously. 'I'm listening.'

An hour later, safely installed back in Melvyn's office, Tibor recovered from his ordeal with a brandy.

'So?' asked Melvyn. 'Is there anything to his story?'

'The diamonds? Yes, I do believe there might be.'

'Then . . . what is my cut?'

'Ho, ho,' laughed Tibor at the unintended pun. He was in a very good mood. 'Half?' he suggested. 'After my expenses, of course.'

The deal was sealed with a firm handshake and another brandy, a Fitzbaudly '37.

Later that day a carriage heavily burdened with luggage strapped to the roof, rattled its way out of the city, heading north, deep into the heart of the Moiraean Mountains. Within it were two men both dressed in the latest fashion, though it must be said one looked far more at ease in his clothes than the other, who was chatting excitedly and clutching at a document with a grip of iron. It was not to be easily yielded.

His companion sat opposite with his hands resting on his cane and his ankles crossed, though not in such a way as to scuff his shoes. He was a firm believer in the maxim that to know what a fellow thinks of himself, one must look at his shoes. He seemed preoccupied, although listening, and every so often he pulled back the blind ever so slightly and looked out at the terrain. Night was falling and the road was steep and uneven, as evidenced by the alarming jolting of the carriage, and at the edge of the road was a sheer drop.

'So,' he said, interrupting his friend's merry rambling. 'How does it feel to be a free man?'

'Marvellous,' the man enthused, and he smoothed down his new velvet coat and tried to see his wide smile reflected in his own gleaming boots. 'I was thinking, mind, that really I would prefer not to return to Opum Oppidulum. Perhaps you could drop me off somewhere along the way. I believe there are plenty of villages.'

'I am sure that can be arranged.'

'Might I say again how pleased I am with this rather fine document?' He held up the stiff page with a smile. Printed across the top in large black letters were the words:

OFFICIAL DECLARATION OF SANITY

'Yes, it is a most useful document indeed,' smiled the other traveller. Then he started and looked down at the man's feet. 'There is a speck of some sort on your boot,' he said. 'Would you like me to remove it?'

'How very kind of you.'

'I have just the thing here.' He reached into his pocket and took out a clean handkerchief. Then he took from the travelling valise at his side a small brown bottle. 'This will bring up the shine like no man's business,' he said, uncorking it. He held the cloth over the mouth of the bottle, tipped it up for a second and in one swift movement stepped across the gap between the two of them, and pressed the cloth hard over his companion's mouth and nose. There was a struggle, of sorts — the upright man had the advantage over the seated — before he went limp. Working quickly, the treacherous assailant dragged his unconscious victim on to the floor, opened the carriage door and heaved him out. He closed the door, tossed the handkerchief out of the window, followed shortly by the document which he had ripped into tiny pieces.

Then he dusted off his hands and sat back with a self-satisfied smile. He took a piece of paper from inside his coat, spread it out across his knees and carefully studied the diagram. The carriage slowed and the driver's face appeared at the window in the roof.

'Everything all right in there, Dr Velhildegildus? I thought I heard a noise.'

'Everything is fine, my good man. The door came open by accident, that is all.'

'I thought there was two of yer?' he said with a puzzled look. 'Hooper, weren't it, the other fella?'

'My companion changed his mind before we set off. He remained at the lodging house. He did not want to continue.'

'Very well, sir,' said the driver. It made no difference to him. The fare had been paid in advance. And with one passenger, well, the horses would go slightly faster.

16

A Book and an Egg

Rex paced the floor like a wild animal behind bars, heedless of the crushed and scattered metal debris underfoot. He felt like a lion preparing to pounce on his prey, his muscles tensed and coiled, but the release never came. And he cursed under his breath and made his hands into fists, for he was exactly where his father had warned him not to be – in the clutches of Acantha.

Barely seconds after his father had been hauled away by the constables Acantha had arrived and marched him back to the house and locked him in his room. 'For your own safety,' she had said, 'in case any more of the lunatics come after you.'

Of course, he hadn't slept a wink that night and was ready and waiting when Acantha came up to see him the next morning.

'Where is Father?' he shouted. 'Take me to him!'

Acantha informed him coldly that Ambrose had died in the custody of the constables.

'It's true, Rex,' said Stradigund, appearing from behind Acantha. He at least had the decency to appear vaguely upset. But it was too late. Rex didn't want to hear anything he had to say and he pushed them both away and slammed his door. He stayed in his room for three days and his disbelief at the tragedy of his father soon turned to utter despair.

Over the next week Acantha locked Rex in his room, with no thought for his grief. She came up to question him over and over about what his father had said to him on the lake shore. Rex had told her quite truthfully that Ambrose had been rambling and had said nothing of any worth or interest. First she had used her wheedling voice, the one she had employed with his father to twist him round her finger, but that didn't last long. Then she tried to be friendly; it didn't come easy to her. She even said once that she wouldn't send him to Reform School. Finally she lost her thin veneer of patience and resorted to violence. 'I'll break every model in here,' she screamed – and she had, one by one, smashed every model to smithereens. That had hurt more than anything but with gritted teeth Rex had stuck to his story.

'He didn't tell me anything.'

But what was it she thought he might know? Something about the mysterious Andrew Faye? Whatever it was, Rex knew she was watching his every move. But he hardly cared any more. His world had disintegrated. He could not get the last sight of his father out of his mind: dragged away like an animal carcass over the shingle, two deep troughs left in the stones by his feet.

But as the days passed his despair was replaced with the realization that he had to take matters into his own hands.

He had to get to Droprock Island.

Acantha relented somewhat and now only locked his room at night. In fact he had heard her turn the key only half an hour ago, but Rex didn't care. With his skills, and his father's picklock, this was hardly his greatest obstacle. Acantha would be sorry she had dismissed him so easily.

Rex had pondered his father's last cryptic words and actions until the early hours. He was determined to carry out Ambrose's wishes and expose Acantha for what she was. In his mind, she was responsible for his father's death and that made her a murderer. But there could be no more procrastinating. Action was required now. The last time he had failed to take action, Stradigund had invoked the Law of a Hundred Days and look what had happened after that.

Stradigund had been over to the house with more legal papers, but there was no sign of Chapelizod. He had not attended Acantha's meal as Rex had presumed the night his father had returned. In fact it transpired he had not been seen since the breakout at the asylum.

Rex thought again of his father's words. *Don't fly too close to the sun.* He knew the Classical reference, to Daedalus and his son Icarus — his father had read him the story many times. In Greek mythology Daedalus had been an engineer too. Trapped with his son in a maze, he had made wings from feather and wax upon which to escape. Icarus's downfall was to ignore his father's warning. 'Maybe that's what Father meant when he said "*On your head be it*",' murmured Rex. If he didn't do what his father said then he would only have himself to blame. But for what? Suddenly Rex's heart began to race. Of course! Why hadn't he thought of it before? He should fetch the book itself!

The book, however, was downstairs in the library.

Rex listened at his door and, certain no one was coming, he crossed swiftly to the fireplace and splayed his fingers on one of the decorative roundels of wood. He turned it twice and it came away to reveal a small hiding place. He reached in and took out a piece of soft cloth which he spread open on his palm. There lay within its folds two items: a diamond the size of a pea and his father's picklock. These were his father's last gift to him that night on the shore. He had hidden them in his trouser cuff until he was safely home. Presumably the diamond was a source of money – for a bribe perhaps, to pay someone to take him to the island.

And I know exactly what a picklock is for, he thought, and merely seconds later his door was open and he was out on the landing. He knew that at this time of night Acantha would be snoozing in the sitting room in front of the fire, sated after dinner and, no doubt, a few glasses of expensive wine. The library was right next to the study.

Shortly after, Rex stood again between the shelves, scanning the spines. He knew exactly where the book would be. It was a rare first edition that his mother had bought for him when he was a baby and it was kept safe here in the cool atmosphere. Rex ran his hand along the tops of the books, delighting in the smell of old leather and paper, until he came to it: an insignificant-looking slender volume with a soft brown cover.

He left the library but paused at the study door. Decisively he turned the handle and entered. It looked much as it had the last time he came in; all that had changed was the thickness of the layer of dust. There was little here at first sight to help Rex in his quest for answers. He opened both desk drawers; one held envelopes and calling cards, ink and quills; the other some old sketches. He gave them a perfunctory look but lingered upon the last. 'I remember this,' he said softly. 'The Perambulating Submersible. I had no idea Father had drawn it in such detail.' He held it up and saw that Ambrose had sketched in one of Rex's own suggestions. 'I knew it was a good idea,' he said in delight.

Rex took the sketch but as he closed the drawer something rolled and bumped inside. He reached in again to retrieve a small oval-shaped brass object. It was smooth to the touch and most pleasing to the eye. Rex let it rest in his palm.

'The brazen egg,' he said with affection, and put it in his pocket. Then with one last look around the room he left.

Once safely upstairs and locked in again, Rex settled on his bed with the book. He realized that he actually felt a little better now, perhaps because he had a purpose. He turned the book over in his hand. It was wrinkled and creased, grease-stained from when he had fingered it after a piece of pie (his father had been very cross with him for not washing his hands) and the pages were dog-eared. The front cover had a line drawing of Icarus, the winged boy who had flown too close to the sun, and on the back there was a drawing of a labyrinth. The book itself was a compilation of myths and tales of ancient civilizations. He knew the stories well. He looked at the flyleaf and read the inscription.

To darling Rex, from Mother

He turned the pages slowly but by the end he was still uninspired. Perhaps it is just something to treasure, thought Rex, and no more than that. Something to remind me of better times. Of before Acantha.

He shook his head slowly at the thought of the woman. He felt deep disappointment. He had been so sure the book held the answer. But perhaps he was looking in the wrong place.

So he turned his thoughts to the island. It wouldn't be that difficult to get across – there was a ferryman – but as soon as Acantha found out he had gone there she would just come to get him. If he hadn't managed to find the evidence his father had left for him it would all be for nothing. Perhaps he should concentrate instead on finding the elusive Andrew Faye. Certainly Ambrose had bristled at the name. Did *he* hold the key to the puzzle? But how to find him, when he was stuck here in a house full of memories waiting for Acantha to decide his future?

Rex sighed heavily and lay back, more conscious than ever of the ticking of the clock beside him.

17

Departure

While Rex slept in the relative comfort of his bed, on the outskirts of Opum Oppidulum Hildred Buttonquail, a girl similar in age to the troubled boy, was not in quite such an enviable position. She stood on tiptoe on the edge of a rickety covered wagon, clinging to the window ledge with her fingers, peering inside. It was a clear night, and cold, and she would certainly have preferred to have been somewhere else.

It was not easy to see anything much but she could make out the curled-up shape of the man sleeping on the narrow cot opposite the window. His snoring was so stentorian that she could actually feel its vibrations through her fingers. And the man from whose throat and nose the noises emanated was Rudy Idolice.

Twenty minutes or so before Hildred looked in at the window, Rudy had been slumped in a thoughtful muddle in his small wagon, sadly contemplating its faded glory. How had it come to this? His bloodshot eyes swept the compact interior of his wooden home on wheels. Where once there had been silks and satins, now he saw only ragged curtains. Where there had been bright colours and polished wood, now he saw cracked and peeling paint. Evidence of his downfall was everywhere. In the moth-eaten rug, the crooked door swinging on its hinges, the window held in place with string. Rudy shifted on his seat; the cushion was worn through and his scrawny cheeks ached. He grunted and with some difficulty stood to look at himself in the cracked mirror. Its decorative gesso edge was chipped and the gold leaf was long gone.

Rudy Idolice was a man who was always on the verge of something. Unfortunately, on account of his love of whisky, it was never obvious exactly what that something might be.

I am as dilapidated as my wagon, he thought.

He brought a bottle to his lips and felt at the back of his throat the burning consolation. But even that feeling was only half what it used to be. 'Where did it all go wrong?' he asked himself, and as is often the case the answer was staring him right in the face. On the floor there was a crumpled flyer stating boldly:

RUDY IDOLICE'S PEREGRINATING PANOPTICON OF WONDERS

Perhaps things'll be better in the next town, he thought, as he did almost every evening at this time. 'Opum Oppidulum,' he said out loud, and he felt a small surge of hope rise in his stomach. 'We'll set off tomorrow at sunrise.'

Now he had a plan he felt better and went to lie on the narrow shelf that acted as a bed and began to snore. He missed, as a result, Hildred's face at the window. And by choosing to snooze Rudy inadvertently set his life on a very different path. Such is the nature of Lady Luck, ever fickle, always unpredictable.

Hildred dropped lightly to the ground and ran in an odd, loose-legged fashion across to another wagon, similar in size to Rudy's and in no better condition. She took the steps in one bound and opened the door to enter the dim and cramped interior, where every available inch of standing room or sitting surface was taken by the crew of travelling performers before her. Undeterred, she squeezed herself into a narrow space on top of a cupboard. If you hadn't seen her there you would have thought it impossible for a person to fit.

'Well?' asked a deep voice.

'Guess what he's up to,' said Hildred.

'Asleep,' rejoined a chorus of voices.

At the other end of the wagon sat the stout owner of the deep voice, sporting a rather thick, luxurious beard through which she ran her fingers, picking out crumbs and occasionally larger morsels of food. When she thought no one was looking she popped them quickly into her mouth. Barbata, the Bearded Beauty – for she was a lady – let nothing go to waste.

Beside her, eyeing the veritable cornucopia of a beard,

half sat, half stood Stanley. He always found it difficult to get comfortable owing to his third leg (a fully functioning appendage). As part of his act he tap-danced with two legs while resting on the third. 'If there was money to be made from snoring Rudy could have retired years ago,' he commented wryly.

'We could all have retired,' said someone else soberly. 'That is exactly the problem. We will be working into our graves while Rudy slumbers on his cot.'

This particular speaker sat near the door. He stood out from the rest of the occupants of the wagon on account of the fact that he appeared to have no physical attributes that might cause a person stop and stare. He was tall, broad-shouldered and muscular. His hair, cut in a classical Roman style, was short and curly, like a shorn sheep, and he sported a soft blonde beard cut close to the chin. Hildred smiled. You could always rely on Mr Ephcott, the only surviving 'centaur' in the world (obviously he was not in his costume right now, which consisted simply of the back end of a horse), to get to the point.

Of all the players in Rudy's show, Mr Ephcott was the most educated. Knowledgeable and well-spoken, he had an ardent fan-base of wealthy ladies. He could talk to them on exactly their level. In fact he could talk several levels above them but his real charm, apart from his deliciously hairy chest, was to make them appear clever. The ladies' husbands were not quite so enamoured of him. It seemed a little odd to them that their wives would pay money to address a bare-chested fellow, but of course, as the ladies insisted loudly, 'He is not a fellow, he is a horse!' And that seemed to settle the matter.

'Friends,' said Mr Ephcott grimly, 'we are here to make a decision. Are we staying with Rudy, to watch the show fall apart and to see what little money we take drunk away? Or are we to cut loose and make our own way in life? There are other travelling shows out there we could join. We're professionals, after all. It's Rudy has let us down. What do you say?'

'Very well,' said another man in the centre of the caravan (he had two heads). 'Both Bob and I agree that Mr Ephcott here is right.' This pronouncement was a great surprise to the listeners: each head had a completely different personality and rarely agreed on any matter. 'We say the time has come to act. Let's go to Rudy, demand what we're owed and leave.'

Hildred smiled wryly and looked around the wagon. Here were all her friends, the people who had looked after her for as long as she could remember. Barbata had always been very kind to her, even when she had pulled her beard. And then there was Matilda, the lady who could bite her own elbow (right now she was sitting quite happily on her hands) – she had treated her as her own. And across from her sat Billy and Rosalyn Dunnet (pronounced 'Doonay': they claimed French ancestry), watching with pride their quadruplets – Lucy, Rebecca, Aina and Tobias – practising outside in the twilight for the next show. Billed as 'The Most Daring Quartet of Quirt Wielders and Whip Crackers' (a quirt, of course, being a whip with a leather thong at one end), what those four could do with whips and quirts would make your eyes water!

Hildred knew she would miss them all, but none more so than Mr Ephcott. This gentle and charming man had taken her under his wing when her father absconded after her mother's fatal accident. He had taught her, with great patience, not only to read and to write but also a thousand other things that he said would one day be useful when she had to go out into the real world.

And now that time had come. Rudy had been given chance after chance but this was the end of the line. The proposal was put to the vote and in Rudy's absence it was unanimously decided that the travelling show was to disband.

'I suppose we won't be going to Opum Oppidulum now,' said Hildred ruefully as she and Mr Ephcott watched the downcast group disperse to their wagons.

'Don't worry, Hildred,' he said gently. 'You will survive. You are talented and smart. You can leave without any guilt at all. Why not come with me to Urbs Umida? I believe it's the sort of place that would greatly enjoy acts such as yours and mine. This is not the end for you, but the beginning.'

Hildred smiled wryly. 'I know, but I cannot help feeling sorry for Rudy. In his own way he has been good to me all these years.'

Mr Ephcott looked her straight in the eye. 'Hildred, you owe Rudy nothing,' he said solemnly. 'You have worked for years in the show, and paid your way.'

Hildred frowned. This life, with the travelling Panopticon, was all she had ever known and the motley players were the closest thing to a family she possessed. But there were other matters to consider. She took a deep breath.

'I don't want to perform any more. After all, you have furnished me with an excellent education, better I dare say than any schoolroom, and I would like to put it to good use. Perhaps I could be a governess or a tutor in a house that does not move from place to place. And I do not wish to be stared at any longer. I think I will go on to Opum Oppidulum after all.'

Mr Ephcott paled. 'You wish to tutor in Opum Oppidulum? Hildred, are you sure that's the only reason? Better let sleeping dogs lie, don't you think?'

Hildred shook her head. 'I want to go. It's important to me – to find out about my real family.' She looked at Mr Ephcott's downcast face and gasped. 'Oh, I'm so sorry,' she said. 'I didn't mean it to sound like that.'

'I know,' said Mr Ephcott. 'I – we – have all done our best, but it's not the same.' He laughed lightly. 'And I also know that once you have made up your mind you will not be swayed. It's not a bad place, Opum Oppidulum, certainly better than Urbs Umida. I believe Lake Beluarum is a sight to behold. The deepest, coldest lake known to man. It is not so far, but winter is approaching. You will need strength and stamina.'

'I have plenty of that,' said Hildred.

'Well, if you will go,' he chided, 'at least let me give you something to help you on your way.' He handed her a small purse heavy with coins.

'I can't take that!' protested Hildred.

Mr Ephcott was also difficult to dissuade from his purpose. 'You must, for my peace of mind,' he insisted. 'I feel partly responsible for your decision. You are very special to me, Hildred,' he said softly, 'and I know it's not always as easy for you as it is for others, but you have overcome much adversity. I couldn't bear it if anything happened to you for lack of something as simple as money.'

So Hildred took the purse and thanked him and gave him a long hug. He was smiling but Hildred could feel that he was shaking.

'I will never forget you,' she said with a small sob.

'Hildred, my dear,' he said kindly. 'I know you will do well wherever you go. How could you not, for I have taught you everything you know!'

18

A Letter to Dr Tibor Velhildegildus

Dr Tibor Velhildegildus relaxed in the luxurious surroundings of his top-floor room in the best lodging house in Opum Oppidulum, all compliments of the town's grateful councillors. He was enjoying his celebrity status as the pioneer of the Lodestone Procedure.

It was about a week since his meeting with the malodorous and dentally challenged Hooper Hopcroft, and he fanned himself with the letter in his hand as if to wave away any lingering smell. The letter was just one of many that had been delivered to his room since his arrival some days ago, but this one was slightly different.

My dear Dr Velhildegildus,
I hope you will forgive my being so forward in
writing to you in this way. I am sure that many
others have already imposed upon your time since
your arrival in our good town, but I beseech you to

spare a few moments to read what I have to say.

My name is Acantha Grammaticus (recently widowed) and I am a resident here in Opum Oppidulum. I have a stepson, Rex, and it is he who concerns me. I have heard (who has not!) that you are a noteworthy Doctor of the Mind, and that your Lodestone Procedure is hailed as miraculous. I believe that my stepson might benefit from your attention.

Since the death of his father, Rex has been acting most peculiarly. He refuses to speak to me, is secretive and shuts himself away in his room. He is destructive – in a fit of childish rage he destroyed many of his father's models – and I know that he blames me for many things that are not my fault – the death of his father, for example – but I cannot make him see this. The situation has become unbearable. I wish to send him away to school in the near future: he is at an age when he needs the discipline of such an institution, but my concern is that once away from the house and the care he receives within its walls (for which he shows no gratitude), he might deteriorate further.

It is possible that you already know that Rex's father, Ambrose Grammaticus, spent the last few months of his life locked up in Droprock Asylum, the very same asylum over which you are to assume control. Naturally, I worry that young Rex is to go the same way, madness, as you are aware, being inherited in many cases. I am grateful that I, not being a blood relative, am wholly immune from any familial anomalies or mental feebleness.

Recently, without my knowledge and wholly against my wishes, Rex's father visited with him very shortly before his death. I am certain that he said something to turn Rex against me. As you can imagine, as a loving stepmother it is heartbreaking to be shunned by the boy whom I consider in so many ways my own flesh and blood. But my only concern is for him. I could bear the pain he inflicts, and indeed forgive him for it, if I knew that there was a cure for his ills.

My question is this: do you suppose that your Lodestone Procedure might be a treatment suited to dear young Rex? I understand that under its influence patients reveal their deepest troubles, thus bringing about peace of mind. Perhaps you could persuade Rex to reveal exactly what it was his father said to him before he died. At least then I would be able to rebut any unjust accusations and demonstrate that I am not the monster he made me out to be (for I am certain his father said terrible things about me – he was completely insane in the end) and then Rex could go off to school untroubled by mental stresses.

Dr Velhildegildus, I throw myself upon your mercy. Help me in my hour of need!

With my warmest wishes,

F.E.HIGGINS

Acantha Grammaticus (Mrs)

Postscript: I will pay, naturally, for your services.

Tibor looked thoughtful. Under normal circumstances he would decline to help; he had many such begging letters but this one was different. Firstly (lastly, to be precise) the lady had offered to pay (this was highly unusual) and, secondly, there was the matter of her name – Grammaticus: now a surname of great interest to Tibor.

He sat back in his chair and played his fingers on the desktop. Something was going on here, a chain of events set in motion, surely, by Fate. Well, if Fate wished to direct his actions, then he wasn't going to ignore Her! So he took out a piece of paper and began to write.

My dear Mrs Grammaticus,
I was intrigued by your letter . . .

19

Article from

𝕿𝖍𝖊 𝕺𝖕𝖚𝖒 𝕺𝖕𝖕𝖎𝖉𝖚𝖑𝖚𝖒 𝕳𝖊𝖇𝖉𝖔𝖒𝖆𝖉𝖆𝖑

AN INTERVIEW WITH
DR TIBOR VELHILDEGILDUS

by
Cecil Notwithstanding

Well, this autumn month draws to an end and the full moon approaches, bringing with it the prospect of Madman's Tide. Yet another lunatic's body has washed up on the lake shore and the whereabouts of Mr Camus Chapelizod remain unknown.

Let us not dwell on that, but instead on the welcome news that the town council has recently secured as superintendent of the asylum the renowned Dr Tibor Velhildegildus. For many years now Dr Velhildegildus has run a very successful practice in Urbs Umida dealing with those who suffer in-stabilities of the mind. His arrival marks a return to more humane practices in the care of the feeble minded as was once commonplace in Droprock Asylum.

I met with Dr Tibor Vel-hildegildus recently in his lodging house and our con-versation is detailed below.

Cecil Notwithstanding *Wel-come, Dr Velhildegildus, to the lakeside town of Opum Oppidulum. Tell me, what methodologies in particular do you practise when deal-ing with those afflicted by diseases of the mind?*

Dr Velhildegildus I believe it is vital to have a whole range of tools at your disposal, and never more so than when dealing with infirm mentali-ties. I am a highly qualified medical doctor with degrees from all the great educational institutions, but my specific skill lies in the treatment of those whose minds are ill at ease as is evidenced by my many triumphs. I recently certified sane a man who had been considered mad for many years.

CN *I have heard that you use magnetite in your treat-ments. This is a relatively new development, is it not?*

Dr V Indeed it is. I call it the 'Lodestone Proce-dure'. To be specific, it is a method whereby I am able to bring great comfort to those who find it difficult to deal with daily life. With the Lodestone Procedure I balance the negative and positive humours in the body and restore equilibrium to troubled minds. *Mens sana in corpore sano*, as they say.

CN *Ah yes, 'a healthy mind in a healthy body'. Is it true with this procedure that you can actually control the mind of your patient?*

110

Dr V Man has free will and chooses his path in life, but certainly with this technique I can tap into the deep recesses of the troubled mind and draw out the true nature of a person. This is vital if I am to suggest to them how best to address their problems.

CN *Fascinating, Dr Velhildegildus, but what of the asylum itself? How long will it be before you can admit patients again?*

Dr V Renovating the asylum is my highest priority. I wish to create a pleasant and soothing atmosphere in which to treat the future inmates.

CN *Doubtless the citizens will be grateful for that! Now I wonder, are you aware of the stories that are associated with the asylum and the lake?*

Dr V *(laughs slightly)* No doubt you refer to the ghost in the maze of catacombs and the monster in Lake Beluarum. I am a man of science, and I do not believe in ghosts. As for the creature in the water, I am neither a sailor nor a fisherman so I think I will be safe.

CN *Many thanks, Dr Velhildegildus.*

Dr V No, thank you!

Well, dear readers, what an honourable and wonderful man! How fortunate we are to have him in charge of the asylum, and we look forward to a long and happy relationship with him.

Now on to my investigation into the ongoing problem of beggars.

Tibor smiled a crooked smile and laid down the *Hebdomadal*. That should keep the nosy parkers away from the island for long enough. He looked again at the diagram for the Perambulating Submersible. He had spent a good few hours copying it out on to decent paper. The original was falling apart and the ink, some odd concoction, certainly of poor quality, was fading. The more he studied it the more he thought it could be done. Imagine! To be the man who built a full-sized working underwater vessel! He would be famous and rich. And what better place to build it than in an empty asylum reached only by a small boat. No one would possibly suspect. And then there were the diamonds. It was almost too much luck! Even the two small ones he had from Hooper (strictly speaking, one belonged to Melvyn Halibutte) were worth a small fortune. Either way, how could he lose? As for the lunatics? Let their families deal with them for once.

He pulled out his pocket watch. Just enough time to polish the Lodestone before the arrival of Mrs Grammaticus.

20

The Lodestone Procedure

From the street below Rex heard hoofs, followed shortly by the sound of knocking at the front door. Subsequently, footsteps on the stairs warned him of Acantha's approach. She was heavy-footed these days. Since dispensing with Ambrose she had been living well and was rapidly gaining in girth. In fact her swollen face was barely recognizable as the dainty young lady his father had married.

Rex counted the steps. Same number every time. The housemaid did it in half as many again, always rushing along like a sparrow. But with Acantha it was a solid thud, thud, thud. There was no knock – she just came straight in. She was wearing her best cloak and Rex could see that she had rouged her face and applied some sort of scarlet lipsalve. Hardly for my benefit, he thought.

'Fetch your coat,' she snarled. 'We've got an appointment.'

✳

Not long after, Rex found himself standing in the plush entrance hall of Walton House, the finest lodging rooms in Opum Oppidulum.

We must be here to see someone important, he thought.

Acantha rang the bell on the desk and a man in a black suit came out from the back room and gave her a lifeless smile.

'My name is Acantha Grammaticus. We are expected by the doctor.'

Doctor? Am I here for a cure? wondered Rex.

'Allow me to escort you to his rooms,' said the man. 'He has taken the top floor.'

Acantha was huffing and puffing after only a few stairs and their diplomatic escort slowed his pace to accommodate her. It struck Rex as they made their way up that if someone could invent some sort of pulling platform to 'lift' them from street level to the top of the building, it would save a lot of time and effort. Or perhaps moving stairs. Was that possible?

'Anything is possible,' he murmured, and made a mental note to think on it further when he had the opportunity.

Finally they reached the top landing and came to a door upon which their helpful guide knocked smartly. The door opened and Rex and Acantha stepped into a luxurious room. A man was sitting in a chair by the window and he looked up at their entrance. Rex's heart sank. He knew who this was – though only from his glasses: the sketch in the *Hebdomadal* was far too flattering to be accurate. This was the mind doctor, the expert who had come to take over the asylum.

Was he, Rex Grammaticus, to be declared insane too?

Rex looked long and hard at the doctor. He was a tall man, with thick dark hair beautifully smoothed back over his square-jawed, tetragonocephalic head. His wire-rimmed spectacles gave him a peculiarly piercing stare through the lenses. Although the bridge of his nose was broad, the tip tapered delicately to a point. He wore a moustache but was clean-shaven on the chin. He stood stiffly with one arm by his side and a hand on his hip.

Tibor for his part was staring at Acantha, apparently transfixed by her; then he seemed to come to life and he smiled. But it was an odd sort of smile. Whereas a smile would usually change someone's countenance markedly, a smile on this man's face seemed to make little difference to his appearance at all. He was the sort of fellow whose thoughts one could only guess at, for his face gave nothing away.

'Welcome,' he said in a voice that somehow made one feel instantly and totally at ease. Rex thought it sounded like a soft paintbrush on a fresh canvas. Dr Velhildegildus took Acantha's hand and kissed it.

She flushed, ever so slightly. 'I am Acantha Grammaticus,' she said with a simper.

Rex gritted his teeth. He hated to hear her lay claim to his family name. Now that his father was gone, he thought she should relinquish it.

'Acantha,' repeated Tibor with a smile. 'My, what a delightful name you have.' He inhaled and then dropped her hand. 'Might I say how deliciously aromatic you are?'

115

'Dr Velhildegildus,' exhaled Acantha. 'You don't look at all like your picture. I am just so pleased to meet you. We have all heard so much about you.' It was true. Everyone knew about the marvellous Dr Tibor Velhildegildus. He was the talk of the town and the toast of the *Hebdomadal*. Despite his fears, undeniably Rex was as intrigued as everyone else to meet him.

There was an awkward silence as the two adults just looked intently at each other. It was Tibor who broke the spell. 'Thank you again for your letter,' he said. 'It was most interesting to me. Now that I have met you, I sincerely hope I can help you.' He turned to Rex. 'You must be Rex.'

Rex held out his hand dutifully. He was not surprised to find that the fellow's hand was cold. He had that look in his eye, like a dead fish, but his words ran like syrup from a dripper.

'So, my young fellow, what do you know of me?'

'No more than I have read in the *Hebdomadal*,' replied Rex, not quite as coldly as he had wished. He was not immune to Tibor's charms either.

'Probably for the best,' said Dr Velhildegildus smoothly. 'I find if a client has too much information it can affect the Procedure.'

Rex's eyes widened. Procedure?

Dr Velhildegildus looked at Acantha with a smile and yet an expression of sincere concern. 'I am afraid, my dear Acantha, in order to achieve maximum effect, I am going to have to ask you to leave. Your very presence could have undue influence. But do not worry, we can have a full and frank discussion afterwards.'

Rex thought Acantha might object but surprisingly she acquiesced. 'I look forward to it, Doctor,' she said, and went compliantly into the adjoining room. Rex had already gleaned that Tibor Velhildegildus was a very persuasive sort of fellow. Now the two of them were alone.

'Well, Rex,' said Tibor, steering him to the couch. 'Please, make yourself comfortable.'

Rex did as he was told, now wholly under the spell of Tibor's mellifluous tones, and lay back on the couch. Dr Velhildegildus turned down the lamps and in the semi-darkness Rex watched him draw a chair up to the couch and sit down. He felt a hand on his shoulder.

'Relax, my dear boy,' soothed Tibor. 'I can sense that you are nervous but this is all for your own good. Do you know why you are here?'

Rex shook his head.

'Your stepmother is concerned for your well-being. She informs me that you have been very upset since the dreadful death of your father.'

Acantha was concerned for him? Since when! This must be some sort of trick. Rex tried to sit up but Dr Velhildegildus pushed him back gently.

'We were very close,' said Rex, and suddenly, inexplicably, he felt tearful. 'I saw him dragged away by the constables.'

'Don't worry,' murmured Dr Velhildegildus. His voice made you think of velvet; it had the same quality to the ear as to the touch. 'I am here to help you to make sense of the things that have happened to you, but you must relax.'

Make sense of it all? Was that even possible? Rex had the feeling that Dr Velhildegildus was taking in everything, watching his every move, and he made up his mind not to utter another word without first making sure it gave nothing away. But as soon as Tibor spoke his resolve seemed to melt away.

'I am going to put you in a state of extreme calm,' he crooned, 'and then I am going to ask you some questions. It is possible that painful memories will be brought to the surface but I will help you to deal with them. All you have to do is watch and listen.'

Dr Velhildegildus reached into his breast pocket and took out what appeared to be some sort of stone on a silver chain. It was shaped like a disc and dark in colour and it twinkled. He held the end of the chain in his right hand leaving the disc to swing on about six inches of chain.

'What's that?' asked Rex.

'My patented Lodestone,' said Dr Velhildegildus softly. 'A disc of solid magnetite. Its qualities of attraction will help to harmonize all the volatile fluids in your body and bring you to a state of calm.' He leaned forward and stared intensely into Rex's eyes.

'Am I to fall asleep?' asked Rex.

'Not asleep, you will still be aware, but on another level of consciousness.'

With a slight movement of his hand Dr Velhildegildus caused the Lodestone to move. Slowly, slowly, it began to swing across Rex's line of vision, right to left, left to right, right to left, along a steady arc.

'Now, Rex,' he whispered. 'Keep your eyes on the Lodestone and empty your mind.'

Rex tracked the movement of the dark disc from side to side. He actually found it comforting. The tension eased in his body and he succumbed to a wonderful feeling of calm. All his troubles were draining away. As instructed he began to empty his mind of all thoughts. In truth it would be a relief not to think any more. One by one he cast them out: his fears, his dreams, his worries, his suspicions, his terror. Rex began to enjoy the absolute emptiness of his mind.

All the time Dr Velhildegildus was speaking in a low, soothing monotone. 'Try to imagine that the inside of your head is filled with a light white gas that floats around in gentle swirls.'

Rex did just that and found the sensation most pleasing.

'Now,' continued Dr Velhildegildus, 'tell me about your childhood.'

Immediately images of his father crowded into the space inside his head. 'I was happy,' said Rex. 'All the time. My mother died when I was an infant, but Father and I, we did everything together. We used to make things, he was an engineer,' he said proudly. 'He built bridges and houses. All sorts of things. And he taught me everything he knew. I can build anything.'

Velhildegildus's right eyebrow lifted very slightly at Rex's claim.

'I sense that something changed.'

Rex screwed up his face. 'Acantha,' he said. 'Father married her, even though he knew I did not wish it. She was only after his money.' Then he leaned up on one elbow and said in a conspiratorial whisper. 'Acantha smells; she smells strange.'

'Calm yourself,' said Velhildegildus, and Rex suddenly had the sensation of soft cream running all over his skin. 'Tell me what happened before your father was sent to the asylum.'

'He went berserk,' said Rex. 'One minute he was eating his dinner and the next he was attacking me. Acantha had him off to the asylum before anyone had a chance to find out what was really wrong.'

'But he came back?'

'He escaped, somehow, when the lunatics took over the asylum. And he had a hook in place of his hand, a dreadful-looking thing. And we went somewhere but I don't know where. I fell asleep. He gave me a diamond.'

'A diamond?' murmured Velhildegildus before he could help himself.

'Yes,' continued Rex. 'And he said, "*On your head be it.*" I think it was a warning to me, to do something, and that I might be in trouble if didn't.'

'What do you think he wants you to do?'

'He said to go to Droprock Island and he told me not to fly too close to the sun.'

'What did he mean by that?'

'I think he means one of my favourite stories, a myth about Daedalus and his son Icarus.'

'Ah, yes, I know of it,' said Dr Velhildegildus. 'Do you think your father wants you to make wings?'

'I don't know,' said Rex. 'I just don't know.'

Tibor was silent and he allowed the Lodestone to slow gradually. Then he waved the flat of his hand across Rex's eyes and back again and finished with a smart clap. Rex opened his eyes.

'Dr Velhildegildus,' he said in surprise. 'How did I do?'

Tibor smiled. 'You did very well indeed, Rex, very well indeed.'

21

A Boating Trip

'Oh, fingerknots!' exclaimed Hildred Buttonquail as she stumbled. 'What on earth!'

She looked down to her feet and her hand went to her mouth involuntarily. She felt slightly ill. And not without good reason. The cause of her near tumble was right there touching the toes of her laced-up boots.

A drenched and lifeless body.

'Oh, dear,' she murmured. Carefully she hooked her foot under the sodden mass and turned it over – it was not difficult, its being merely a bundle of bones and rags – to stare into the dull eyes of a dead man. At least he suffers no longer, she thought.

There was nothing she could do so she said a silent prayer and continued on her way along the misty shingle shore of Lake Beluarum. When the body was well behind her she chose a sheltered spot, a dip in the shore, and sat down to enjoy her last piece of bread and a boiled egg. It had taken longer than she'd thought to bid farewell to all of her friends at the Panopticon and she hadn't left until after lunch. Mr Ephcott had accompanied her as far as the rim of the Porridge Bowl and she was grateful for that much, but it had taken the rest of the afternoon to descend to the lake. Already it was twilight and being so deep in this natural bowl, she guessed that night would fall quickly. She was glad to see the outline of Opum Oppidulum ahead in the foggy distance.

Hildred pulled her cloak tight, raised her hood and brushed down her front. She thought of Barbata; she would not have discarded the crumbs so quickly! She scrunched up her toes a few times in an attempt to get the blood flowing again. Her feet were blistered and her bones ached. She looked towards the town. The large houses overlooking the shore were hardly the sort that would take kindly to someone knocking on the door looking for work. Tonight she would have to spend some of her money on lodgings.

She walked to the water's edge, enjoying the feel of the shifting shingle beneath her feet. She could hardly see more than a few yards across the lake before the mist became so thick as to be an impenetrable wall. She wondered if the water was safe to drink. She cupped her hands and dipped them in and gasped at how cold it was.

To her right the shore curved away until it met with a sheer cliff that stretched for what seemed like miles. There was nowhere to go in that direction. With a resigned sigh she trudged off towards the town. As she got closer the fog lifted somewhat and she saw a small wooden jetty and a boat bobbing alongside. Then she gave a little gasp of fright. A man, hunched over, was sitting on the jetty dangling his legs over the side.

'Hello there,' he called, looking up. 'What are you doing out on such a cold and foggy evening?'

Hildred's instinct was to run but she resisted. This fellow might be able to help her. As if sensing her hesitation the man reached for the lantern beside him and held it up. Now she could see his face properly. He was old, his head was very small, almost too small for his body, but his eyes were bright, and lively.

'Don't mind me,' he said. 'I mean you no harm. Stay where you are if it makes you feel safer.'

'Who are you?' asked Hildred boldly. Mr Ephcott had always told her to be brave and confident no matter how she felt inside. The man straightened and looked directly at Hildred.

'Why, I'm Walter Freakley,' he said proudly. 'I'm the ferryman.'

'Ferryman?' repeated Hildred.

'I go to Droprock Island,' he said, gesturing out to the middle of the lake. 'You can't see it now, and sometimes you can't even see it in the day. There's a mist comes and goes on that lake that's as thick as a Mrs Runcible's pea soup. But if you're lucky tomorrow it might be clear.'

'I hear the lake is very big,' said Hildred, and the boatman laughed.

'It's enormous,' he said. 'I mean, it's so wide you can't see the other shore even on a good day. And they say it is so deep that it would take a month to reach the bottom. That is if you were even able to get there.'

'Perhaps in the right sort of vessel,' suggested Hildred with inadvertent prescience.

'Whatever the vessel, you'd never make it,' said Walter firmly. 'You'd be eaten before you knew it.'

'By what creature?'

'A monster,' said Walter, 'of proportions unknown to man.'

He pursed his lips and began to whistle – a piercing, high-pitched, repetitive tune that Hildred didn't recognize . . . but there was something oddly enticing about it. He stopped and spoke again.

'So, my dear. You haven't even told me your name, let alone your purpose. It's not many young 'uns come to this place without a very good reason.'

Hildred regarded Walter with a practised eye. Was this a man she could trust? 'Well, I recently left a position I held for many years, to seek a different life.'

'Were you in service?'

'Oh no,' said Hildred. 'I hope to be a tutor. But to be honest, Mr Freakley,' she confessed, 'tonight I need somewhere to stay, then I can consider a job.'

'You need no more than many,' said Walter drily. 'Well, perhaps your luck is in. After all, as soon as the asylum is back to rights—'

'You mean the asylum on the island?' interrupted Hildred.

'You've heard of it?'

'Oh yes. Opum Oppidulum is well known for it.'

'Well, I'm sure Mrs Runcible would be grateful to have some help over there. She's a marvel, that woman, does everything; cooking, cleaning. She could use an extra pair of hands. She was only saying the other day it's too much for one.'

'You would help me?'

'Why not?' said Walter kindly. He stood up and Hildred could see that he was only just as tall as she was. He stepped down into the boat and it rocked violently on the water. He seemed not to notice. 'Hop in,' he said, 'and I'll take you over. I'm expected for supper anyhows.'

Hildred only hesitated a moment before jumping into the boat. Nothing ventured, she thought, and took her seat opposite Walter.

Walter began to row and now that she was so close to him Hildred could see that he had a small snake tattoo on his neck. His face was deeply lined, so deep in fact that there was dust in the cracks. He was smiling to himself. 'It's my greatest pleasure to row,' he said absent-mindedly.

Walter rowed with even pulls, his strength belying his age, and the boat progressed quickly across the glassy water. It was only a matter of minutes before they were in the midst of the fog and Hildred could no longer see the shore. Neither could she see where they were heading. Walter was whistling again, that same eerie tune, and it seemed to her that the fog echoed it. Her feet crunched something on the floor of the boat and she noticed a chain under Walter's seat. Walter saw her looking. In the shifting mist his face had taken on a spectral quality and she watched his lips as he spoke.

'Gotta chain the boat up sometimes,' he explained. 'In case it's stolen.'

'What about the monster?'

'It's *in* the water, and we're *on* the water. We'll be safe enough.' He resumed his disjointed, haunting whistle and as an accompaniment she could feel the oars bumping against their rests.

'What did you mean when you said the asylum was back to rights?' asked Hildred after a while.

'Well,' said Walter, 'it's like this. When people is locked up for long enough they wants to escape. You know, like an animal that needs to be free, and the time came when the people—'

'The patients?' suggested Hildred.

Walter shrugged. 'Call 'em what you like, they wanted to be free and they escaped. I took a few of 'em ashore, the more sensible ones. The others, well, they tried to swim to Opum Oppidulum and of course they drowned. The water is too cold. You couldn't survive more than a minute or two.'

'I saw a body on the beach,' said Hildred, and Walter shook his head sadly.

'Some people, you just can't tell 'em.'

'Who was supposed to be in charge? Were they not being looked after?'

'A man called Mr Chapelizod was the superintendent, but he was a nasty piece of work. Subjected them poor fellas to all sorts of terrible treatment – bloodletting, torture, beatings. 'E 'ad 'em chained up all day and night. It weren't right what he was doing to them poor souls. Some of 'em weren't even mad. Just stuck in there by their families who didn't want nowt to do with them any more. Still, this new fellow, Dr Velhildegildus, sounds a fair enough man. He's due over tomorrow. We'll give him a chance.'

'What about Chapelizod?'

'No one knows where he is,' said Walter, 'and no one cares.' The boat seemed to rise on a swell but Walter was unperturbed. He began to whistle again and the mournful tune echoed all around them in the mist.

22

Thoughts of the Monstrous Creature

Way down in the darkest depths of the lake, a distance off-shore, the monster sensed that there was something in the water overhead. It had heard these noises before, and recently more and more often. They did not disturb it but they did arouse its curiosity.

The creature, a primitive teratoid, glided smoothly through the numbingly cold waters of Lake Beluarum. It might have lacked the senses of a more evolved fish, if fish it even was, but it could still feel the water against its glittering scaly outer flesh and the sensation was pleasing to it. It used its two huge front flippers, each with six webbed and clawed toes, to propel itself lazily along. Its rear flippers hung motionless out behind it. Three eyes, the largest on the top of its lumpy head, and one on either side, gave it almost 360-degree vision. They were huge, as was normal with creatures that spent their lives in tenebrous depths. Despite the darkness, it could still make out shadows on the surface above. It knew this particular shadow well: longer than a fish, even the biggest fish in the lake. It had two flippers — at least that's what they looked like to the creature's rather limited imagination — dipping in and out of the water, propelling it along. Perhaps it was another one of those strange creatures, the ones that flailed about making odd noises. They had been tasty, a welcome change from its usual diet of deep-living dwellers.

It went to investigate.

As it swam to the surface a solitary fish came into view — *Salpa salpa* a scientist would later name it — and within a split second the creature had flicked out one of its many suckered tentacles, wrapped it around the fish and reeled it back into its cavernous mouth. Five rows of serrated razor-sharp teeth sawed at the fish and the creature shivered with delight as the blood washed over its palate and the shredded flesh was drawn down the back of its throat on its way to its enormous belly. It had an odd taste and for a while after eating it the creature felt slightly out of sorts, but in an enjoyable way.

Satisfied for the moment, the creature turned its attention once more to the shadow above. But as it swam closer it was distracted by another sound, a tuneful pentatonic call. The sound was pleasing to the creature and by quickly pressing its huge tongue against the roof of its mouth and then releasing it, it echoed the tune back up through the water. Soothed by the music, it rested its fins and allowed itself to sink slowly back down. It had lost the urge to hunt. It would look again another day. Besides, the numerous parasites in its skin were beginning to feed and the creature was starting to feel unbearably itchy. It knew where to go to get relief so it tipped up and headed, with instinctive purposeful intent, nose down towards the bottom of the lake where recently a large fissure had burst open in the lake bed, spewing forth strong gases and glittering stones.

23

The Third Party

Locked in his room again, Rex stood by the window, rolling over and over in his hand the brazen egg he had taken from his father's study. It was in fact a small brass prototype that he and his father had been working on before his life had become so complicated. His eyes were drawn as ever to Droprock Island where the asylum rose above the mist in the distance. The light in the upper window was on intermittently but since the breakout had been discovered the rest of the asylum remained in darkness.

Rex still felt a little odd from the Lodestone Procedure the previous day. He could hardly remember what he had talked about while on the couch. Afterwards, as he lay there in a sort of daze, Acantha had returned to the room and she and Dr Velhildegildus had spoken in hushed tones. He heard brief snatches of their conversation; they were talking about him, but he also heard mention of someone called Meredith. He noted that they seemed very much at ease with one other, laughing softly as they discussed his fate.

'And you intend to send him off to school?' asked Dr Velhildegildus.

Acantha nodded. 'Next week,' she replied. 'I can't think what else to do.'

'Well,' mused Tibor. 'I think I might have a solution to the problem that will benefit both of us.' He looked over at Rex and then ushered Acantha back into the adjoining room and Rex heard no more. When they had eventually returned home Rex had been overwhelmed with fatigue and had slept like a log all night for the first time in weeks. Now, however, he was making plans of his own. Whatever scheme Dr Velhildegildus and Acantha were cooking up, he wanted no part of it. Acantha was busy tonight – she was having another one of her suppers – and as soon as the guests arrived he was going to take off. He had decided to take a chance and go to the asylum. He would find what his father had left and take it to Cecil Notwithstanding. After that? Well, he wasn't entirely sure. He might not be able to stay in Opum Oppidulum. But he would cross that bridge when he came to it.

Earlier there had been another delivery from the butcher and in the last half-hour the cook, the housekeeper, the maid and the bootboy all left together to enjoy a free evening. As the time of his departure drew near, Rex's excitement and fear grew in equal measure.

Just then two carriages arrived in quick succession; from the first stepped Mr Stradigund – Rex would recognize

133

that stoop anywhere — but from the second a dark-cloaked stranger emerged. Hmm, wondered Rex. Could this be Andrew Faye? The man who held a vital piece to the puzzle of his father's madness; the man who linked Acantha with her conspirators. This might be his last opportunity to find out more about him. If he could perhaps talk to him somehow, ask him about his father, maybe he could shed some light on the whole mystery.

I think perhaps I should take a look, thought Rex.

Acantha still had no idea about his picklock, and what great pleasure it gave him to know something that she didn't! It was only a matter of moments before he was down in the hallway. He could hear his stepmother and her guests below in the kitchen. The aroma of something meaty and delicious came wafting up towards him. Rex crept down the stairs and along the narrow hall that led to the kitchen. He drew up at the door, which was slightly ajar, and stood quietly in the shadows.

Rex had always thought Acantha's supper nights rather unusual, but then he also knew not to expect the ordinary from his stepmother. It was an eerie scene upon which he gazed. The low-ceilinged room was lit by one large candelabrum in the centre of the table, holding six tall candles. Three places were set, each laid with the best silver and crystal and a shallow but capacious dish. Stradigund was already seated while Acantha was busy at the stove. The third member of the party was just out of sight. Rex could see only the tips of his shoes, polished and pointed. Step forward, Mr Faye, urged Rex silently. Come into the light! But he remained tantalizingly out of view.

Acantha was tending to a huge black pot, stirring its contents around and around. 'My, my,' she said, turning to her companions with a smile, 'I think I have surpassed myself this time.'

The pointed shoes made their move.

Yes, thought Rex, at last!

And there stepped into view none other than Tibor Velhildegildus. A smile crossed his wide face. He leaned over the pot and sniffed deeply; his eyes were shining and saliva glistened on his lips.

Dr Velhildegildus! thought Rex, completely taken aback. He was both surprised and disappointed. He had been so sure it was Andrew Faye.

'Dr Velhildegildus, you will find that Acantha is an excellent cook,' said Stradigund.

'Well, I am simply delighted to be here tonight,' said Tibor. 'What a happy coincidence that we met, Acantha, and can do each other such favours.'

Acantha tutted. 'That boy, he is like a thorn in my side.'

'Not for much longer. Just send him on over to me on Droprock Island. As we discussed yesterday, he will not be idle. I will send you reports of his progress.'

'And I will look forward to them,' grinned Acantha.

Rex frowned. So that was what they had been planning. So now he was going to the island, not to Reform School. He undoubtedly felt relief, but why the change of heart? What exactly would he be doing in an empty asylum? More questions, still no answers. Stradigund was becoming impatient. He took a large mouthful of the opaque ruby liquid in his crystal glass and smacked his lips. 'Acantha, put us out of our misery! Let us have some stew!'

Acantha wrapped two great thick cloths around the handles and lifted the pot from the stove to place it in the middle of the table. 'It's a different cut this time,' she remarked. 'Not so lean.'

'Well, it's the fat that gives meat its taste, and as long as that taste is good, who cares which part of the beast it comes from,' said Stradigund. 'As they say, beggars can't be choosers!'

Acantha and Stradigund laughed out loud at this and Velhildegildus took up his spoon and pretended in an exaggerated way to dip it into the pot. Acantha smacked him playfully on the wrist with the ladle and he withdrew to lick the gravy from his skin.

Rex watched this little drama with confusion and interest. It was odd to see Acantha so light-hearted; she was like a different person. 'But that was always your strength,' he muttered. 'To appear as one thing but to be another entirely.' Wasn't that how she had convinced his father to marry her?

Suddenly the mood changed tangibly. Acantha, by the mere action of taking the ladle in her right hand and supporting the pot at an angle with her left, caused a hush to fall over the table. The diners watched with naked hunger in their eyes as she ladled out generous amounts of the dark meaty stew into each dish. Velhildegildus wiped away a pearl of spittle that had appeared at the corner of his mouth and Stradigund was visibly quivering with anticipation.

Acantha finally dished out her own portion and took her seat. She raised her sparkling glass and with a triumphant smile she proposed a toast. 'To the members, old and new, of the Society of Andrew Faye,' she said.

> *'Here and now I raise my glass.*
> *Let not this meal be our last.*
> *Let not a portion go astray*
> *Raise your glass to Andrew Faye.'*

At her signal her companions dipped their spoons and scooped up a mouthful of the deliciously sapid stew.

'Ah,' they murmured in unison, and fell to the meal with a voracity that was quite startling to watch. There was something rather obscene about their edacity. It was only a stew! Acantha paused for a moment to speak again.

'I think it is only proper that I mention our dear friend, Mr Cadmus Chapelizod, at this time. Wherever he is, I am sure he would have wanted us to remember him this way.'

'Hear, hear,' they mumbled, and then silence descended over the table again.

Rex couldn't stand the slurping any longer. He took a final look and retreated to his room.

Rex sat thoughtfully on his bed. Yes, he was disappointed that he had not met Andrew Faye, but he had not come away from the bizarre feast empty-handed; this turn of events, the fact that he was going to the island, was an absolute godsend. Unwittingly Acantha and Dr Velhildegildus had provided the answer to his problems. Now he didn't have to make his own way to the island – he had an invitation! Rex hugged himself with glee. At last, something was going his way!

Suddenly he realized that he hadn't locked his door, but when he felt in his pocket for the picklock it wasn't there. He must have dropped it downstairs. He couldn't go without it – it was invaluable, and who knows what locked doors he might face in the asylum? So he spent the next two hours listening for sounds that the guests were leaving. But the carousing just got louder and louder. At midnight he lay on his bed. 'I'll just close my eyes,' he murmured. 'For a few minutes . . .'

Rex woke to the rattle of carriages in the street; Stradigund and Velhildegildus were going. Shortly after came the familiar thudding up the stairs, even slower than usual. He waited until they had passed and then hopped out of bed and retraced his earlier steps by the light of his chamber candle.

He found the picklock on the floor outside the kitchen and when he bent to retrieve it the aroma of the stew tantalized his nose. It seemed to have matured over the hours and was now quite literally mouth-watering. Rex licked his lips and suddenly he was overcome with hunger. So, against his better judgement, he crept into the kitchen.

In the light of the glowing fire he could see that the table had not been cleared. The plates were clean, almost as if they had been licked. Whatever it was that Acantha had cooked, it must have been very tasty indeed. The pot was still on the table. He tilted it slightly, rupturing the skin on the dark sauce that covered the bottom. Unable to stop himself, Rex dipped his finger in and scooped up a thick meaty globule. It was without doubt the finest, richest stew he had ever tasted.

And then he bit down painfully on something very hard. He cursed. A piece of bone he thought, and he spat out a small lump of meat into his hand, but before he could examine it a gruff voice took him by surprise.

'Looking for something?'

Rex jumped and turned around, slipping the bone into his pocket. Acantha was standing at the end of the table, her bloated face flushed and greasy, her lips dark red.

'How did you get down here?' She didn't give him time to answer. 'No matter. You'll be gone tomorrow. To where you belong, Droprock Island! Dr Velhildegildus is going to sort you out for once and for all. And when you get back, then you're going to Reform School.'

Rex could smell her. She stank of meat and wine. 'Anywhere's better than here,' he said through gritted teeth.

'There's gravy on your chin,' said Acantha with mock concern. 'Your father liked my stew too.'

Rex snarled and pushed past her. But all the way up the stairs he could hear her laughter.

24

The New Superintendent

Dr Tibor Velhildegildus clambered rather ungracefully out of the wooden boat to stand on the end of the projecting rock that acted as a natural landing place on Droprock Island. He smoothed back his hair (the mist had made it rather unruly) and brushed down the seat of his trousers. He looked around him at the uninviting shore. It looked far more likely that he would find dead fish here than jewels. But even young Rex had a diamond so he was confident that there was still something to Hooper's story.

He had to shield his eyes against the weak winter sun. With his back slightly arched and his other hand on his hip he looked up at the building that was to be his new home. A self-satisfied smile spread slowly across his face and he stroked his clean-shaven angular jaw in contemplation.

The Droprock Asylum for the Peculiar and the Bizarre was not the most interesting place to behold. It was un-doubtedly showing signs of age, having been built two

centuries before and, thought Tibor, whoever this Chapelizod fellow was, he had certainly not paid any attention to
the fabric of the exterior during his stewardship. He sincerely hoped that it would not be as bad inside. He was
well aware of the saying that one mustn't judge a book by
its cover. After all, how many seemingly sane people had he
come across in his profession who, after a light probing, had
in fact proved to be completely mad? From where he stood
now, the building looked hardly tenantable. He gloomily
suspected in this case that the cover was a very good indica-
tion of what was on the pages between.

Built on the highest point of the island, the asylum
sat directly above him, defiantly gazing across the lake at
Opum Oppidulum. It was a large square-fronted building, dark grey in colour with thick green ivy covering
much of the walls. On either side, set slightly back, the
west and east wings extended out towards the perimeter
wall. At first glance the building looked as if it could be an
ordinary functional dwelling, but the windows gave away
its true purpose. They were small and all iron-barred with
the exception of those on the top floor. Presumably if an
occupant had attempted to escape from up there, death
was considered inevitable and no impediment to the
escape was thought necessary.

Nonetheless it was an imposing edifice. Tibor, slightly daunted now that he was finally here, patted his breast
pocket wherein rested Hooper's diamonds and the plan for
the sub-aquatic vessel. He steeled himself for what was to
come and reminded himself of the path that had brought

him here. He was a great believer in Fate and the evidence of Her existence in this case could not be disputed. He counted off the coincidences on his fingers: first to meet that loon, Hooper; then on the same day to have an offer of a job in the very place Hooper had found the diamonds; and finally the boy, Grammaticus, and his father's design for the unique underwater vessel. And add to the mix the marvellous meal last night . . . It was many years since a woman of Acantha's unique culinary talents and attributes had cooked him such a hearty meal. It quite stirred him up inside.

Tibor truly felt as if the stars had suddenly all aligned in his favour. Whatever discomfort he had to suffer here, it was going to be worth it.

The sun had gone in and creeping yellow fog was all around. It had a strange smell to it, a sort of sweetness, but the sweetness that one usually associates with rot.

'It comes off the lake,' said Walter Freakley helpfully when he saw the look on his passenger's face. Tibor glanced back at the few feet of dark flat water that was still visible and noted that there was no evidence of their arrival, no eddies, no disturbances on the surface. It was as if Freakley's oar had never touched it. Strangely enough, though, he thought he could still hear the echo of the man's tuneless whistling.

'Not always so flat,' said Walter. Tibor thought that the oarsman's face seemed to have caved in in the middle, a little like a button stitched into a chair with tight radiating creases.

'Once a month, at the full moon, the water rises and

afterwards there are all sorts of things left behind. They call it Madman's Tide.'

'What sort of things?'

'Dead creatures from deep in the lake, teeth, bones and the like.'

And diamonds? thought Tibor.

'That's why they built the asylum so high up,' explained Walter. 'In the past the water has risen halfway up the cliff. There's a water mark.'

Tibor looked to where Walter was pointing and saw clearly the brown mark on the rocks. 'Only at the full moon, you say?'

'Guaranteed,' said Walter. 'You'll see it for yourself soon enough.'

'Is this the way to the asylum?' hinted Tibor, anxious to go, nodding towards the rocky steps at the base of the cliff.

They climbed what felt like at least a hundred steps to stand on the flat top of the rock facing the wall of the asylum. It presented a huge unscalable obstacle. And if by some miracle someone had managed to get to the top of it the surface was deliberately set with jagged razor-sharp stones upon which skin would be quickly shredded to pieces.

And where indeed would you even go? Tibor asked himself. The island was not particularly big. The only way to the mainland was across the cold dark lake. There was only one landing point, the remainder of the island being sheer cliff face. There were two gates in the wall, huge wrought-iron constructions, but they were already open.

'There's no one to keep in,' explained Walter.

Weeds intertwined themselves around the gates and straggled across the path, once paved but now cracked and distorted, that led to the main entrance. If he had looked up Tibor would have caught sight of a pale face at one of the windows observing his ingress, but he didn't and so, blissfully unaware that he was under intense scrutiny, he climbed the steps to the imposing doors. A man came out and managed the briefest of smiles.

'So you are the famous Dr Velhildegildus,' he said. 'Welcome. My name is Gerulphus. I am the asylum caretaker.'

Tibor looked at the tall, pale, abnormally thin fellow before him and nodded slowly. 'Gerulphus, eh?' he said softly. 'I knew a man once called Gerulphus. Long time ago.'

'It's a common enough name.'

'Well, Gerulphus, and, Walter, I believe that it has been a trying time for you both.'

'Oh, it certainly has,' agreed Walter with feeling. 'Poor Mrs Runcible, the cook, has been most unsettled by it all. Though with everyone gone her workload is not what it would have been. But I brought over a young girl the other night to help out in the kitchen. Hildred's her name.'

'So how many staff are there?' asked Tibor.

'Well, there's myself, the girl and the cook, and Gerulphus here. The warders left after the escape.'

'Not surprising, I suppose,' said Tibor. 'After all, a bunch of lunatics can be quite an intimidating sight!'

'You're telling me,' said Gerulphus with something approaching levity.

'I was half frightened to death by them,' said Walter. 'Out of their minds they were.'

'Well, that's all in the past,' said Tibor.

'Allow me to show you around,' offered Gerulphus. 'You'll see what it's been like here.'

'Hmm,' mused Tibor. 'Very well, a brief tour, and then take me to my quarters. I should like to see Chapelizod's books. I believe he has a substantial library to do with my profession.'

Gerulphus smiled briefly. 'Ah, yes, your profession, the mysteries of the mind. Mr Chapelizod did indeed have a comprehensive collection. I think you will be pleased.'

'Oh, have no fear about that,' said Tibor. 'Have no fear.'

Walter looked at the two men quizzically. There was an odd tension between them. He shrugged. He was the boat-man. He was not interested in how the place was to be run.

Gerulphus proved to be an efficient, if uncommunicative, guide and he took Tibor quickly around the building and then to Chapelizod's office as requested. Tibor noted on the way that the damage to the asylum, largely in the west wing, was mainly superficial – broken furniture, up-turned tables – but seeing as it was such a bare, cold place there was not much around to actually destroy. There was evidence of a fire in one of the rooms, but even that had been reasonably confined.

'The lunatics were a little cold,' explained Gerulphus.

They crossed the hall to enter the rather more lux-urious surroundings of the east wing. Here were the superintendent's rooms: a lounge area, a dining room, a library, a bedroom suite and finally a spacious and well-appointed study. At the study door Gerulphus handed Tibor a large key from the bunch he carried on his belt.

'Thank you, Gerulphus,' said Tibor, 'and please rest assured that I am not going to interfere in any way with your usual duties so you may carry on as normal.'

Gerulphus nodded and Tibor watched until he turned the corner before he entered the study and closed and locked the door. He hardly paused to look around before going straight to the bookcase behind the desk. Without any hesitation at all he pulled out a green-bound volume of Gibbon's *Decline and Fall*. Seconds later the entire bookshelf slid silently two feet across to reveal a small opening in the wall, just big enough for a person to fit through. And right now that person was Tibor Velhildegildus. He stepped through, the shelf slid back again and there was not a sign that anyone had ever been there at all.

25

Settling In

From her room Hildred could just make out the lights of Opum Oppidulum. She was still getting used to the fact that, for the time being at least, she did not have to spend her days travelling from one place to the next.

Upon landing earlier that week Walter had taken Hildred directly to the asylum and straight down to the kitchen to meet Mrs Runcible. She in turn had given Hildred a very warm welcome ('Oh, how lovely to have someone young around the place,' she'd said. 'I always wanted a daughter of me own') and had taken great pleasure in serving her up a filling, if not particularly tasty, hot meal. During the meal Mrs Runcible had chatted non-stop. Hildred only managed to catch half of what she was saying, but she had the feeling she wasn't missing much. And then Mrs Runcible had insisted on reading her tea leaves.

Later Gerulphus had come in and briefly acknowledged Hildred's presence before settling down by the fire with a copy of the *Hebdomadal*. ('He's not one for chat, our Gerul-phus,' said Mrs Runcible.) He had read the paper from front to back but remarked only once that Cadmus Chapelizod was still missing. Mrs Runcible didn't seem to think this was particularly important.

'Dreadful fellow,' she had said to Hildred with a con-cerned shake of her head. 'Now, finish up and come with me.'

Hildred had followed Mrs Runcible out of the kitchen and back up to the large stone-floored entrance hall from which all areas of the asylum could be reached. Dr Velhil-degildus was to have a suite of rooms to himself in the east wing of the asylum but Hildred's room was tucked away up several flights of stairs at the top of the building. It was small, with a bed, a trunk for clothing and a fireplace.

'Now, dear,' Mrs Runcible had said. 'Settle yourself in and tomorrow we'll sort out a few jobs for you. The place is in a bit of a state, you see; the lunatics really were quite careless. Dr Velhildegildus is coming in a couple of days so we'll try to make it nice for him. He's a very important fel-low by all accounts. And of course, once the place is ready, then we'll have more patients and you'll be able to help out properly.'

'I shall look forward to it,' said Hildred, but she was quite glad when Mrs Runcible left, worn out by her incessant chatter. No wonder Gerulphus hid behind the *Hebdomadal*. She'd lit the fire, folded her clothes neatly in the trunk and then slipped into bed.

Hildred had spent the next two days trailing around

after Mrs Runcible and acquainting herself with the asylum. It was hardly the most welcoming of places. It was built with its purpose in mind and there was little extraneous decoration. The floors were tiled in grey stone and the lower half of the walls was painted brown. There were no pictures, only rudimentary curtains, the long corridors were dark and smelly and all the doors were ominously solid.

'Ooh, it's a horrible old place really,' Mrs Runcible had said more than once. 'I stays down in the kitchen mostly, at least it is warm down there.'

Hildred had just listened. It was not easy to stop Mrs Runcible when she was in full flow. There was evidence everywhere of the breakout, but Hildred could see that the damage was not as bad as it looked.

'It looks as if they were burning books,' she'd remarked when they came upon the remnants of a fire. And indeed there were very obvious remains of books in the ashes. Hildred retrieved one of the rather less damaged ones.

'Oh, well, you know, they were cold,' said Mrs Runcible vaguely.

'So how long were they at large?' asked Hildred.

'Long enough,' replied the cook. 'Until one of them suggested trying to swim over to Opum Oppidulum. Of course, that was the end of them. But that's enough about all of that. I don't like to think about it really.'

Hildred put the burnt book down. 'I'm sorry,' she said, and changed the subject. 'I heard that there are haunted catacombs beneath the asylum.'

'Dunno about ghosts,' said Mrs Runcible with a shrug, 'but there's certainly a maze of tunnels,' and that was about as much as she would say. Hildred got the distinct feeling that Mrs Runcible preferred not to think about the past. She had then volunteered to make a start on clearing up the mess from the fire and Mrs Runcible retreated happily to the kitchen where she was generally perfectly content among her pots and pans.

When Dr Velhildegildus had finally arrived he came down during the course of the day to the kitchen to meet Mrs Runcible. Hildred noticed how she and Walter, but not so much Gerulphus, seemed to latch on to every word he said and were visibly relieved when the doctor said that he had no intention of interfering in their business. Hildred thought him an interesting character. Certainly his face was unusual but she felt disinclined to have much to do with him.

So tonight she lay on her bed and considered her new life. It was a pleasant introduction to the world of normal folk, folk who didn't have to earn their living from their freakishness. If she was completely honest with herself, it had not been as easy as she made out to leave the Panopticon, and more than once in the last few days she had wished with all her heart to be back among her family.

'Sometimes it's important to try things that scare you,' Mr Ephcott had said, and Hildred knew that he was right. Well, this isn't too scary, she thought, and it is only temporary.

And then she pulled on her cloak, took a small lamp and went off into the night to explore further the recesses of her new home.

There was a boy arriving the next day and he might well interfere with her plans.

26

A Proposition

Rex stood on the jetty and watched as Walter Freakley rowed his boat towards him. Its silent motion barely caused the water to stir, as if it was on a great lake of dark treacle, and only if he listened very hard could Rex hear the soft lap of the water. There was a small bag at his feet containing clothes and his precious book. In one pocket he had the diamond and his picklock, in the other his little brazen egg.

'Ahoy, there,' called out Walter over his shoulder. He approached the jetty in a series of rather awkward manoeuvrings, bumping heavily against a post and causing the flimsy structure to shudder violently. Rex was both unsteadied and unnerved at his unusual technique. After all, he was going to have to cross to the island in this man's care. Walter flung a rope out, which Rex caught and looped over the post.

Walter grinned and his face crumpled as if it was

collapsing in on itself. 'Are you young Rex Grammaticus, coming over to the asylum?'

'I am,' said Rex.

'Not afeared, are you?'

Rex shook his head. 'Not at all, it will be a relief to get away from the town.'

Walter didn't question this. He took Rex's bag, and then Rex climbed in and they set off across the dark water.

'What brings you to the island?' asked Walter.

'I have been told I am to work with Dr Velhildegildus,' replied Rex. 'But I am not sure what it is exactly that he wishes me to do.'

'Probably to help out in the kitchen with Hildred.'

'Hildred?'

'Young girl, works with Mrs Runcible the cook,' said Walter. 'About your age, she is. She'll be glad enough to see you.'

'Oh,' said Rex. He had not thought who else might be there. Then he asked, 'How long have you been the ferryman?'

Walter smiled. 'Oh, long enough,' he said. 'But it's not as easy as it looks, you know.' He changed the subject. 'I met your father once,' he said. 'Seemed a nice enough chap.'

'Did he say anything about me?'

'He did. Very proud of you he was.'

'But did you think he was mad?' pressed Rex.

Walter frowned and shook his head. 'Your father, 'e was different, certainly he was troubled, but I don't know if he was as mad as they made out.'

F.E.HIGGINS

'I don't believe he was mad,' said Rex. 'Did he tell you about his hand?'

'The hook? Yes, told us 'ow 'e'd lost it in an engineering accident.'

Rex sighed and rested his elbows on his knees and his chin in his hands. He looked down at his feet and saw something on the bottom of the boat. He picked it up.

'Careful, lad,' warned Walter. 'It's as sharp as a cut-throat.'

'What is it?'

'It's a tooth, from the monster in the lake; you find them on the shore occasionally.'

'You mean there really is something there?'

'Oh, most definitely there is,' said Walter, and he began to whistle.

Rex was in no doubt that Walter believed the creature existed. It certainly looked like a tooth, triangular in shape and yellowing, and very large indeed. Freakley continued to whistle and Rex was almost certain he could hear someone whistling back. A trick of the night, he thought, but before he could say anything else there was a violent jolt. They had reached Droprock Island.

Rex followed Freakley carefully, counting the steps – one hundred and fifteen in all. He thought again of his idea about the elevating machine. By the time they reached the top Rex was wet from the mist and feeling the cold. He shivered and looked up. The asylum stood silently before

154

him, filling his field of vision. Enveloped as it was in the mist, it looked even more unearthly than he could have imagined. Dread washed over him. This was the place wherein his father had lived out his final days. The sight evoked in him a mixed reaction: great sadness; a sense that some of his journey was over; and mounting horror as he relived in his mind that terrible night back in Opum Oppidulum. Rex touched his head. He could still feel a slight ridge where he had cut it on the shingle. He made a great effort to put the dark thoughts from his mind. He was here with a purpose: to prove that his father wasn't mad and that Acantha was, at the very least, a common thief and at worst a treacherous murderer.

Don't fly too close to the sun or on your head be it, thought Rex. From constant repetition, his father's words had begun to run together.

Walter led Rex up to the formidable double doors just as a tall, pale, freakishly thin fellow came out.

'Master Rex,' he said. 'Dr Velhildegildus is waiting for you.'

Walter bade Rex goodbye. 'Gerulphus here'll look after you,' he said, and crossed the hall to disappear through a narrow archway.

Rex followed Gerulphus, all the while marvelling at how wan and emaciated the man was, in the opposite direction. Unnaturally sensitive these days to its odour, Rex thought he could smell fish. They passed under a wider archway and travelled down a long carpeted corridor. There were pictures on the walls, landscapes and portraits, and the rug underfoot was of good quality.

Perhaps it wasn't so bad for Father after all, thought Rex, and he felt a little better.

Gerulphus walked on, unsmiling – he rarely smiled, as Rex was soon to discover – and he said as little as he could get away with. Finally they came to a halt outside Dr Velhildegildus's study.

'Knock,' said Gerulphus.

Rex knocked timidly. He was surprised to find that his mouth was dry and that his knees were trembling. He steeled himself for his second encounter with Dr Velhildegildus.

'Enter!'

The study was large and light and warm. Tibor himself was standing by the fire holding a glass of brandy. He was wearing a burgundy velvet smoking jacket, a paler silk foulard around his neck and dark trousers. The fire reflected in his polished shoes. Rex felt a shiver down his spine at the thought of their last meeting. He had still not wholly recalled what he had said under the influence of the Lodestone. He wondered if he ever would.

As soon as Tibor saw him he placed his glass on the mantel and approached with his big smile.

'Dear boy, how marvellous to see you again,' he said agreeably. 'You needn't look so worried – my Lodestone is safely packed away!'

Rex managed a smile. From hearing just those few words he realized again that so much of Tibor's power lay in his voice. It was creamy like a healing unguent, soporific like a sedative, persuasive like temptation.

Tibor continued, 'Did you have a safe journey? I must say it's not such a pleasant thing to cross that lake in the mist. Old Freakley seems to know what he's doing though. Take a seat. Would you like some refreshments?'

Rex sat by the fire and Tibor pulled the servant's bell. A minute or so later a young girl walked in. Perhaps 'walked' isn't quite the right word — she had an awkward loose-limbed gait — but her blue eyes were quite startling in their intensity.

'Hildred,' said Tibor, 'meet young Rex. He is to stay here with us for a while. Perhaps you could bring a drink for the young man.'

Rex gave her a smile, which she returned with warmth before leaving.

'Now, Rex,' said Tibor, sitting opposite and leaning forward. 'I have been most anxious to see you again. Have you any idea at all why you have been sent here to me?'

Rex chewed on his lip. 'I believe my stepmother thinks I am troubled over my father's death,' he ventured cautiously.

'Ah, good, good,' said Dr Velhildegildus smoothly. 'Certainly that is what she intimated to me, and there is no doubt I can help you with that, and of course that will be a priority, but while you're here I . . . er, see no reason not to take advantage of your other skills.'

'My skills?'

'I know that you are a talented boy, Rex, you are your father's son after all, and actually, heh, heh, I have other plans for you.'

'Oh?' said Rex. Was anything what it seemed these days?

'I'll get straight to the point. I have come up with a rather marvellous invention. I am in quite a fever about it and I do so want to build it. Alas, I am a doctor of the mind, not an engineer like your poor father was. I will need some help.'

At the second mention of his father Rex paid even closer attention to Dr Velhildegildus's hypnotic voice.

'Rex, I need *your* help.'

'I should be glad to look at it,' said Rex carefully. This was not at all what he had expected.

'But there is a condition. You must not tell anyone what we are doing,' he warned. 'Can I trust you?'

'Of course.' Rex was now absolutely intrigued by Dr Velhildegildus's creation – whatever it might be.

'You see,' continued Tibor, and although his face remained impassive, his voice altered and his honeyed tones were now spread with the thinnest layer of menace, 'I realize that your stepmother has your best interests at heart, but I also understand that you have no wish to return to her. Well, as long as you are here you are, how shall I put it . . . safe from Acantha, which, you might recall, you told me is what you say your father wanted. But I have undertaken to assess your troubled mind and to report back to her on your progress. I can take as long or as short a time as I wish. But if I cannot trust you then I will have no choice but to send you back to your stepmother immediately. Do you understand?'

'So,' said Rex slowly, but thinking rapidly, 'if I help you with your invention, and tell no one about it, then I can stay here as long as I wish?'

'Absolutely,' said Tibor.

'Then let me see this invention,' said Rex.

27

A Mystery

Rex watched excitedly as Tibor unfolded a piece of stiff paper on the desk and flattened it out. He saw immediately that it was a plan for some sort of vessel, by the looks of it an underwater vessel, and it caused his heart to beat a little faster. Thinking hard, he pored over it for a long time, tracing the lines with his fingers, his lips moving as he made internal calculations, lingering over some parts but not others. All the while he was acutely aware of both the brazen egg in his pocket and the sense that Tibor's eyes were firmly fixed on him.

'I see from your face that you are surprised by this,' said Tibor at last. 'Perhaps you did not think a man such as I could be capable of such creativity?'

'It is not that,' said Rex, struggling to master his emotions. 'It's just . . . well . . . a Perambulating Submersible? It's incredible.'

'But do you think it is possible? Do you think that we – you and I – can do it?'

Rex looked Tibor confidently in the eye. 'Yes,' he said. 'I believe we can.'

'Marvellous,' exclaimed Tibor, and his face was a picture of pure delight. 'Well, then, let's not beat around the bush. *Mox nox in rem*, as they say.'

Rex wished again he had paid more attention in his Latin lessons.

'Get on with it,' urged Tibor.

So *that's* what it means, thought Rex. 'Right,' he began, 'this is a relatively simple design. It relies heavily on levers and cogs and wheels. The power needed to move it is generated at a low level in one source and increases rapidly as it moves through the internal workings. I should imagine it will be reasonably quiet and also slow, but it should be sturdy and reliable. As long as we make sure all the welds and seals are watertight I see no reason why you shouldn't be able to take an underwater voyage very soon.'

Tibor clapped with glee at Rex's conclusion. 'First things first,' he said excitedly. 'Where can we get the necessary materials to make it? Do you know?'

'Of course,' said Rex confidently. 'I know plenty of metalworks that will supply us. They all know my father's name.'

'Then you must make a list of everything required and we will send for it straight away.'

Rex nodded. He looked around the study. 'But we will

need some sort of workshop. The vessel will be quite big when it is finished.'

'Don't worry about that,' said Tibor. 'I know exactly the place.'

'And where will we launch it?' continued Rex. 'The island is so rocky—'

'No problem,' said Tibor. 'It is all in hand. Oh, just think of it. It will be magnificent!' he cried. 'I do have one question. Do you see this box?' He pointed to a square on the paper. 'In the key I have called it a "Re-breather". I . . . er, just wanted to check that you knew what it was and how it works.'

'A Re-breather? Yes, I was a little surprised to see that,' said Rex.

'Surprised?' queried Tibor.

Rex looked pensive. 'Well, you see, it is a fairly new invention and in truth I would not expect to come across it in a plan such as this. You must have taken good advice from somewhere.'

Tibor puffed up with more than a little pride. 'Dear boy, I took the very best advice, as any sensible person would do. This Re-breather was recommended to me by, um . . . an expert in the field. But I will admit that I am not quite sure how it works. And in all honesty I am far better at designing than building, which is why I need your help. Can you make it?' asked Tibor anxiously. 'It is, after all, the linchpin of the success of the machine. There are no hosepipes for the air.'

Rex smiled. 'Yes,' he said slowly, 'I do know how to make

it. It is a simple enough idea but very effective, but I won't go into the difficult scientific explanation—'

'Good, good,' interrupted Tibor. Scientific explanations were the last thing he wanted.

'It's enough for you to understand that it works by absorbing the toxic gases that we breathe out and replacing them with the gases that we breathe in. It can convert the toxic gases into harmless ones so you can *re*-breathe them. Obviously there is a time limit to how long it can do this without an external air supply. But I should imagine –' Rex looked again at the diagram – 'that certainly in a vessel the size of this one, you should be able to get three or four hours out of it.'

'What a marvellous invention! It looks as if I was very well advised!'

'You were, indeed,' said Rex thoughtfully. Then he asked, 'Does my stepmother know about the Perambulating Submersible?'

'Oh no,' said Dr Velhildegildus firmly. 'That is our little secret.'

'But what about the Lodestone Procedure? What did you tell her of that? She did pay you after all.'

Dr Velhildegildus nodded his head slowly. 'Your stepmother is convinced that your father left something for you here on the island. I told her what you said to me, and explained that as far as I could tell it was merely the ravings of a lunatic – no offence intended. To please her, however, I agreed to bring you over here and to keep an eye on you. But, as you can see, I have much more important things to do! Whether there is any truth in your father's words is of no importance to me. Now stop worrying about Acantha, take the plan and make a list of the parts. The sooner we have the equipment, the sooner we can start.'

'There is just one other thing,' said Rex as he stood up.

'Oh yes, and what is that?'

'If I do help you to build this machine, surely it is not unreasonable of me to ask that you allow me to go free and not send me back to Acantha at all?'

Tibor looked a little surprised. 'Er . . .' he faltered. 'I suppose that is a possible outcome. Let us see when it is all built and ready to go. Perhaps I could say you escaped.'

'Perhaps?' said Rex. 'I am afraid that is not good enough.'

'Oh, very well,' agreed Tibor. 'You may go free. You have my word. Now, what else will you need?' he asked, moving swiftly on. He pulled open one of the desk drawers. 'Take these.' He handed Rex a pile of paper, an ink bottle, an inkwell and a selection of quills and some blotting paper. Finally, he handed him a smaller copy of the plan and began to usher Rex out of the room. 'We start work tomorrow. And remember, Rex,' he warned. 'Tell no one.'

'You have *my* word,' said Rex.

'What is the saying?' murmured Tibor. 'Give me a lever and I will move the world.'

'Archimedes of Syracuse,' said Rex. 'The greatest mathematician who ever lived.'

'Impressive,' said Tibor. 'I knew you were right for the

job. Together let us see what we can move.'

Rex smiled and took off up the corridor.

Tibor closed the door and let out a sigh of relief. He was over the biggest hurdle. *He had just managed to pass off the stolen plan as his own.* It was as he suspected: Ambrose Grammaticus must have come up with the plan in his cell; the boy had not seen it before. And, of course, he had transcribed it all in his own handwriting, which made it even more unlikely that Rex would make the connection.

Besides, his main concern is to get away from Acantha, poor fellow, he mused. Well, we shall have to see about that.

Further down the corridor, Rex found that he was filled with enthusiasm, just like the old days when he worked with his father. He was elated at the thought that he was to do something useful again. As he rounded the corner he ran straight into Hildred.

'Hello, Rex,' she said shyly. 'Mrs Runcible has supper ready for you.'

Deep in thought, Rex followed Hildred to the kitchen. He had a lot to think about and it tempered his mood. Dr Velhildegildus certainly appeared to be on his side, but could Rex really trust him? It was obvious that the doctor's priority was the Perambulating Submersible, but that didn't change the fact that he had made promises to Acantha. He would have to tread very carefully indeed. If he did find the information his father had left then he had to make sure to keep it hidden from Tibor until he could get it off the island.

'I can trust no one,' he said to himself.

And there was one other thing troubling him. How on earth had Dr Velhildegildus got hold of his father's plan for the Perambulating Submersible in the first place?

28

Tea Leaves and Secrets

'Oh my,' exclaimed Mrs Ida Runcible, and chewed nervously on her lip. She sat at the kitchen table busily swilling the dregs of her tea around the bottom of her cup. She turned the cup first this way and that, and then this way again, and then put it down and peered in. It was still there.

'Oh my,' she repeated softly, for there at the bottom, clearly visible in the dark brown tea leaves, for the third time this week, was the ominous and unmistakable shape of a monster. Unmistakable at least in Ida Runcible's eyes. Gerulphus could not see it at all.

'It's there, I tell you,' she insisted, but Gerulphus merely raised an eyebrow and continued to drink his vegetable soup.

A woman of great superstition, Ida Runcible rarely did anything without taking advice from the leaves. First thing in the morning, even before a bite to eat, the water was boiled and the tea was stewing. This was her fifth cup today and so far she had seen doom, gloom, bad tidings, misfortune and now the monster.

When Hildred and Rex came in she was still busy poring over the leaves. As soon as she saw Rex she immediately showed him the cup.

'Er . . . I think I can see something,' said Rex non-committally but it was all Ida needed. She looked at Gerulphus as if to say, 'I told you so.' Then she turned back to Rex and gave him a crooked-toothed smile. She smoothed down her frizzy hair in an apparent attempt to make herself more presentable but it sprang back again in defiance. Rex thought he had never seen a cook so skinny or with such wild eyebrows.

Rex was still mulling over the growing niggle about the Perambulating Submersible, but he couldn't ignore the fact that he was hungry. He sat down and Hildred brought him over some soup and a slice of bread. He began to eat under the watchful eye of Mrs Runcible and Gerulphus. Hildred smiled at him reassuringly.

'So,' said Mrs Runcible conversationally. 'What exactly is it Dr Velhildegildus wants you to do?'

'Can't you tell from the tea leaves?' sneered Gerulphus in his low monotone.

'Er . . . I am to help him fix up the asylum,' said Rex. That was the story he and Tibor had agreed on. 'My father was an engineer, you see, and a designer. I know all about making things, so I am to be his assistant.'

'How interesting,' said Hildred, cracking her knuckles.

There were lots of things Rex had already noticed about Hildred, knuckle-cracking being one of them; she was rather plain, her brown hair was unremarkable and she walked very oddly, but none of this mattered when you looked at her wide-set blue eyes, and experienced the way she stared directly at you when you talked. Strangely enough, Rex didn't find it unnerving. In her penetrating gaze you felt as if you were really being listened to. It made him feel good to have someone who paid him attention. Like his father used to.

'Any idea is better than the way Chapelizod used to run the place,' tutted Mrs Runcible. 'A devil he was in disguise. I should have seen it in my tea leaves, but of course I didn't have any then.'

'Did Mr Chapelizod not let you have tea?' asked Rex. Nothing would surprise him about the man now.

Gerulphus shot a look at Mrs Runcible. 'The boy doesn't need to know about that,' he said sharply, and Rex sensed something pass between the two.

Mrs Runcible looked a little remorseful but continued gaily, 'Oh, how my tongue runs away with itself! I heard that there will be new rooms for the patients, bigger ones, with proper beds and everything.'

'Proper beds?' queried Rex, but Mrs Runcible was in full flow.

'Wonderful man he is. He'll probably win some sort of prize.'

Gerulphus snorted. 'We'll see. He doesn't seem to be in any great hurry to get the place filled again. There are no inmates at present, unless you count us, of course.' At this Mrs Runcible broke out in nervous laughter. Gerulphus ignored her and continued. 'They all escaped; even the warders fled.'

Rex smiled wryly. 'Yes, I saw in the *Hebdomadal* that the bodies were washing up on the shore.' Out of the corner of his eye he saw Hildred shudder.

'It really was a terrible thing,' sighed Mrs Runcible. 'They were quite, quite mad. They decided to swim but of course the water is so cold. I tried to tell them but they wouldn't listen.'

'Even the warders?' asked Rex, but she was busy looking in the teacup again.

'Well, at least now you only have to cook for four,' said Gerulphus.

'Five,' Hildred corrected with a nod to Rex.

Rex took another mouthful of soup. It wasn't the best he had tasted but it was filling. 'So, Dr Velhildegildus has promised to fix up the asylum and then reopen it?'

'Exactly,' said Gerulphus. 'The Mayor and the town council are paying him well. Though why he has chosen a boy to help him . . .' His voice tailed off.

'I am very good at, er . . . renovating,' Rex defended himself.

Hildred laughed and left the table. 'Come on, Rex, finish up and I'll show you around. I have readied a room for you.'

Rex wiped his bowl with a last piece of bread and followed Hildred out of the kitchen.

'Oh, look,' they heard Mrs Runcible screech behind them. 'It's not a monster . . . it's a big fish.'

Outside the kitchen Rex looked at Hildred with raised eyebrows. 'I think Mrs Runcible actually believes those tea leaves. She probably believes in the monster in the lake, too. Walter Freakley certainly does.'

'There are stranger things in the world than a monster in a lake,' said Hildred. 'That Chapelizod fellow sounds evil. Walter told me all about him. He was wicked. It's a blessing that he's gone. Now that you are assisting Dr Velhildegildus I'm sure things will be back to normal soon.'

'That's our plan,' said Rex carefully. 'Is that why you came? To help run the asylum?'

'Yes. In fact this is my first proper job.'

'What did you do before?'

Hildred looked a little awkward. 'Don't make fun,' she said, 'but I used to be with a travelling show. I don't suppose you've heard of Rudy Idolice and his Peregrinating Panopticon?'

'I have,' said Rex, but he didn't say that what he'd heard was that the show was going steadily downhill and did not enjoy half the reputation it used to. 'What was your act?'

'I was a contortionist!' In an instant Hildred had twisted herself into such a knot of limbs, accompanied by ominous cracking sounds, that Rex feared for her health. But quick as a flash she was back to normal. Well, nearly normal. Her left shoulder was still dislocated and it took a second or two for her to snap it back into place. Rex didn't quite know how to react and he just stood staring dumbfounded while Hildred looked a little uncomfortable.

'One of the reasons I left,' she said quietly, 'was I didn't want to be looked at any more.'

'Sorry,' said Rex, and he averted his eyes to the ceiling.

Together they ascended the stairs from the kitchen to the main entrance hall. Taking up a position with the front doors behind him, Rex had a proper look around. The hall was large and airy but plainly decorated. The walls were half panelled in dark wood, above which they were painted white. There were some pictures hanging from the picture rail and a floral tapestry. On his right was the wide-arched hallway that led into the east wing where Dr Velhildegildus had his own rooms and his study. Directly opposite, the main staircase rose diagonally against the back wall leading up to the first floor. 'There are lots of rooms up there,' said Hildred. 'That's where Walter and Mrs Runcible and Gerulphus sleep.'

'And what's through there?' asked Rex, pointing at two hallways side by side in the far left corner.

'One leads down to the underground cells,' said Hildred matter-of-factly.

'Cells? Sounds like a prison,' joked Rex, but Hildred didn't answer.

'And the other leads up to our rooms,' she finished. She turned to give him a smile. 'Come on.'

'I heard there was a ghost roaming around in the catacombs under the asylum,' he said.

'It's true there is an underground maze, but I haven't

found it. And I certainly haven't seen any ghosts.'

Rex followed Hildred along the narrow corridor, at the end of which was a rickety set of wooden stairs. They climbed three flights before reaching a small square landing with two doors. 'You're in here,' said Hildred, 'and I'm just opposite.'

Rex looked to where she was pointing and saw into her small room. She had stuck newspaper cuttings and leaflets to the wall, about the Panopticon in its heyday, and on the table beside her bed was a small framed silhouette – of her parents, he presumed. He entered his own room. It was painfully bare by comparison. He had a bed, a chair, a table and a trunk for his clothes. The walls were grey, unpainted, and the plaster was crumbling in places.

'I did my best,' said Hildred apologetically, 'but . . .'

'It's fine,' said Rex, and laid his bag on the bed and sat down heavily.

Hildred hesitated. 'You don't look very happy. Are you all right?'

Rex looked into her eyes and before he knew what he was doing, he blurted out, 'My father . . . he died just recently.'

Hildred nodded. 'How utterly dreadful for you.'

Rex realized that these were the kindest words he had heard in many days. A mist came up over his eyes and his nose began to sting. Hildred patted his shoulder and then, rather strangely he thought, settled cross-legged on the floor looking up at him. 'Tell me what's wrong.'

Rex couldn't believe that he was so quick to pour out his troubles, but it was the first time since his father had died that someone seemed to be genuinely listening. Now that he had started he wasn't sure that he would be able to stop.

'He was here, in this asylum, but he wasn't mad. I'm sure my stepmother had something to do with it. Father was fine before he met her and then suddenly he went completely crazy. She drove him mad. He attacked me and . . . and . . . well, it was just terrible. I try to forget it. Look, I have a scar.' He held out his arm and Hildred examined the raised red mark carefully.

'Your poor father,' she said gently. 'What happened to him?'

'He escaped from the asylum and came back one night to the house. He was trying to tell me something but he was ill and couldn't say much. He left me some clues, but they don't make any sense. I want to find out what really happened and I think the answer is here in the asylum.'

'Is that the real reason you are here?' asked Hildred intuitively. She saw Rex's hesitation. 'You mustn't worry,' she said. 'I can keep a secret. Tell me the clues. I'm quite good at this sort of thing – perhaps I can help.'

Rex sighed. What harm would it do? So he told her about the book and seeing Mr Sarpalius, about Acantha and about Andrew Faye . . . almost everything, in a muddled jumble of words. And the whole time Hildred listened intently without speaking a word.

'So, you see, Father told me to come here,' he finished, 'but I didn't know how to get here without Acantha knowing. And then Tibor asked for my help.' Should he tell her about the Perambulating Submersible? He decided not just yet. He didn't like the deceit but he had given his word. 'Luck I suppose.'

'Or Fate?' said Hildred thoughtfully.

'I don't know if I believe in Fate,' said Rex with a bitter laugh. 'She hasn't been kind to me.'

Hildred got to her feet. 'Being sad won't bring your father back. You need to clear his name. It's just a puzzle. When we have all the pieces the picture will become clear.'

'I suppose so,' said Rex doubtfully. With a deep sigh he stood up and began to unpack his bag. It didn't take long – a few spare clothes, another pair of boots and at the bottom the book he had taken from the library. When he pulled the brazen egg from his pocket Hildred pounced on it immediately.

'What's that?' she asked.

'Just something I made with my father.'

Hildred examined it carefully. It was smooth all over, even at the joins. Rex set it down on the table and pushed a button at the top and she watched in delight as four legs unfolded from out of the sides. It rose up and began to move slowly across the surface with regular clicking noises. It looked like some sort of fat-bodied insect.

'Oh, it's delightful,' she said, and placed her fingertips gently on the table as it made its mechanical progress towards her. 'It's so delicate you can hardly feel it moving. How does it work?'

Rex smiled, enjoying the satisfaction of seeing something that had started out as a jumble of discrete pieces of metal and screws being brought to life as a whole. 'Magnets mainly,' he said, 'and a few other things. I made lots of models like these, but this is my favourite.' he said. 'Acantha smashed the rest of them.'

Then from somewhere deep in the heart of the building a bell jangled. 'What's that for?' asked Rex. Hildred, engrossed as she was in the mechanism, didn't seem to hear. Rex touched her on the back and she jumped.

'What's the bell for?'

She put her hand to her mouth. 'Oh, it's Dr Velhildegildus. I completely forgot! I'm to take him his supper.' She hurried to the stairs. 'I'll come back later, and we'll make a proper plan. I love mysteries.'

'But you won't say anything to him about this, will you?' said Rex anxiously. 'The egg, I mean. I have little else left to remind me of my father. Dr Velhildegildus seems kind enough but for all I know—'

Hildred shook her head. 'We all have our secrets,' she said simply, and then she was gone.

Rex lay down on the bed and looked up at the dusty cobwebbed ceiling. This was certainly a far cry from his father's house on the shores of the lake. And Acantha. He'd looked it up once, her name. It meant 'thorny spine'.

'How true,' he murmured. He was tired now. He felt as if he had been on a long journey. And Mrs Runcible's soup was weighing him down. He picked up the brazen egg and smiled. It was only one small thing but it meant so much.

Yes, he thought. We all have our secrets.

But what was Hildred's?

29

Ghost?

Rex woke suddenly from a deep sleep. He sat up and his breath clouded on the cold air — which was strange: usually there would be a fire in the grate. He pulled his blanket around him and wrinkled his nose at the smell. He ran his hand over it, and it was rough to the touch. And then he remembered: he wasn't in Opum Oppidulum any more, and he wasn't in his own bedroom.

Neither was he alone.

In his sleep-befuddled state he called out 'Father?' before realizing that it couldn't possibly be him. But there was definitely a figure in the doorway and now it was moving towards him.

'It's me,' whispered the figure.

'Hildred!' He recognized her voice but also that swaying gait. He leaned over and fumbled to light his candle. 'What time is it?' he asked, holding up the light to see her shining eyes.

'Oh, around midnight. I told you I'd come back.'

Midnight? How long does it take to give someone supper, he wondered.

'I've been thinking about what you told me,' said Hildred. 'We should try to find your father's cell. He might have left something there for you. I can take you there if you like.'

'Now?'

Hildred was already at the door. Rex pulled on his boots and went after her. As he descended the stairs behind her he caught the faintest whiff of something, like ashes from a fire.

If Rex had thought the asylum gloomy by day, he decided that by night it was positively creepy. He kept close to Hildred. She seemed unworried by the darkness and the eerie creaks and groans of the building.

'Did you hear that?' he hissed, pulling Hildred's sleeve.

'What?' Hildred held her lantern up high so she could see Rex's worried face.

'That moaning.'

'It might be the ghost,' she said, and then laughed. 'It's probably the wind. This building is very old. If you put your hand on the walls sometimes you can feel it move.'

Rex flattened his palm against the wall but he felt nothing. 'How well do you know this place?' he asked.

'Hardly at all,' replied Hildred. 'I've had a look around and it's easy to see that Chapelizod lived very well in the east wing. The patients were not so lucky. Now come on.'

Rex followed Hildred down to the entrance hall and then took a sharp right under the arch into the second corridor until they came to a flight of steep descending steps.

'My father said that his room was upstairs,' said Rex. 'I used to watch the light at night.'

Hildred shook her head. 'Most of the rooms are empty up there. Perhaps you saw Mrs Runcible's light.'

'But what about the lunatics?' asked Rex.

Hildred hesitated for a moment. 'Rex, the patients were all kept underground.'

She started down the steps and Rex followed somewhat reluctantly. Already he could smell dampness in the air, and something else: an increasingly foul odour. Down they went and down, deeper and deeper, and the atmosphere thickened with every step and the smell was almost unbearable. Rex was more and more unnerved.

'Surely this can't be right,' he said half to himself and half out loud as he reached the bottom and looked around in dismay. This was no longer part of the building. It was as if they were in the heart of the rocky island itself. The smell was terrible and the air was choking. Hildred was further on, struggling with a door that was hanging off its hinges. 'Damaged in the breakout,' she explained, finally dragging it open.

Rex helped to prop it up against the wall and they went through into a low-roofed rocky tunnel. And in their lanterns' light the full horror of the place was revealed.

'Oh my,' breathed Rex. His words echoed off the craggy walls. He felt sick to his stomach. How could his father have survived down here? How could anyone survive down here?

All along the tunnel there were cells on either side. The iron-barred doors were wide open and Rex looked inside the forbidding subterranean chambers. Each was tiny, almost too small for a man to stand up in, and the uneven floors were wet and water puddled in the dips. The walls were running and long streaks of green slime clung to the surface. Bold and curious rats stared up at him, their little eyes shining in the darkness, seemingly unafraid.

No wonder the lunatics had jumped to their deaths in the lake. Its freezing embrace would have been more comfort than this.

'Chapelizod kept everyone down here,' said Hildred, watching him intently. 'Walter Freakley told me.'

Rex took a deep breath. 'Are you telling me that my father was kept in one of these?'

'It's possible,' said Hildred, and then she saw the look on his face. 'Oh, Rex, I'm sorry. How thoughtless of me. I should have warned you.'

Rex swallowed hard. He felt as if he was choking. 'How do I know which cell was my father's?'

'I don't know,' said Hildred. 'Was he alone?

'He had a friend, a fellow called Hooper,' said Rex hoarsely. He was finding it hard to speak.

'Then let us look for a cell with two beds.'

'Beds!' he snorted. 'You mean two piles of straw.'

So they looked into each cell, Rex feeling increasingly

180

nauseous, but most had two flattened piles of straw rather than one. Rex was unwilling to enter the cells – it was just too horrible.

But why did Father say he was upstairs? he asked himself. He was trying to protect me, he realized, and his heart burned. All that time he had wasted, trusting Stradigund to help, just waiting, and meanwhile his father had been kept down here, like some sort of animal. He would never forgive himself for his inaction. And if he ever found Chapelizod he would not be held responsible for what he might do to him. He felt as if his heart had broken up inside his chest.

'There's nothing,' concluded Hildred, having scattered straw and examined the corners in every cell. 'Some poor soul was marking off the days in here but it's impossible to tell who. We'll have to look elsewhere.'

Rex had reached the end of the tunnel and was met by a wall of rock. There was a door to his right – solid wood, not barred like the others – but it was closed, and when he tried the ring-handle he found it was locked.

'Strange,' he murmured. 'It looks as if this door has been rehung.' There was grease on his fingers. He felt in his pocket for his picklock but realized he had left it in his room. Hildred came up behind him.

Suddenly he started and Hildred saw. 'What is it?' she asked.

'Can't you hear it?'

'No.'

'Voices. I think I can hear voices.' Rex cocked his head and listened intently.

Hildred placed her head against the wall and flattened her hands on the slime-covered, dripping rock.

'You're right. There *is* something,' she said. 'I can feel it.'

Both listened closely and from the other side of the wall came the unmistakable sound of moaning and wailing. They looked at each other quickly.

'It's the ghost,' said Rex. 'We must get out of here!' Without another word the pair turned and ran.

30

Down to Work

Over breakfast the next morning Hildred and Rex exchanged glances, both recalling, with mixed emotions, the events of the previous night: their midnight foray into the depths of the asylum, the tunnel of cells and of course the wretched groaning.

Breakfast was substantial: porridge (burnt), toasted bread (burnt) and butter (slightly off), an egg (very hard-boiled) and tea (stewed). Rex tucked in ravenously regardless and said not a word until he had finished. As he drained his mug Mrs Runcible called over from the stove, 'Don't drink your leaves! I want to read them!'

After breakfast Mrs Runcible took Hildred away, under instructions from Dr Velhildegildus, to continue the clear-up the breakout had necessitated.

So, thought Rex, Dr Velhildegildus is at least making it *look* as if he might reopen the asylum.

With Hildred otherwise occupied, Rex decided to make

a start on the list for the Perambulating Submersible. The thought excited him – he was as keen as Dr Velhildegildus to get to work – and it took his mind off the disturbing revelations of the previous night. So he returned to his room and settled on the floor to pore over his copy of the plan.

The list of materials and equipment was extensive, but the beauty of the design, as he had explained to Dr Velhildegildus, was that nothing was too complicated. Cost didn't seem to be an issue – Tibor had waved his hand in the air dismissively when Rex brought it up – but it did make him wonder just how much a person earned from being the superintendent of an asylum. After a couple of hours he added the final item, a drum of lubricant, preferably whale oil, and looked it over with great satisfaction and a degree of anticipation. It comprised, among other things: levers, springs, clamps and nut-spinners; headbolts, deadbolts, mauls and mallets; cogs, leather, grommets and filters; buckles, rods, toggles and tappetshims; jacks, switches, tacks and tin strips; kerosene, tallow and whale oil.

Droprock Island wasn't quite as pleasant a place to live as Opum Oppidulum, but it had one major advantage: no Acantha. Freed from her pernicious influence, Rex felt more positive than he had for a long time. To have the opportunity to make the Perambulating Submersible, and perhaps even to pilot it, was like a dream come true. But Rex still didn't like to think how Tibor had acquired the plan; he suspected by foul means rather than fair.

The motive was simple enough: money. The Perambulating Submersible was unique. It would be sought after all over the world. Tibor was going to be famous. Rex wasn't sure how he felt about this either, but there were more important things to worry about than fame. And as long as Dr Velhildegildus was occupied building the underwater craft then he couldn't conduct any more Lodestone interrogations, and in the meantime Rex could investigate the meaning of his father's cryptic last words.

Did he trust Dr Velhildegildus? 'Hmm,' mused Rex. It was an odd thing. When he was in the same room as him, listening to him speak, he believed that he was a man of his word. It was only afterwards that he was not so sure. But they had a deal and it was to neither's advantage to break it.

A shadow fell across the page and Rex looked up to see Hildred in the doorway. Startled again by the intensity of her eyes, he wondered if he would ever get used to them.

'What are you doing?'

Rex quickly folded up the plan. 'Er, I'm not really supposed to say.'

'I promise not to look.'

'I'm finished anyway.' He picked up the list and Hildred sat down opposite him with her legs tucked neatly under her. Rex could see that her boots were grubby and her fingernails were black.

'Did Dr Velhildegildus say anything about when the asylum would be ready again?' she asked.

Rex laughed. Bearing in mind Dr Velhildegildus's other

priorities, he thought it might be quite some time before they saw any new faces. 'Are you anxious for more work?'

Hildred shrugged, and it was quite a sight to see. 'Maybe it's because I'm not used to the emptiness. When I was with the Panopticon there were people around all the time.'

'What about your mother and father?'

'My mother died in an accident a long time ago, and Father, well, he left the Panopticon after that. I haven't seen him since. Besides, your father is so much more interesting. Tell me again about the man with the serpent's tongue.'

'Mr Sarpalius,' recalled Rex. 'I remember having a drink – I'm sure now that it was drugged – and I fell asleep. The next thing I knew, I was lying beside the lake. Oh, and I'd hit my head.' He put his hand up to his skull. The wound was still tender. 'That's when Father said he couldn't take me with him.'

Hildred frowned. 'But he didn't want you to stay with Acantha either.'

'I watched them drag him away,' said Rex quietly. 'The doctor said he died from a lung disease, something he caught in the asylum. If he'd never come here he would still be alive.' A note of bitterness had crept into his voice. 'The night he went mad he said he'd found out something about Mr Chapelizod, and that he wasn't to come to the house any more. Acantha just watched him, as if she knew what was going to happen, but I can't prove that she did.'

'It certainly looks as if she has something to hide,' said Hildred. She was cracking her knuckles, as she always did when she was thinking.

'After that Acantha took me to Dr Velhildegildus and he used his Lodestone Procedure on me.'

Hildred's eyes widened. 'What on earth's that?'

'It's a sort of interrogation. It's very hard to resist. Dr Velhildegildus is so persuasive. He has a way of making you say stuff even though you don't want to. It's like a dream – you don't know what's real and what's not.'

'I doubt he would get anything out of me.'

Rex snorted at Hildred's confidence. 'I wouldn't be so sure. I barely remember what I told him!'

Hildred chewed thoughtfully on her lip. 'And then he asked you here to help him out? Don't you think that's a coincidence?'

'I suppose so,' said Rex cagily. 'He knows I'm a Grammaticus. I'm good at making things, and that's exactly what he needs, for the asylum, I mean.'

Rex looked at Hildred's grave expression. She seemed determined, even more so than he, to work out the mystery.

'What about the book your father gave you?' she asked.

'I know all of the stories inside out. My favourite is Daedalus and Icarus – they were stuck on an island with a maze too.'

'Maybe *that* means something.'

'Well, I'm hardly going to make wings and fly away!'

'What about the warning?'

'*On your head be it*?' said Rex. 'It sounds as if I have to do something, but I just don't know what.'

They both fell silent. Rex looked over at Hildred. He

wanted to unburden himself completely, to tell her what he was really doing with Dr Velhildegildus, but he stopped himself. 'It's hard to know who to trust these days,' he said quietly.

'You can trust me,' said Hildred. 'You have no reason not to.'

Rex smiled. 'I do believe I can.'

'You know,' said Hildred, 'I'm really glad you're here. Apart from anything, what on earth would I do on my own? Let's face it, Mrs Runcible is plain odd, Walter Freakley spends all his time messing about with his boat, and as for Gerulphus! I don't know what he does all day. Have you noticed how he keeps disappearing?' Then she jumped to her feet. 'Enough talk. Let's go see if we can hear those voices again. I'm sure it won't be so bad in the daytime.'

31

All Part of the Job

The question of what Gerulphus did at the asylum was indeed a valid one. While Rex was busy with his list and Hildred was with Mrs Runcible, Gerulphus was enjoying a light snooze, and the peace, by the kitchen fire. Mrs Runcible chatted incessantly. 'Enough to drive a fellow mad,' he murmured.

From under the *Hebdomadal* he considered his current situation. As far as Tibor Velhildegildus knew, he was just Gerulphus, the asylum caretaker. Dr Velhildegildus seemed happy with that; Gerulphus certainly was, and what Tibor Velhildegildus didn't know wouldn't harm him! In fact there were lots of things it was not necessary for the 'mind doctor' to be aware of for the time being; namely what Gerulphus had done before the breakout and how after the breakout he had seized the opportunity to change his life. Who wouldn't have in the same situation? It had all worked out very well indeed. After all, Mrs Runcible was perfectly happy in the kitchen – she had always loved to cook – and Walter Freakley enjoyed his job as boatman. So why shouldn't he, Gerulphus, take the chance to have a little satisfaction too?

Hildred was right. He did spend much of his day out of sight. Mainly he spent his time wandering the empty asylum corridors, taking immense pleasure from the fact that there wasn't the noise there used to be. He had always found the shouting, screaming, moaning, complaining and general cacophony of the inmates most unpleasant. Gerulphus enjoyed his own company, and always had, even as a little boy. He had never been particularly sociable. Just as well; few wished to spend time in his company. To others, he didn't look right – people were so judgemental! But no one cared about that here. He thought about his present companions – hardly his intellectual equals but at least they accepted him. Sometimes Mrs Runcible would not see him from morning until evening but she never said a word. Her meals were as hit and miss as his appearances for them; when it came to cooking, enthusiasm was no substitute for skill.

Gerulphus sighed and the paper flapped gently on his nose. Yes, weighing up his past life and his present position, there was no doubt that he was now in a far better place. He knew that he had to make the most of his relative freedom. Now that Dr Velhildegildus was in charge, his days here were numbered. But he had come to view all obstacles as opportunities.

'Ah, well,' he murmured, 'all good things must come to an end.' Whatever the doctor was up to, and Gerulphus

knew he was up to something, he would not let it interfere
with his own plans. He had been very interested to hear
that young Rex was to come over. It was a shame about
Rex's father. Of all the lunatics in the place he seemed the
least mad. He had tried to help him, and Hooper, during
those difficult days, but Fate had other ideas. Tired of thinking, Gerulphus laid down the journal and roused himself.
There was *one* job he had to finish before he left.

A short time later Gerulphus was standing at the end of
the tunnel of cells, as had Rex and Hildred the previous
night, in front of the last door. He pulled a long chain from
under his shirt upon which there were two keys. Using the
larger one he unlocked the door. It opened with ease – he
had oiled the hinges – and once inside he made sure to lock
the door behind him. This cell was much bigger than the
others and in the centre there were two tables side by side.
On shelves around the room, and against the walls, there
were glass jars and pots and miscellaneous oddments, but
Gerulphus paid them no heed.

On the wall behind the door there was a panel of wood.
Ostensibly its purpose was to provide hooks upon which
to hang old branding irons, but Gerulphus knew better. He
pushed aside one of the irons to expose a keyhole. He put
the second key in the hole, turned it and the panel swung
out like a door, revealing a dark hole in the wall behind it.
Gerulphus climbed through and the panel closed slowly behind him, leaving not a trace of his presence.

Gerulphus had entered the underground maze.

※

Gerulphus stood with his lantern and listened for a moment. All was quiet. He strode off with the confidence of one familiar with his surroundings. As he went along the subterranean passageways he passed at intervals the grinning skulls and skeletal remains of previous occupants of the asylum above. For it was here, down in this labyrinth of catacombs, that the bodies of the lunatics were laid to rest when they passed on. They were not given a coffin or even a simple wooden box, merely placed in roughly hewn shallow cavities in the walls, where down the decades they dried out and turned to dust. Gerulphus was not in any way unnerved by his silent and desiccated companions; he lacked the imagination to be.

This was where in a moment of weakness he had taken Ambrose and Hooper, to protect them from the rampaging lunatics – they really were completely mad! When it was safe, Freakley had been more than happy to row them over to Opum Oppidulum.

Gerulphus's confident stride was deceptive. In truth, it was possible to get utterly lost down here and Gerulphus knew of at least three skeletons that were seated on the ground rather than lying in their proper resting place in the wall. There was also a lone skull. Perhaps they had been mistakenly laid to rest and then revived – only to die anyway. Or perhaps they were one of the many lunatics abandoned regularly in the labyrinth by the cruel warders . . .

Ticking off the turns on his long fingers, and taking great care to avoid a very deep hole in the middle of one

passageway, Gerulphus eventually rounded one final corner and stepped out into an enormous chamber to enjoy a
sight that was nothing short of spectacular. The whole space
was lit by a strange luminescence emanating from the rocky
walls and convex ceiling. Some sort of lichen, he had concluded, that cast an odd blue glow across the place, which
was reflected and intensified by the sheet of sparkling water
that greeted the eye. Water? Yes, for in this underground
chamber, by means of prehistoric underwater passages,
Lake Beluarum lapped gently on a sparkling sandy shore.

During the lunatics' breakout, genuinely fearing for their
lives, the warders themselves had hidden in the tunnels but,
in an ironic twist of fate, they had met their death at the
hands of a lunatic who was already in there.

A sort of poetic justice, thought Gerulphus. He might
be the asylum caretaker but he had little sympathy for the
warders. They were no better than Chapelizod.

But the underground lake wasn't the only thing Gerulphus had discovered. He went towards the water's edge,
dropped to his knees and began to rake through the pebbles.
After a few minutes he picked out one which shone quite
unlike the others. A diamond. Just recently there were always one or two to be found in the pebbles, and he made
sure to collect them every day. And with the advent of the
full moon and the rising water they seemed to be washing
up with increasing regularity. Gerulphus smiled and put it
in his pocket to add to his collection.

Next he crunched purposefully towards a rocky ledge
that ran around the wall just above the surface of the water

and climbed up on to it. About halfway around, part of the ledge projected out into the water. Gerulphus walked to the end and picked up a stick that was lying there. He knelt at the edge, his pale blue reflection looking back at him, and began to hit the surface of the water rhythmically. The noise echoed around the chamber, a sort of watery slap, and he continued for some minutes. Nothing happened but he kept going. It made him smile to think that if anyone were to look at him now they could be forgiven for thinking they might be in the presence of a genuine lunatic.

And then he stopped. On the far side of the chamber, where the rocky ceiling came down in a curving arc to meet the lake, a ripple spread slowly across the surface. And then another and then another. Gerulphus watched with bated breath, the stick suspended before him, until finally a huge, dark and triangular scaly fin broke the surface and cut through the water.

'Ah, here you are, my lovely,' whispered Gerulphus, almost, but not quite, with affection. 'Ready for your snack?'

As it approached, the true size of the monster became apparent. It cruised back and forth for a while, with each pass coming ever closer to the end of the rocky promontory. Then in one smooth and graceful movement it rolled over on its side and looked at Gerulphus with an enormous left eye. And its skin glittered with the hundreds of delicate diamonds that were pressed into its fleshy scales.

32

An Unexpected Encounter

Rex thought he would never get used to the smell in the tunnel of cells and he hated inhaling the damp and fungal odour. This time, he avoided even looking into the tiny rooms and went straight to the locked door at the end. Hildred was already there with her hands flat on the wall again. She certainly has strange ways of doing things, thought Rex.

'I can't feel anything,' she said. 'Yesterday, I could feel reverberations in the rock. Now, nothing.'

Rex pressed his own ear to the rock and they both stood silently for a few more minutes, concentrating intently.

'It must have been my imagination,' said Rex finally. 'But I'll tell you what is real – the smell of fish! Mrs Runcible was cooking some this morning and the stink seems to have made its way down here.'

'Forget the fish,' said Hildred impatiently. 'Let's see what's behind this door. Have you got the picklock?'

195

Rex was surprised to find that his hands were shaking, and the simple task took longer than usual. It didn't help that Hildred was breathing down his neck in anticipation. When the lock finally sprang he pushed the door open into the coal-black room.

Hildred smiled. 'That's a good trick,' she said, and went straight into the darkness.

Rex followed. 'You know,' he said, 'we can't both have imagined it.'

'Imagined what?' said a deep voice from the shadows.

Rex dropped the lantern in fright and Hildred grabbed at it before it hit the floor. Then both she and Rex near leaped out of their skins as a ghostly figure came out of the darkness towards them.

'Gerulphus!' exclaimed Rex with a mixture of relief and fear.

Hildred gripped Rex's arm and he could feel that she was shaking.

'I'm intrigued,' said Gerulphus in his familiar monotone. 'What is it you think you imagined?'

'We heard noises down here yesterday,' said Hildred, recovering. 'We came to have another look.'

'But today it is quiet?'

'Yes.'

'Then maybe it *is* all in your head. Or it could be the ghost.'

Was that a smile on his face? wondered Rex.

Hildred spoke first. 'So what brings you down here? Dr Velhildegildus does not plan to use the cells again, does he?'

'I would not allow it,' said Gerulphus firmly, and his voice was tinged with sincerity and his face showed what passed for an expression of sadness. 'Some terrible things were going on here under Mr Chapelizod and to this day it is my greatest regret that I didn't do anything to prevent it. But Cadmus Chapelizod was a clever fellow. He and the warders were all in on it together. In fact the head warder was almost as bad as he was. They went to great lengths to hide what they were up to. As caretaker, I wasn't even allowed down here. Chapelizod insisted that I spend my time in the grounds. As for Mrs Runcible and Freakley, she was in the kitchen and he was in the boat.'

'Don't worry,' said Hildred kindly (rather too kindly, thought Rex). 'You mustn't blame yourself. You weren't to know.'

Rex did not find Gerulphus as convincing as Hildred did, and he couldn't help remembering the state of the asylum grounds when he had arrived. They didn't look as if they had been titivated at all.

'Now, if you look around in here for example,' continued Gerulphus evenly, 'you will see what I mean.'

He closed the door fully and took up a position with his back to the panel.

'As you can tell,' he said, 'Mr Chapelizod was not a man to suffer fools gladly.' He lit his own more powerful lantern and in its spreading light Rex and Hildred watched with growing horror the shapes that emerged.

'Oh my word,' breathed Rex finally. For there was no

doubt about it. This was not a cell; it was a medieval torture chamber.

Rusty chains strung through metal hoops looped across the walls. Manacles were riveted to posts buried in the floor. There were racks of long-bladed knives and sharp irons rested in the corners, as if just left there casually. Even the tables, innocent in the dark, once fully revealed conspired in the horror, with handcuffs at one end and ankle straps at the other. The floor was strewn with stained straw and wet with brown puddles. And, like all the other cells, there were rats biding their time in the shadows. The shelves on the back wall were crammed untidily with corked brown bottles of unidentifiable liquids. A large bell jar sat at one end of the bottom shelf and, unable to help himself, Rex went closer, only to recoil in disgust when he saw that it was filled with slow-moving, dark-skinned, mottled, writhing creatures.

'Leeches,' said Gerulphus. 'You see why I keep it locked. Indeed, I thought it was. How did you get in?'

'You must have left it open,' said Rex innocently.

'Evidently. I will have to be more careful. This is not the sort of place a child should see.' He gestured to the door. 'Shall we go? I believe Mrs Runcible is waiting for you both in the kitchen.'

Hildred and Rex were only too happy to leave this squalid and sinister place. Gerulphus secured the door and the sober threesome made their way towards the stairs.

'Well, it's all in the past now,' said Gerulphus as they ascended. 'A new era is dawning with Dr Velhildegildus. But I think you should stay out of here. It's damp and cold; there could be disease down here. Have you seen the size of the rats?'

'Big as dogs, some of 'em,' said Hildred. She laughed lightly but she was holding Rex's arm tightly. It struck him that this was the longest conversation Gerulphus had ever engaged in.

Once upstairs, Gerulphus declined to go down to the kitchen and as soon as he was out of sight Rex began to talk, very quickly, still slightly shocked by what he had seen, but also puzzled. 'I don't believe Gerulphus couldn't help the inmates,' he said. 'And did you notice how quick he was to excuse Mrs Runcible and Walter? And what he was doing in that horrible place in the dark?'

'Maybe it was his voice you heard the other night,' said Hildred. 'Maybe he was in there, behind that door, all the time.'

'Oh Lord,' said Rex quietly. 'My father might have been taken there. Strapped to one of those tables and . . . and who knows!'

'Try not to think about it,' said Hildred.

Rex shook his head slowly. 'I don't ever want to go in that room again.'

Hildred placed a comforting hand on his shoulder. 'But we have to,' she said. 'Don't you understand? Gerulphus wasn't just advising us to stay away – *he was warning us*. It can only mean one thing: there must be something down there he doesn't want us to see.'

33

Article from

𝕿𝖍𝖊 𝕺𝖕𝖚𝖒 𝕺𝖕𝖕𝖎𝖉𝖚𝖑𝖚𝖒 𝕳𝖊𝖇𝖉𝖔𝖒𝖆𝖉𝖆𝖑

MAKING GOOD PROGRESS
by
Cecil Notwithstanding

How pleasing it is to see a man keeping his word. I write of course of Dr Tibor Velhildegildus, the new superintendent of Droprock Asylum. It has been duly noted that he has already begun the renovations that he promised when last I spoke to him. Certainly judging by the amount of equipment he has been taking over to the island this week, he has some innovative ideas.

With the impending full moon, conditions on the lake are not as conducive as usual to all the toing and froing. The water seems quite disturbed these days and it looks as if the tide this month is going to

200

be unusually high. The last record-breaking Madman's Tide was over fifty years ago – the high-water marks are still on the rock.

As the solution to one problem is found, however, another proves rather more elusive: that of the beggars.

It could not be denied that once Dr Tibor Velhildegildus made up his mind to do something he threw himself into it with unbridled energy and enthusiasm. Almost as soon as Rex delivered the list, equipment began arriving, generally transported across the lake by Walter Freakley, who grumbled constantly about the weight, and his boat, and how they were mismatched. Indeed there were a few near misses when he overestimated the capacity of his craft. Eventually it was arranged for the larger parts to be put on a separate boat and pulled behind. The spectacle was watched with great enthusiasm by well-wishers on the jetty, all of whom were looking forward to the grand reopening of the asylum. And if the jetty could hardly take the strain, one suspected that the well-wishers too were under a lot of pressure, namely from mad relatives in their houses.

Gerulphus did his fair share of laconic grumbling, as with each new delivery he was commandeered into lugging whatever it was, big or small, up the steep steps to the asylum. For his part Dr Velhildegildus watched from the rocks, shouting instructions and telling them to take care. 'It's for the patients,' he kept saying, 'treat it with respect.'

Everything, regardless of size, was taken to his study and

Rex's time was spent hauling the goods along the east wing corridors. Hildred appeared intermittently on the first day but he hardly saw her after that. He did knock on her door at night but she didn't answer. He looked in once but could see that she was curled up under the blankets so he went to bed without disturbing her.

By the end of the third day everything was in. Tibor sent Rex off for supper and he went gladly, ravenous after all the hard work. On his way back to the study he spotted Hildred tripping sinuously down the main staircase. 'What are you doing up there?' he called out but as was often her habit she declined to answer. He waited at the bottom for her. 'You needn't worry,' he joked, 'it's all done now.'

Hildred didn't look as if she got the joke. 'I've been busy too,' she said defensively. She certainly looked as if she had been busy. In fact she was rather dirty, and Rex was certain he could smell ash again. There was a smudge on her forehead where she had wiped her hand across her brow.

'You have your hands full,' she remarked as Freakley dragged one last crate across the floor. 'But I can't see how any of this is suited to an asylum. Where are the beds and the mattresses? The medicines? And –' she lowered her voice – 'if you are engaged in this . . . project, how will you possibly have time to find what you are looking for?'

Rex shrugged. 'Maybe it will all have to wait,' he said carelessly.

'Have you forgotten your father might have suffered torture here?'

'Rex!' called Tibor from somewhere down the passage.

'I have to go,' said Rex. Hildred raised an eyebrow and walked away.

Rex instantly felt ashamed of his offhand behaviour. He knew that he had upset her. He almost went after her but something held him back. In truth the torture chamber had disturbed him much more than he let on. He had been glad of the distraction of all the arrivals, and he looked forward to building the Perambulating Submersible. Seeing all the boxes and crates had made it very real. And for all that he didn't quite trust Dr Velhildegildus it was obvious that he too had a passion for the machine. And there was always the feeling that his father was watching over him, a feeling made all the more intense because he was to build the submersible in the place where his father had suffered so badly.

Apart from all that, Rex was especially keen to work on the Re-breather, something that was of particular interest to him. He resolved to talk to Hildred tonight. Perhaps he might even tell her exactly what was going on. He felt he owed her that much. Could it really do any harm to be honest?

Standing in Tibor's study, Rex looked at the boxes and crates, the piles of metal, the containers of nuts and bolts, the tools, the panels and one hundred and one other things that were stacked in front of him. He shook his head in disbelief. There was hardly room to move.

'What on earth are we to do with all of this?' asked Rex. 'We cannot make the vessel here.'

Tibor, standing between two barrels of whale oil lubricant, looked very pleased with himself. 'Never fear, my dear boy,' he said. 'It's all in hand.' Unable as he was to actually go to the window, he pointed instead to the waxing moon in the night sky.

'I wish the vessel to be completed by the next full moon. The water will be at its highest level, making it most propitious for a launch. They are saying it will be an exceptionally high Madman's Tide.'

'That's only a matter of days,' said Rex incredulously. 'Dr Velhildegildus, if we really are to finish this in such a short time, I wonder if we should allow Hildred to work on it too. She is very clever, and her fingers are nimble. I know you wish it to be a secret, but she has no one to tell. Her mother is dead; her father hasn't been seen for years. Besides, she is already suspicious. Anyone can tell this equipment is not necessary for an asylum. And the quicker we finish, the less likely it is that people from Opum Oppidulum will start to poke their noses in.'

'I suppose it might not be such a bad idea,' said Dr Velhildegildus slowly. 'Time *is* of the essence. I can see that you and the girl, Hildred, have become friends. But still we must be cautious. Believe me, I know just how charming young ladies can be! Are you certain you have given nothing away?'

'I haven't said a word,' said Rex solemnly, crossing his heart.

'Then let me think on it.' Once again Tibor's voice had taken on that sinister quality that reminded Rex he was dealing with a character who was not necessarily as straightforward as he might appear.

'And you remember your side of the deal too?' Rex prompted.

'But of course,' replied Tibor, almost offended, and once again his words flowed like satin over polished wood. 'But now I have something very important to show you.' He went to the bookshelf behind his desk, hooked his finger over the top of Gibbon's *Decline and Fall* and pulled the book forward. The bookcase moved slowly to one side to reveal once more the opening in the wall.

'Oh my,' exclaimed Rex, most impressed with this clever engineering. He had not been expecting this!

'Take a lantern,' said Tibor, 'and follow me.'

Rex unhooked a lantern from the wall and stepped into the tunnel where Tibor was waiting.

'Welcome to the catacombs of Droprock Island' said his enigmatic guide. 'This way.'

Tibor kept up a running commentary as they descended the steep tunnel. 'The catacombs have been here since the asylum was built. There is nowhere else to bury the dead on the island, and generally their relatives want little to do with them. Which is why they're here in the first place, I suppose.'

At least Father had a proper burial, thought Rex. Acantha had to do that much for him. Apparently Cecil Notwithstanding had insisted.

Tibor was moving at a fast pace. 'Keep up, Rex,' he warned. 'And don't stray from this tunnel. It's a veritable maze down here. If we get separated you might never find your way out.' Rex had no intention of getting lost and he kept as close to Tibor as he could in the narrow passage-way.

They passed other tunnels on the left and right but Tibor continued down the central aisle. And all the time Rex was acutely aware of the dehydrated, ragged-clothed bones of lunatics in the wall cavities.

Well, at least there's no smell, he thought. And why would there be? All of these skeletons looked as if they had been there for years. Had no one died recently? Up ahead Tibor took a blind bend and disappeared from sight. In a moment of panic Rex broke into a run and rounded the corner to emerge unexpectedly into a large rocky chamber with a high ceiling. The whole place was bathed in an odd blue light. And right in the middle of the chamber, Rex could see – though at first he didn't quite believe it – an expanse of dark water. The ground beneath his feet was a mixture of pebbles and small rocks and sand.

'It's Lake Beluarum,' said Tibor. 'It comes in under the asylum.'

Rex stood on the spot, taking it all in. The water was as flat as a mill pond and blue-black, giving no hint of its depth. He saw how it went right up to the walls on the left and right. He saw the narrow ledge that ran around the water and the rocky promontory. He saw too on the opposite side of the water a number of roughly hewn tun-nel entrances.

'More catacombs,' said Tibor with a nod towards them.

'And just as labyrinthine, if not worse, than the ones behind us.'

Rex calculated quickly. Obviously they had descended to the level of the lake outside. He and Tibor had approached from the east wing, so the catacombs on the other side of the water must be under the west wing, possibly right under the tunnel of cells. If he was right, then it would make sense to have an entrance on that side too, for when the prisoners died. But where? He and Hildred had met only with a dead end.

Tibor's excited voice cut into his thoughts. 'I plan to make my vessel here,' he said, gesturing enthusiastically around the space.

Listen to how he says '*my*', thought Rex, and it galled him to hear it. How proud he is of *his* design. Maybe this wasn't going to be as easy as he had first thought.

'It's a good spot,' he observed neutrally. 'And when it is finished the water is only a matter of feet away.'

'And soon it will be even closer,' said Tibor.

'But won't we have to bring all the equipment down first?'

'That is our next task.'

Rex tried a second time. 'Dr Velhildegildus, if you really want to launch the vessel on the night of the full moon, we must have more help. Gerulphus is unwilling—'

'I wouldn't ask him anyway,' said Dr Velhildegildus sniffily.

'Mrs Runcible, well . . . and Walter is just too old. It only leaves Hildred . . .'

Tibor seemed to be weighing it up. 'Yes, I've certainly noticed how flexible she is. Another pair of hands could be useful. But can she be trusted, Rex, to keep it secret?'

Tibor didn't wait for an answer but returned to the tunnel from which they had emerged, and Rex noted for the future that its entrance was the largest of them all.

Stepping back into Tibor's study, Rex was glad to be in the fresher atmosphere. He watched the bookcase slide back noiselessly and wondered briefly how Tibor knew about it, before pondering its mechanical workings.

'We'll start tomorrow morning,' said Tibor. 'Be here at seven.'

Rex tried again. 'And Hildred?'

Tibor seemed distracted, muttering to himself and touching all the boxes and crates within his reach. 'What? Oh, very well,' he said. 'Bring the girl too.' He rubbed his hands together with pleasure and there was look of wild excitement in his eye that Rex had not seen before.

It was the look of a man possessed.

34

Wanderings

Hildred sat on the edge of her bed. It was nearly midnight and she hadn't seen hide nor hair of Rex for hours. She was still stinging from her earlier dismissal and was more than a little disappointed that her only ally on the island had found it so easy to shut her out – and just when they had discovered the torture chamber, a possible breakthrough in his quest for answers.

And now he has abandoned me! It would never have happened when I was with the Panopticon, she thought. Mr Ephcott was *always* there for me.

Unusually for her, Hildred allowed herself to indulge in a few minutes' self-pity, giving in to the pangs of loneliness that she had felt on and off since arriving at Droprock, and succumbing for a moment to self-doubt. Had it been a mistake to come here? Should she have gone with Mr Ephcott to Urbs Umida?

'Absolutely not,' she said resolutely. 'Urbs Umida sounds

like a foul place and Rex isn't the only one with secrets and mysteries.' She felt a sudden burst of anger. Did Rex think she was stupid? She could read the words on the boxes, she could hear the clinking and clanging from within. This stuff was not needed for fixing up the asylum. The asylum needed beds and paint and curtains. And a decent cook, she thought wryly, but immediately felt guilty. Poor Mrs Runcible, she wasn't *that* bad. Hapless in the kitchen, yes, but none could dispute that she was a cheerful person who did her best for one and all, and that went a long way these days.

'*And* Rex said he trusted me,' said Hildred to herself. 'But obviously he doesn't, or he would tell me what he and the doctor are planning to do.' She remembered when she had gone to his room, and he had been working on that plan on the floor. Maybe she should go to look for that. 'No,' she scolded herself. 'How can I accuse him of not trusting me and then snoop in his room!'

She stood up and pulled on her dark hooded cloak. 'Perhaps I can't solve his mystery,' she said with determination, 'but maybe I can solve my own.'

And off she went.

In another part of the asylum Gerulphus too was mulling over recent events. He sat on the edge of his own bed (larger and more comfortable than Hildred's: he was in a superior room) in a state of indecision. There was more to Dr Velhildegildus than met the eye. A lot more. But the question, however, was not what the doctor was up to, but how his clandestine activities might affect Gerulphus. He sighed deeply. He had so wanted to stay here just that little bit longer before venturing out into the real world again, but now things were getting too complicated. Already the doctor's antics were attracting far too much attention from across the water in Opum Oppidulum. The *Hebdomadal* was reporting on the recent acquisitions and it was not beyond the bounds of reason to expect that soon there would be visitors, councillors at the very least or, worse, nosy journalists from the paper. Cecil Notwithstanding in particular. When he wasn't writing about beggars – his latest theory was that the beggars were somehow disappearing – he seemed to have an unhealthy interest in Droprock Island. And, if that wasn't bad enough, the cheek of Dr Velhildegildus, expecting Gerulphus to lug things back and forth like some sort of workhorse!

With a clenched jaw Gerulphus got up and cloaked himself, and emerged from his room. He had better things to do with his time.

Like shadows in the night Hildred and Gerulphus passed along the narrow, unwelcoming corridors of Droprock Asylum, sensing all around them the tortured spirits of previous inmates, missing each other only by moments, unaware that they were not alone in their meanderings. And as Gerulphus descended to the very bowels of the asylum Hildred made her way up to its heights.

Rex, unwittingly completing the trio of nocturnal peregrinators, was also at large.

He still felt guilty at how rude he had been earlier and was looking forward to telling Hildred she could help with the Perambulating Submersible, hoping that it would not only please her but also go some way towards her mollification. With this intention, upon leaving Dr Velhildegildus's study he went straight to her room.

'Hildred,' he hissed as he had done for the last couple of nights, but this time he prodded the mound of blankets on her bed – only to discover that was exactly what they were: a mound of blankets.

Hildred was gone.

Now where on earth could she be? he thought. Undeterred by the hour, determined to tell her the good news, he went quickly to the entrance hall. It was from here that all the parts, good or bad, of the asylum could be reached, like a sort of crossroads, and there was a very clear dividing line between one side and the other. The east wing – light, superior in comfort and decor – was designed for the guardians; the west wing – dark, uncomfortable, insanitary – was for those who needed to be guarded.

Rex, reluctant to go down into the cells during the day, was even less inclined to do so at night. As he tried to pluck up his courage, light footsteps alerted him to another nocturnal wanderer.

Speak of the devil, he thought, and shrank back into the shadows just as Gerulphus appeared. Rex watched him disappear down one of the corridors. Off to the cells? he thought. Well, that made up his mind for him: if he couldn't go down, then he would go up.

He climbed the main staircase quickly. The first floor was a long corridor with rooms on either side. He could hear snoring from one (Mrs Runcible) and whistling from another (Walter Freakley). A third door, presumably Gerulphus's room, was locked (Rex couldn't resist trying the handle). All the others were empty and Rex noted signs that their owners had left in a hurry. Furniture was overturned, drawers appeared to have been ransacked and in one Rex saw draped over a chair a dark grey jacket, with some sort of red badge on it. A warder, he thought bitterly, cruelly reminded of the two uniformed men who had taken his father away.

At the end of the corridor was another flight of stairs leading up to more rooms. These were much smaller, for maids and bootboys and kitchen staff. Finally, he came to one last set of narrow winding stairs, at the top of which was a small landing and a closed door. A thin band of light underneath alerted Rex to the possibility of an occupant on the other side.

Well, he thought, I know it isn't Gerulphus, and it's hardly Dr Velhildegildus, and ghosts don't need light.

Thus reassured as to the unlikelihood of danger, he turned the handle. The door gave with a creak and opened into a dusty attic, with criss-crossing beams and a pitched roof. In the poor light – its source was a chamber candle set atop a stool – he could make out pieces of randomly stacked broken furniture, three-legged tables and seatless chairs, broken-hinged trunks and damaged tea crates. It smelt of bats and birds' nests and dead animals. And ash.

And there in the middle of the dust and the cobwebs sat Hildred. Her back was to Rex and she was wholly absorbed in whatever it was she was doing.

Rex smiled and exhaled, unaware until then that he had been holding his breath. 'Hildred! So this is where you go at night.'

When she failed to react he reached out and tapped her on the shoulder. With a little shriek Hildred leaped up and turned, and it seemed to Rex that her head swivelled nearly the whole way round before her body followed. It was unnerving to watch.

'Oh, Rex,' she exclaimed. 'You gave me such a fright. Don't sneak up on people like that!'

'Didn't you hear me come in?'

'Obviously not,' she replied tartly, quickly recovering her composure. 'Your great friend Dr Velhildegildus has certainly been keeping you busy. I'm honoured to see you.'

Rex flushed. 'I know. I'm sorry. I was really rude to you earlier. That's why I came, to apologize, and to tell you something. Dr Velhildegildus . . .' He stopped. 'But what's all this?'

On the floor in front of her there was a stack of books and a pile of handwritten pages. From her expression it was obvious Hildred was trying to decide whether or not to tell him. Finally she said, 'I'm looking for information.'

'About my father?' asked Rex, wide-eyed. 'I *knew* you were up to something.'

Hildred chewed on her lip. 'Did you?'

'Of course. I've hardly seen you. You weren't in your bed and you're always covered in cobwebs. But you should have told me. I would have helped you.'

'Would you?'

Rex knew immediately what she meant and began a halting apology. She interrupted before he could finish.

'It's not about your father, it's about mine.'

'Oh.' Rex took a step back. 'But you said you hadn't seen him for years.'

'I haven't, not since my mother died. That's why I'm looking.'

'But why would you find it up here, in these books?'

Hildred stared at him coolly and remained silent. Rex gasped, suddenly understanding. 'He was here? In the asylum?'

'Yes,' said Hildred defensively. 'And what of it? It was nearly ten years ago.' She knelt down and picked up the open book. 'Mr Ephcott told me, when the Panopticon disbanded. He thought I was old enough to know. You see, when my mother died my father blamed himself. He lost his mind and was committed to the asylum. We were so near to Opum Oppidulum I had to come, to see whether he was still alive.'

Rex was incredulous. 'In this place? After a decade under Chapelizod?' Hildred frowned deeply and Rex immediately regretted his insensitivity.

'Well, obviously I arrived too late,' she said. 'Everyone was gone, but I wondered if maybe there were records somewhere.'

'And these are record books?'

'Yes,' said Hildred. 'At least, what remains of them. Somehow most of them were burned during the breakout. I salvaged what I could from the ashes and brought them up here so I could look at them in private. But you have found me.'

Now that he was closer, Rex could see that the books were indeed in a sorry state, badly charred, and the loose pages were brown and powdery.

'What was your father's name?' he asked, sitting down beside her.

'Arthur Buttonquail, but there's nothing here.' Hildred couldn't hide her disappointment.

'You did your best,' said Rex, putting his arm around her bony shoulder. 'You were just too late. Anyhow, this doesn't prove anything. There might be other books, other records. Who knows, your father might even have been let out. Perhaps he's in Opum Oppidulum right now, alive and well.'

Hildred pasted a smile back on her face. 'Maybe that's where I should go, then. I have no reason to stay now. I only came for this.'

Rex's face fell. 'You can't go. Dr Velhildegildus said that you can help us if you want.'

'With the asylum? But I want to be a tutor.'

'Er . . . not exactly.'

'Then what?'

Rex looked her straight in the eye. 'OK, I'll be honest with you. Dr Velhildegildus has a plan for an underwater vessel, a Perambulating Submersible, and he wants to make it here. I did want to tell you, from the beginning, but I made a deal. He's asked me to help because he knows that I am good at making things.'

Hildred looked surprised but there was no hiding her interest.

'So . . . will you stay and help us to build it?'

Hildred laughed. 'Why not? It sounds fascinating.' She pushed the fragile books and pages to one side, then she stood up and dusted herself off. 'Tell me more.'

Hildred asked questions all the way back to their rooms. 'You mean this will really work underwater? But how will you breathe? Through pipes? But they will limit the range of the machine. And what if they break? People have been trying to make underwater boats for centuries, you know. Mr Ephcott told me. The air supply was always the sticking point. This Re-breather sounds just the thing. If it really works, Dr Velhildegildus will be famous. Though I don't suppose he'll want to run the asylum any more.'

Rex answered all the questions, keeping as close to the truth as possible; he knew that was the best way to lie.

'And did you show him the egg?' she asked finally.

'No,' said Rex. 'The egg is . . . special. I *will* show him, just not yet.'

'I won't tell him,' said Hildred with a shrug.

Rex hadn't realized just how much he wanted Hildred to stay until he thought that she might not. But his pleasure was tainted by the strange gnawing at his insides, like something eating away at his belly. What Hildred said was true. If Dr Velhildegildus was to claim all the credit for his father's design he really would be famous.

There was a part of Rex that wanted to tell Tibor that he knew about the plan. But he didn't trust him yet. It was better at this stage to say nothing. Perhaps he might even admit it later.

'What's that smile for?' asked Hildred looking at Rex's strangely twisted mouth.

'Nothing,' he said.

Hildred felt sure that Rex was still keeping something from her. And the only way to find out was to help.

35

Mox Nox in Rem

The clock struck seven. Rex knocked.

'Enter!'

Rex and Hildred found the geometrically jawed doctor warming his legs by the fire's flames.

'Hildred,' he said smoothly. 'I believe Rex has let you in on our little secret.'

Hildred nodded. She found this man odd to look at. He had a curious way of speaking, his lips forming his words into strangely exaggerated shapes.

'I think it is a wonderful idea,' she said.

'Excellent,' said Tibor with a slight smile. 'But I hope he has impressed upon you the need for secrecy.'

Rex, hearing the slightest suspicion in Tibor's tone (how that voice got under his skin!) reassured him hastily. 'I have.' He glanced over at Hildred but she seemed unmoved by Tibor's nuances.

'Then let us go.'

It was with delight and trepidation that Hildred followed Dr Velhildegildus and Rex through the secret entrance behind the bookcase into the long tunnel beneath the asylum. And when they emerged into the blue light of the underground chamber she stood and stared in wonderment at the beautiful vista before her.

'Rex,' she breathed. 'How could you keep this from me?'

Rex smiled apologetically. From the sidelines Dr Velhildegildus was watching the two of them intently. *It seems the boy is telling the truth*, he thought. He stroked his broad jaw with his fingers, and his lips moved rapidly as he talked to himself. 'There's work to do,' he said shortly. '*Mox nox in rem.*'

Rex groaned.

'Soon the night, get to business,' translated Hildred, with a knowing smile.

Rex spread the plan out on a large crate and the three of them pored over it.

'Where do you suggest we start?' asked Tibor, and both he and Hildred looked to Rex for guidance.

Rex's heart swelled. He thought of his father. All those years he had spent at his side, listening, learning and, more importantly, actually creating. This was exactly what Ambrose had prepared him for. It was in his blood. And it was for his father's blood he was doing this now.

Rex took a deep breath and began.

'Hildred, you start with this part. It's small, but important, and needs to be put together accurately.

Dr Velhildegildus, you can work with the panels. They can be assembled now, and then fixed together later. I will begin work on the Re-breather.'

'Yes, sir,' said Hildred with a laugh and a mock salute, and even Tibor managed a smile.

For the next five days, and on into the nights, the unlikely trio – Rex, Dr Velhildegildus and Hildred – worked away in the underground chamber creating the vessel that for one of them was ultimately a matter of greed; for another a labour of salvation and healing; and for the third of little consequence at all.

It was by no means an easy job and all of them found it exhausting, both mentally and physically, but particularly Rex. With every turn of the screw, every downswing of the hammer, every pounding of the mallet, he felt as if his father was in the chamber with them, watching over his work, silently judging.

Tibor was the most keen, to the point of obsession, if not the most talented. He would have been perfectly content to put the whole machine together himself but, lacking the required practical and mechanical knowledge, and limited by the time constraint he had placed upon the work, he allowed Rex to take charge. And the boy had proved from the outset that he was more than capable of managing the task.

Dr Velhildegildus was a quick learner, and what he lacked in skill he made up for in enthusiasm. He had no qualms about taking a greasy spanner to a nut or a dusty cloth to a piece of glass. Rex had not thought a man of his social standing and reputation would have been so ready to get his hands dirty. It was a side to the doctor that he found surprising.

Tibor had brought down (well, more accurately, Rex and Hildred had carried) a large supply of food and drink to the chamber, but he himself seemed hardly to need sleep or nourishment. If it wasn't for Rex or Hildred stopping occasionally, Rex doubted Tibor would have taken any food at all. But Tibor's energy, a sort of superhuman madness, was contagious and soon Rex and Hildred too found themselves less and less inclined to halt. Instead they threw themselves into the project with the same obsessive compulsion as the doctor.

As for Hildred's contribution, undoubtedly she had skills that were needed in his project. Mr Ephcott had impressed upon her the importance of logical and sequential thinking and she proved well able to follow the plan without any help whatsoever (Tibor, whose mind seemed rather less organized, needed regular reassurance). Her nimble fingers were invaluable when it came to tricky and awkward parts, and her ability to contort to any shape meant that she could reach into places that neither Rex nor Dr Velhildegildus could ever hope to access. But she became so deeply absorbed in what she was doing that Rex lost count of the times he had had to repeat what he said to her.

Nut by nut, bolt by bolt, panel by panel, the Perambulating Submersible grew before their eyes. Rex knew that it was going to be a truly beautiful piece of machinery, unrivalled anywhere in the country, perhaps even the world.

How he wished his father could be there to see it. How he wished he could pilot it. How he wished that people would know the truth of its inception . . .

'What are you going to call her?' asked Hildred on the afternoon of the fifth day as they took a moment to stand back to examine their work. It was now so close to completion that it did not take much imagination to see that the Perambulating Submersible was to be a spectacular vessel. 'She must have a name.'

'I am as yet unsure,' said Dr Velhildegildus.

'*Indagator Gurgitis*,' said Rex without hesitation. He laughed when he saw the expressions on Hildred's and Dr Velhildegildus's faces. 'It means "Explorer of the Deep".'

'You told me you hated Latin,' said Hildred with narrowed eyes.

Tibor stood up. '*Indagator Gurgitis* it is,' he declared. 'Now, seeing as we are so far ahead of schedule and that my vessel requires little more than a tweak here and a tweak there, a good polish and the installation of the Re-breather . . .' Here he looked enquiringly at Rex.

'It will be ready, Dr Velhildegildus,' said Rex confidently. 'I will fit it myself on the day of the full moon.'

'Excellent,' continued Dr Velhildegildus. 'Then I propose that we return to the asylum for the rest of the day.'

Hildred was very pleased to hear this. Fascinating as she found the project, she was longing for fresh air. 'And to get away from the constant clanging and pounding,' she said. 'Everything echoes dreadfully down here. It hurts my head.'

Rex was equally pleased. He felt he had reached a point of fatigue beyond which he thought it impossible to go.

And so it was with great relief on all sides that the three returned to the study. Tibor sat down gratefully by the fire.

'There's a letter here for you,' said Hildred. She picked it up from the desk and handed it over, but not before Rex had seen the seal — *the unmistakable blue seal of Grammaticus.* His heart skipped a beat. How he hated to think of Acantha in his father's study using his letterhead and his seal. But, more worrying, why was she writing to Tibor?

Tibor broke the seal, unfolded the single page and glanced quickly at the contents, his lips moving all the time as he read it. He refolded it and put it in his pocket.

'Off you go, then,' he said, gesturing to them to leave. 'I'm sure Mrs Runcible has an excellent lunch for you. I need to go to Opum Oppidulum this afternoon, to, er . . . attend to a few urgent matters. And I have visitors this evening so I suggest you both keep out of the way.'

'Do you still intend to reopen the asylum, Dr Velhil-degildus?' asked Hildred at the door.

Tibor looked a little surprised at the question, but he considered it before replying. 'My dear friends,' he said solemnly. 'What do you think a madman is?'

Rex could only stare at the corner of the letter in Tibor's pocket while Hildred considered the question.

'I have heard it said that it is someone who repeats the same action every day but always thinks there will be a different outcome,' she said.

Tibor steepled his fingers and smiled, causing his face to widen even more. 'If that is the case, we are all touched by madness, are we not?'

'Then should we all be locked up?' asked Hildred.

Tibor laughed. 'There are plenty of lunatics under lock and key who would be perfectly at ease in the real world,' he said. 'And there are plenty of madmen who are free who should not be. But who is the judge? People fear what they do not know, what they do not understand, and they want to hide those things away. Some things are best left like that. Hidden. The real lunacy would be to continue to enquire into what doesn't concern you.'

The hint was hardly subtle, and Rex and Hildred left the study. As soon as they were out of earshot Rex grabbed Hildred by the arm. 'I have to see that letter,' he said. 'It's from Acantha.'

'I know,' said Hildred.

'You know?' Rex was aghast. 'How?'

She hesitated. 'I was close enough to see the writing through the paper.'

Rex took her hesitation as embarrassment that she had read private correspondence. 'So, what did it say?'

'Well, if I recall correctly,' said Hildred, 'Acantha wrote, "My dearest Tibor, Urgent news. I suspect a certain person is a little too close for comfort. I have suggested that he and I come to the asylum for a meal. I shall bring provisions and we can resolve this matter for once and for all. I do believe a resolution needs to be found now if we are to continue. With fondest wishes, Acantha".'

Rex looked at Hildred in astonishment. 'You read all that through the paper? Is there no end to your talents?'

'Apparently not,' replied Hildred with a chuckle.

Rex was not so light-hearted. 'This cannot be good,' he said. 'It sounds like some sort of secret message. Who is the "certain person" and what is this matter they need to resolve?'

'I agree that it is a little mysterious,' said Hildred. 'But don't you think we should concentrate on your father's secrets now that we have a little time in hand?'

Rex knew Hildred was right, but he was worried. Acantha and Tibor seemed a little too friendly for his liking.

36

A Pipe and a Pest

In the kitchen Mrs Runcible was as cheerful as ever, cooking fish again, and Gerulphus was reading the *Hebdomadal*.

'Early today,' she said as burnt fish spattered all around her. 'And I thought Dr Velhildegildus to be a hard taskmaster!'

'He says he has things to do.' Gerulphus spoke from behind the paper. 'Freakley is taking him to town this afternoon.'

'And he has company tonight, but my services are not required,' said Mrs Runcible dolefully. 'Dr Velhildegildus doesn't wish me to cook for his friends.'

Gerulphus shook out the *Hebdomadal* noisily. 'Cecil Notwithstanding is still writing about those "missing" beggars,' he said as if she hadn't spoken. 'I can hardly imagine why. Good riddance, I say. That committee should be commended for doing such a fine job.' He dropped the paper on the table as he left the kitchen and Hildred picked it up.

'Rex, come and see me when you're finished,' said Hildred pointedly, as she too left. 'I've got something to show you.'

Mrs Runcible smiled after her. 'Lovely girl, that Hildred,' she said. 'But I can't make head nor tail of her leaves!'

Intrigued by Hildred's cryptic message, Rex rushed the remainder of his food. Burping gently as he crossed the entrance hall, he caught sight of Tibor out of the window. He was with Walter Freakley. He watched through the dusty glass until he saw the boat heading out into the misty lake and then hurried on to join Hildred in her room. She was waiting impatiently at the door for him. As soon as he came in she locked it and turned her face to Rex in that way peculiar to her.

'Look,' she said, holding up the *Hebdomadal*. 'I saw it when Gerulphus turned the page.'

Rex could see some sort of promotional panel, a few lines of dark print within a black ink drawing of a serpent. Slowly he read the text aloud:

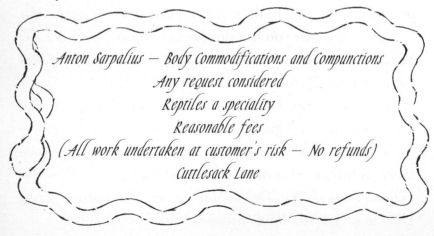

Anton Sarpalius — Body Commodifications and Compunctions
Any request considered
Reptiles a speciality
Reasonable fees
(All work undertaken at customer's risk — No refunds)
Cuttlesack Lane

'Commodifications and compunctions?' said Rex. 'Now where have I heard that before?' He recalled the weather-worn sign over Mr Sarpalius's shop and the missing letters. '*Body commodifications*,' he repeated excitedly.

'Your Mr Sarpalius is a tattoo artist,' said Hildred triumphantly. 'Do you have a tattoo?'

'No,' said Rex. 'Of course not.'

'Then your father must have one,' she said with indisputable logic. 'I think it's time we paid Mr Sarpalius a visit.'

'But I'm so tired,' moaned Rex, falling back on the bed.

Hildred spoke sharply. 'I thought you wanted to find out what really happened to your father. Now all you're interested in is building that stupid machine.'

Rex, taken aback at this unanticipated attack on his beloved *Indagator*, protested quickly, 'It's not stupid! It will be worth a fortune.'

'Not to you, it won't,' said Hildred matter-of-factly, 'even though you're putting in all the work. Dr Velhildegildus doesn't know what he is doing – I can see that – but you, you're different. If I didn't know otherwise I would think that you had drawn up the plans yourself. Dr Velhildegildus is set to make a mint. How much of it will come our way?'

Rex jumped up. 'I didn't realize you were doing it for the money,' he said indignantly. 'That's not what it's about.'

'Then what is it about? You should hear yourself down there. You think you're in charge but you're not. "Yes, Dr Velhildegildus." "No, Dr Velhildegildus." "Anything you say, Dr Velhildegildus." You've turned into Tibor's lapdog.'

'It's not like that,' said Rex hotly, but in truth he was stung by her mimicry and the look of disdain on her face and by the creeping suspicion that everything she said was true. 'It's the way he talks. It's sort of . . . irresistible. Haven't you noticed?'

'No, I haven't,' said Hildred bluntly. 'I think you're hiding something, and if you want me to stay to help you in this awful, awful place then you have to tell me what's going on. Do you think it was easy for me to tell you that my father was put in here? And, worse, that he really *was* insane? Your father wasn't.' Hildred narrowed her eyes. 'Or so you say.'

'OK,' said Rex at last, with a gesture of resignation. 'I'll tell you, but I don't see how it will make any difference. You're right, I already know of the plan. It's my father's and mine.'

'I knew it,' said Hildred with satisfaction. '*Indagator Gurgitis*! You already had the name, didn't you? But why on earth did you give the plan to Dr Velhildegildus?'

'That's just it. I didn't. I don't know how he got hold of it,' replied Rex, and what a relief it was to finally tell the whole truth.

'Then ask him!'

Rex covered his face with his hands and let out a long sigh. 'You don't understand.'

Hildred pulled his hands away from his mouth. 'You're mumbling,' she said and then stopped abruptly. 'Oh Lord, you're scared,' she whispered. 'You're scared to ask.'

Rex's dark-ringed eyes were like stains on his pale

face. 'Yes, I am, because I'm afraid that he did something terrible to get it — maybe he stole it. And I don't know what he would do if he knew that I knew. We've made a deal. If I help with *Indagator* then he won't send me back to Acantha. I don't want to do anything to upset him, not yet.'

'All right,' said Hildred slowly. 'I think I understand. But that doesn't stop us seeing Sarpalius. Let's go now. We can take the boat.'

'Freakley's taken the boat,' said Rex, momentarily relieved to think that they couldn't go. But Hildred's smile told him the lack of boat was no obstacle to her plans.

'You forget. There's the other boat, from when they brought over the equipment. It's still down at the landing place. We'll be there and back before anyone misses us.'

The yellow mist was cool against their anxious faces as Rex and Hildred clambered into the spare boat. Rex pushed off with one oar and Hildred took the other. Quickly they settled into a smooth rowing rhythm and they made fast progress across the dark lake.

'Keep the asylum in front of you,' said Hildred, 'and then we should be on course for the shore.'

Rex looked at Hildred beside him. She seemed lost in thought and oblivious to all about her. It was odd the way she seemed to dip in and out of the world. Sometimes talking to her was like talking to a tree trunk. But then, when she looked at him with those penetrating eyes, he felt as if no one else was getting any attention.

'Can you hear that?' asked Hildred suddenly. 'A sort of whistling.'

Rex shook his head. Hildred laid down her oar and dropped her arm over the side to let her hand dangle in the water. 'I can feel it,' she said, turning to Rex, her eyes shining.

'Are you mad?' he laughed. 'You can't feel whistling.'

'*I* can,' she said simply, then picked up her oar and began to row again.

The town clock was striking the half-hour when they caught sight of the wooden jetty. They had veered across slightly and it was a little way up to the left.

'Freakley's there,' said Hildred. And indeed he was, perched on the jetty and whistling.

'Just row down the shore a little more,' said Rex. 'We'll drag up the boat; he won't see us.'

Once again Rex walked the gloomy streets, distinctly unwelcoming in the low winter's light, this time with Hildred at his side, making their way deeper into the shabby, less salubrious areas of Opum Oppidulum. There was talk that this end of town was going the way of Urbs Umida. They were bothered once or twice by beggars but unusually they seemed loath to persevere once rebuffed.

Rex slowed as they turned into Cuttlesack Lane and reached Mr Sarpalius's shop. Everything was as it had been that night, weeks ago now. The creaking sign, the missing letters, the cobwebbed window. Rex raised his fist but it remained suspended.

'Aren't you going to knock?' asked Hildred.

'I can't,' muttered Rex shakily. His mind was playing havoc with his nerves.

So Hildred knocked confidently on the door. The panel slid across and a pair of eyes looked out.

'We're here to see Mr Sarpalius,' said Hildred.

'Is he expecting you?'

'Tell him it's about Ambrose Grammaticus.'

It seemed an age before the door opened and they were ushered in. Hildred looked around with interest, Rex with fear. Inhaling again the odours of the shop was almost too much for him to bear. Hildred reached for his shaking hand.

'He's last curtain down on the left,' said the man behind the counter. 'He'll see you but only for a minute. He's busy in the afternoons.'

In silence the pair passed down the corridor, listening to intermittent muffled groans of pain on either side of them. The smell was different this time, thought Rex, tinged with a cloying sweetness. It made him feel a little light-headed.

Hildred drew back the last velvet drape to see Anton Sarpalius reclining on a couch so large that it only just fitted in the small space. He was dressed in dark satin and surrounded by plump cushions. His eyes were bloodshot and his pupils were large, bright spots burned on his cheeks, but he looked very much at ease.

'You again,' he said, not unkindly, when he saw Rex hovering behind Hildred. In his right hand he held a long pipe from which he inhaled deeply before resting it in the ebony holder beside him. 'What do you want?'

'We want to know about Ambrose Grammaticus,' said Hildred, unperturbed by the man's lizard-like face. Rex was struck mute beside her. 'Did you give him a tattoo while Rex was asleep?'

Anton yawned lazily and showed his split tongue. 'Asleep? Out like a spit-snuffed candle you were,' he said.

'Did my father tell you anything?' asked Rex, finally finding his voice.

'About what?' It seemed as if Anton had only a tenuous grip on reality.

'A maze, a boy with wings, a diamond.'

'Very particular about his letters, your father. He paid me with a diamond,' said Anton slowly, and took up the pipe again. The blue aromatic smoke curled up his nose and he half shut his eyes. 'Have you one too?'

'Let's go,' said Hildred, dragging Rex away. 'He can't tell you anything and whatever he does tell you, you can't believe it.'

'Leaving so soon?' called Anton after them. 'What about your skull?'

Outside on the street Rex and Hildred took deep breaths of the cold air and walked briskly to shake off the heavy atmosphere of the room. The light was fading fast and they didn't want to cross the lake in the dark. Rex was annoyed with Hildred but even more so with himself, for being so useless, so feeble. 'Why did you drag me away?' he asked irritably.

'He's been smoking opium,' said Hildred. 'He doesn't know what he's saying.'

'But he said something about my skull. Could that mean something?'

'Did he? I didn't hear. Maybe he meant where you hurt your head.'

Involuntarily Rex touched the wound. 'I don't think so,' he began, but was immediately distracted by a cart that had pulled up alongside them. It kept pace with their walking and the driver looked down at them, but then he made a clicking sound with his tongue. 'Ho, Blackbird!' he called, and with a crack of the whip he took off.

'Blackbird?' muttered Rex. Then it dawned on him. 'That's the man who delivers the meat to Acantha. He's the butcher.'

Hildred stared after him. 'Butcher? It says "Pest Controller" on his cart. The man is a rat catcher.'

'Ugh,' laughed Rex. 'Maybe that's what's so special about Acantha's meat.'

'Perhaps he does two jobs,' said Hildred, but she was doubtful. It was not an ideal marriage: rats and meat.

When they reached their boat they saw that Freakley was still waiting at the jetty.

'You know, we don't have to go back,' said Hildred carefully, almost as if she was testing him out. 'We could go somewhere else. Forget the whole business.'

'You can,' said Rex. 'You said it yourself. There's nothing for you at the asylum. I understand if you want to leave, to find your father, but I have to return, to finish *Indagator*.'

'Surely Tibor could fit the Re-breather, couldn't he? We're getting nowhere with the clues.'

'I want to do it,' insisted Rex. 'For *my* father.'

Hildred smiled. 'Good,' she said. 'And I want to help. You're right, I don't have to, but I will,' she said decisively. 'I want to finish what we started. Everything. But you can't keep any more secrets from me.'

37

Thoughts of the Monstrous Creature

Primitive as it was, the monstrous creature was not wholly insensitive to its environment. It could see the light of the growing moon, as it had many times down the centuries, and it knew instinctively what it meant. It anticipated the change in the water with a sort of pleasure.

This time something was different. The water was moving faster, the current was stronger, it had to swim harder against it. It was an exhilarating feeling. The creature was reminded of the time many, many years ago when the water had swollen so high that it had filled the chamber under the rocky island. The same chamber where that strange upright animal fed it. Not fish, but something else, a little like those animals it had found recently flailing on the surface of the lake. They were juicy, if lean, and it had swum up and down many times since, looking for more, but it seemed they were all gone. The others would do for now.

In the moonlight the creature could see up through the

water and make out the shape again of that strange fish above. It watched the broad flippers going back and forth, back and forth, and it waited for the call. But none came. Neither had it answered earlier. The creature was confused, anxious, and began to call again. But still there was no reply.

38

On the Trail of the Elusive Mr Faye

'Take care, Acantha,' warned Tibor as he took her stiff-fingered hand and helped her out of the boat. 'You know what happens to those who fall into Lake Beluarum!'

'Indeed I do, Tibor,' she tittered. She was holding a string-tied wax-papered package under one arm and the boat rocked violently as she clambered awkwardly on to the rock. Walter gave her a helpful shove from behind, for which she shot him a dirty look.

Rex and Hildred, crouching down in their own boat, were only a short distance away. They had just tied up when they heard Walter Freakley's unmistakable whistling behind them. Instinctively they had climbed back into the boat and hidden under the seat.

'They won't see us in the mist,' Rex had whispered as Walter's boat hit the pier with more force than usual. It was sitting very low in the water on account of Acantha's increasing bulk and the fact that it carried not three but four people: Tibor, Acantha, Walter and a bearded man of modest proportions. He stepped on to the pier, hooked his thumbs in his waistcoat pockets and looked around.

'Well, Dr Velhildegildus,' he said with satisfaction, 'I've been looking forward to this visit.'

'I'll lead the way,' said Tibor.

Hildred, tidily squeezed into her confined space, watched as Tibor and his two guests went on ahead. Walter secured the boat before following. As soon as they were out of sight Rex crawled out and stretched his arms, complaining of cramp. Hildred eased herself out with little difficulty and had no such complaints, but she did roll her shoulders with an alarming cracking sound. They waited, deeming it important to give the forward party time enough to reach the asylum.

'So that's Acantha,' said Hildred. 'You described her well. But who's the other fellow?'

Rex smiled triumphantly. 'It's Andrew Faye,' he said. 'Didn't you hear Tibor?'

'No.'

'He said, "I'll lead, Mr Faye." What a stroke of luck. It must be another meeting of the Society of Andrew Faye and this time he's turned up in person.'

'That's why Mrs Runcible won't be cooking,' said Hildred. 'Come on, let's go. I want to have a look at this Mr Faye.'

They made for the steps but Rex stopped suddenly and stared hard at the ground.

'What is it?' asked Hildred.

Rex knelt and wiped his hand across the rock. Sticky strings of a dark red liquid hung between his fingers. 'It's blood,' he said.

'Acantha's package,' said Hildred. 'The meat for tonight. Here, someone's dropped a handkerchief.' She picked up a folded piece of material from the ground. 'You can wipe your hand.'

But Rex wasn't listening. He was transfixed by the substance on his fingers. Before he realized what he was doing, he brought them to his mouth and began to lick them.

Hildred looked at him in utter astonishment. 'Oh, fingerknots! Rex, what in the world do you think you are doing?'

'I . . . I don't know,' he stammered, looking confused and dismayed and surprised all at once. 'The smell was so strong and I just wanted to clean my fingers.'

'Well, at least wait until it's cooked next time.'

They climbed the steps in silence. Rex was worried. He had tried to laugh off his odd behaviour but inside he was as shocked as Hildred. And not because he had licked the blood. But because he had liked the taste.

There was no sign of Dr Velhildegildus and his visitors when they reached the asylum but they bumped into Mrs Runcible in the entrance hall.

'Where've you two been?' she asked. 'It's early supper tonight, so's Dr Velhildegildus can have the kitchen.'

'Where is he now?' asked Hildred.

'They're all in his study.'

Rex was glad. He didn't want to see *her*, just Mr Faye, and preferably on his own.

During supper (cold meat and bread with watered down ale – a reasonably palatable meal; there was little that the good-natured cook could do to ruin it) Mrs Runcible, still miffed at the perceived insult to her cooking, sat mournfully at the end of the table swilling the leaves in a cup.

'It's the lady's,' she said. 'I don't know her name, the doctor hasn't introduced us, but there's lipstick on the side you see. She drinks dainty she does,' she continued. 'You should see the way her little finger sticks out. Sign of breeding.'

Rex shuddered at the scarlet stain on the lip of the cup: Acantha's trademark. 'What do her leaves say?' he asked.

'Difficult to tell,' said Mrs Runcible. 'But give me another few cups and I should be able to say.'

After supper, Hildred and Rex went to Hildred's room and sat debating their next move. Hildred wanted to go back to the torture chamber, as they now called it, but Rex didn't. He wanted to spy on Tibor and his guests. 'I want to get a proper look at Andrew Faye first. I'm certain there's a connection between him and my father and the other clues.'

'We can do both,' suggested Hildred.

Reluctantly Rex agreed.

'See? No moaning,' said Rex tetchily as they made their way down the stinking tunnel to the rocky end wall. He was already regretting agreeing to see the cells first. He could hardly bear to be there, and he was most anxious

242

to eavesdrop on the supper in the kitchen above.

'Be patient, I just want to have a look,' said Hildred. 'I'll only be a minute or two.'

'But what if Andrew Faye leaves tonight? I might never see him again.'

'I shouldn't worry about that. They'll drink too much and then go to Tibor's study, have a few brandies and probably fall asleep by the fire. You might catch him in the morning.'

'But—'

'Besides, I don't think that fellow is your mysterious Mr Faye.'

Rex was momentarily silenced. 'Then who is it?'

'Cecil Notwithstanding.'

Rex snorted in disbelief. 'How on earth do you know that? You've never even seen him.'

'I'll admit it's a bit of a wild guess but I do have some evidence.'

'What evidence?' Rex found Hildred's logic exasperating at times.

Hildred reached into her pocket and produced a large square of white linen stained blue and red. 'Remember this?'

'The handkerchief,' said Rex disdainfully. 'What does that prove?' But then he saw the initials on the corner: 'C.N.'

'Cecil Notwithstanding,' said Hildred matter-of-factly rather than triumphantly. 'And did you see the state of the man's fingers? Black and blue from ink. Is that not the true sign of a journalist? Remember that letter from Acantha?'

she continued. 'I think Cecil is the fellow who knows too much.'

Rex had to admit that she was probably right; she was nothing if not logical. He tried to play her at her own game. 'Then the real question is, what does he know? That's why we have to see him.'

But Hildred had her ear to the wall again. 'Absolutely nothing,' she said with a disappointed shake of her head. She nodded to the locked door. 'I think we should have another look in there.'

Rex hung back.

'Mr Ephcott always said in cases like these that it is vital to eliminate every possibility. You said yourself you saw Gerulphus come down here the other night. There has to be a reason. You've got your picklock, haven't you?'

Rex was tempted to say no, but he could see that Hildred was not to be swayed from her quest so he opened the door. 'Though I don't know what she thinks she's going to find in there,' he muttered to himself.

The room was as before: pungent and dank, like something from a living nightmare. Hildred went around the walls, holding her lamp up high, looking at everything on the shelves, feeling all the tools of torture. There was a large empty barrel in one corner and she peered into it for what seemed like an age. Rex stood by the door, distinctly ill at ease, becoming increasingly agitated. 'This is a waste of time,' he said. 'I *really* don't want to be down here. Can't we go?'

Hildred ignored him and continued with her silent examination of the room.

'Oh, for heaven's sake,' Rex exclaimed. 'You're not even listening!' And with that he turned on his heel and walked out, leaving Hildred alone in the chamber.

'I don't care what she says,' he muttered as he stomped up the tunnel. 'I'm going to see what they're up to with Cecil Notwithstanding.'

39

Eavesdropping

It was a few moments before Hildred even noticed that Rex had gone, but when she realized that she was alone she too was furious.

'I don't believe it!' she exclaimed, looking down the tunnel. 'He's gone and left me down here. After everything I've done for him. What an ungrateful . . . pig!' At the door she tutted with exasperation. 'How stupid can you get? How can I lock the door without a key?'

She noticed a light approaching from beyond the bend down the tunnel, and immediately felt remorseful at how quick she had been to condemn Rex.

But it wasn't Rex up ahead – it was Gerulphus. Luckily, on account of the fact that he sneezed as he rounded the corner, his eyes were closed so he failed to see Hildred stepping hastily back into the chamber of horrors.

Hildred didn't want to be found down here again. Gerulphus might tell Tibor and there was *Indagator* to think about now. Annoying as Rex might be, she didn't want to ruin his chances of finishing the project or, of course, solving his mysteries. Thinking quickly, she stepped into the empty barrel and tucked herself into a tight ball.

Upon arriving at the chamber, Gerulphus was surprised, and suspicious, to find that the door was unlocked. He held up his lantern and looked around. Nothing had been disturbed.

'Those children,' he muttered as he locked the door. 'It's time for a padlock. Unless it's Dr Velhildegildus? Perhaps he has found a key.' What matter? His time was nearly up on Droprock Island.

From her hiding place Hildred's eyes followed Gerulphus's every move. She was nervous but also excited. What exactly was it that brought this laconic oddball back here again and again? She watched with fast-beating heart as he went to the panel with the branding irons. She heard the turn of a key, saw the panel swing open and then, to her great surprise, Gerulphus was gone. But this was no magic trick; Hildred didn't believe in that. There was a logical explanation for everything. So, with no thought for her own safety, only for her curious mind, she crawled out of her hiding space, ran to the closing panel and just managed to slip through before it silently shut.

While Hildred was in pursuit of Gerulphus, Rex was creeping down the stairs to the kitchen. Assailed on his descent by the delicious aroma of Acantha's stew, he licked his lips constantly. Unfortunately his plan – if plan it could be called, so flimsy was its premise — was immediately thwarted. The sound of chairs being pushed back across stone and loud voices put him in a panic and he turned tail, raced back up to the hall and dived for cover under the main stairs.

Barely seconds later Acantha and Tibor and their bearded guest appeared from below. Of the three, the stranger (Rex was still not wholly convinced he was Cecil Notwithstanding) seemed the worst for wear. Unsteady on his feet, he needed support on both sides from his fellow diners.

'This way, Cecil,' said Tibor, dispelling in one fell swoop Rex's lingering doubts. 'We'll go to my study for an early nightcap.'

Rex gritted his teeth. How come Hildred was always right!

'I think I musht have had a little too mush of that fine wine,' slurred Cecil. 'A Fitzbaudly bottle, you say. A very good year, but powerful shtuff!'

Acantha and Tibor, exuding an aromatic cloud of mouth-watering smells, exchanged sly glances behind Cecil's head as they passed by the hidden watcher. Unaware of Rex creeping along in their wake, the two of them half carried, half dragged Cecil all the way to Tibor's study, his limp feet leaving parallel lines in the pile. Knowing this really was Cecil Notwithstanding brought little comfort to Rex. He was unsure what to make of it all. This was the man his father had said to trust — yet here he was, dining with his arch-enemy, Acantha, and Tibor, the man who had promised to liberate him from said enemy. Something didn't add up.

The study door closed and Rex put his ear against it. I had never thought to be such a regular eavesdropper, he mused. Perhaps I should invent some sort of machine that is able to listen through doors.

He cupped his hand and listened intently but in truth he didn't hold out much hope. The dinner conversation would surely have been more enlightening, but Hildred's insistence on going down to the tunnels had prevented his catching that. So Rex was resigned to hearing little more than the chink of the brandy bottle and snoring.

But he was to be surprised. Very surprised indeed.

'Now, Mr Notwithstanding,' he heard Tibor croon. 'You just settle yourself down here. You say you are interested in my Lodestone Procedure. It's a very relaxing experience. What was that? Safe? Oh yes, perfectly safe, I assure you. Perfectly safe indeed!

Lodestone Procedure? thought Rex. He had not expected this!

Hildred was some distance behind Gerulphus but was able to track him by the light of his lantern. Lacking her own, she couldn't afford to let him get too far ahead. Neither could she afford to be squeamish as, in a flash of inspiration, she broke a bony hand from one of the many skeletons in the cavities, and placed a joint at each turn to mark her ever descending path.

After a short while, and many turns left and right, and a near miss with a deep hole, the light ahead remained steady.

What's he doing? wondered Hildred, but she didn't dare

go any closer. Then the light was on the move again, but slower this time, dipping rhythmically as if Gerulphus was hauling something along in short bursts of effort.

At the next turn Hildred just caught sight of Gerulphus taking a left in the distance. He *was* dragging something but she couldn't see what. She walked on quickly and came to an open iron-barred door. Another cell, and all the way down here! The floor was covered in fish bones and there was a small piece of embroidered red cloth caught on the door. She took it then hurried on. Gerulphus's light was no longer visible but she could still see, for now she was bathed in the familiar blue glow of the underground chamber.

We must be nearing the lake, she thought.

She slowed at the final bend. The blue light was stronger now and she could smell the water. Her hands were sweaty and her heart was racing as she stood just inside the exit. Ever so slowly she inched her head around the rock. She saw the lake, the water higher now than before, and there on the ledge was Gerulphus, still dragging his awkward burden.

He went all the way to the end of the rocky promontory before dropping it. There was something in the way it fell and its shape upon the ground that struck a chord with Hildred. 'Oh Lord,' she breathed. 'It's a person! He must have taken him from that last cell.' She prayed that whoever it was was long dead, for she had an ominous feeling that what she was about to witness was not going to be pleasant.

Gerulphus picked up a stick and began to beat on the

water, causing a ripple to spread outwards to the middle of the lake. Nothing happened. Hildred cocked her head to one side, listening intently, though to any other ears no sound could be heard. Seconds later a large scaly fin split the water like a knife. Gerulphus smiled and dropped the stick.

Hildred could hardly bear to look but she couldn't help herself. So she saw the very moment the monstrous creature broke the surface of the water, its scarlet, yawning, dentiferous mouth, its overlapping scales glittering in the blue light. She saw Gerulphus take up the man, for bag of bones he might be but he was still a man, and involuntarily she covered her eyes with her hands. But it wasn't enough and through the gaps between her fingers she watched as, with a great expulsion of breath, Gerulphus flung the body into the maw of the monster. It sank back down and disappeared, the only trace of its existence being the rapidly subsiding undulations on the surface. And in her very marrow Hildred could feel the reverberations of its teeth crunching into the dead man's bones.

'So, Mr Notwithstanding,' crooned Tibor, 'what exactly have you been looking into recently?'

Tibor's voice was at its smoothest. Even through the door Rex could feel his head beginning to swim. He shook it hard and bit his knuckles in an attempt to stay focused.

Concentrate, he urged himself. This was not the time to yield to Dr Velhildegildus's persuasive tones. Cecil Notwithstanding, however, had succumbed.

'The beggars,' replied Cecil easily. 'Certainly there are fewer now than before but there are reports that they are disappearing under strange circumstances. And the asylum superintendent, Cadmus Chapelizod – well, there were some very unpleasant rumours about him. I'm sure there is some sort of connection.'

'Do you know of Cadmus Chapelizod's whereabouts?' continued Tibor. Rex bit harder and warm salty liquid oozed from his knuckle.

'No,' replied Cecil dreamily. 'No one has seen him since news of the breakout reached Opum Oppidulum. It's most infuriating. I wanted to speak to him, about the beggars. I warned Ambrose Grammaticus that something was awry before his tragic . . . And, of course, I wanted to talk to you, Mrs Grammaticus, seeing as you are on the committee looking into the problem of the beggars. It was such a happy coincidence that you invited me here tonight.'

There was a long pause then Tibor spoke again, slowly, very deliberately. 'And what of Andrew Faye?'

Rex's ears immediately pricked up.

'Andrew Faye?' repeated Cecil. 'Not as yet. But, rest assured, if he is in any way involved in this, I, Cecil Notwithstanding, in the interests of truth and justice and the *Hebdomadal*, will find him and expose his crimes!'

There was a long silence and then the sound of deep snoring. Cecil Notwithstanding, under the influence of alcohol and the Lodestone, was enjoying a truly relaxing experience.

Rex knelt, carefully pushed up the keyhole cover and peered in. He could quite clearly see Cecil fast asleep on the couch by the window. Tibor and Acantha were staring down at him. 'What do you think?' asked Acantha.

'I think he is a danger to us all,' said Tibor. 'I will deal with him.'

'What about Rex?'

'I have a plan for him, and the girl. I don't think it's safe to let either go. Even though he admitted little under the Lodestone I have my doubts.'

Behind the door Rex stifled a gasp. Tibor's unguent tones could not soften this betrayal. He continued to listen with a hardening heart.

'Does *he* know about Andrew Faye?' asked Acantha.

'I'm not entirely sure.' A grin appeared like a dark crevice across Tibor's square jaw. 'But I think we will have to induct them both into the Society, after the full moon. That should satisfy their curiosity!'

Acantha laughed. 'You are such a devil, Tibor. The years haven't changed you a bit. Ambrose Grammaticus wasn't a patch on you, the old fool. If you had seen him that night! He might have been a clever inventor, but he wasn't clever enough for me. What a shame we ever parted. But now that I have you back again it was almost worth the pain!' She flung her arms around him and gave him a long, loud kiss on the cheek.

Tibor laughed. 'Fate has seen fit to bring us back together,' he said. 'And now for your surprise, the one you have been waiting so patiently for.'

Acantha clapped her hands in delight. 'At last! Are you certain I will like it? I am *so* difficult to please!'

'Dear, dear Acantha,' said Tibor. 'You most certainly will. Thanks to *my* invention, we will both be rich beyond our wildest dreams.'

He pulled out the copy of *Decline and Fall* and once more the bookcase slid aside, but he hesitated on the threshold. 'You must promise me one thing.'

'Anything, anything,' said Acantha girlishly.

'No fish!'

'Never! Only the best of meat from the finest butcher.'

Tibor gestured into the darkness with his hand. 'After you,' he said gallantly.

40

The Perambulating Submersible

Rex was waiting in Hildred's room when she ran in. She was shivering and her face was grey. She looked, he thought, as if she had suffered a monstrous shock and he felt dreadful that he had left her alone. 'At last,' he said. 'Where have you been? You won't believe what I just heard.'

'And you won't believe what I just saw,' blurted Hildred. 'Gerulphus fed a person, a *person*, to some sort of lake-dwelling monstrous creature.'

'What?'

Hildred then recounted exactly what she had seen and heard. Rex's eyes widened impossibly and his mouth hung open throughout. At intervals he exclaimed, 'No!' and 'I don't believe it!'

'This proves that Walter Freakley's right,' said Rex at last. 'There *is* a monster in the lake.'

Hildred chewed on her lip nervously. 'When I was in the Panopticon I got used to all sorts of things. There was a

255

woman who could bite her own elbow, a fellow with three legs – but I have never seen anything so vile as Gerulphus throwing that man to the monster. The crunching. I can still feel it!'

'He was . . . dead, wasn't he?' asked Rex.

'Oh, Lord have mercy, I do believe he was. There's another cell deep in the catacombs; I think he was kept in there. Maybe it was him doing all that moaning.'

Rex was licking his knuckles. When he saw Hildred looking he wiped them on his trousers.

'The monster,' he said, changing the subject. 'What do you suppose it is?'

Hildred looked dumbfounded. 'Some sort of ancient fish perhaps? Its scales were huge and they seemed to glitter. Gerulphus actually touched it before it submerged. I think he was stroking it!'

'But how did you get back?' asked Rex.

'Well, when he finished with the creature, I hid in a side tunnel until he went past. I thought it would be safer to go back through Tibor's study and take my chances that he wouldn't be there; I knew it was getting late. I went around the lake. It was horrible; there were bits of clothing floating in the water. Just as I reached the *Indagator* I realized that Acantha was coming – that woman walks like an elephant – so I hid behind the whale oil barrel and Acantha *and* Dr Velhildegildus came out. He wanted to show her the *Indagator*. You should have heard his boasting! He was making all sorts of promises, about money and the future. Not a word about you or me. She even tried to go inside but she couldn't fit through that hatch. As soon as they weren't looking I raced back to the study. I nearly died of fright when I saw Cecil Notwithstanding, but he was fast asleep on the couch.'

Hildred fell silent, reliving in her head the all too recent horror. 'What about you?' she said eventually. 'Where have you been . . . since you left me?'

Rex flushed. 'It's not half as bad as what you saw, but it concerns both of us. Tibor carried out a Lodestone Procedure on Cecil Notwithstanding. He wanted to know about beggars and Andrew Faye. I swear, Hildred, Andrew Faye is the answer to all of this. We have to find that man.'

He was pacing up and down now, his fists opening and closing.

'But that's not the worst of it. Tibor isn't going to let me go, or you. He said that you and I were to join the Society, and it sounded like a terrible threat. And then –' he shook his head in disbelief at the thought – 'Acantha kissed him!'

Hildred tutted. 'And your father is hardly cold in his grave!'

'By the sound of it they have known each other for years. I'm certain now the two of them are in this together. Acantha as much as admitted she sent my father mad. And in my book that's the same as killing him. For all I know Dr Velhildegildus was in on it too. Is there no one I can trust?'

Hildred raised an eyebrow meaningfully.

'I know,' said Rex, flushing again. 'And you can trust me. I promise I won't run off on you again. But is it even safe for us here any longer? Maybe we should just take the boat now while we still have a chance.'

'Let's not be hasty,' cautioned Hildred. 'You can't let them get away with this. Isn't that what your father wanted, to expose her? Whatever he has left here for you, it will reveal the truth about her. And think about it. Tibor won't do anything until the *Indagator* is finished. You're still working on the Re-breather, aren't you?'

'The Re-breather,' murmured Rex. 'Yes, you're right. It's the only piece that really matters.'

'Well, just make sure you don't finish it until the very last minute. That will give us a little more time. Tibor won't dare do anything to you until it's ready.'

'We have three days,' said Rex. 'And then it will all be over.'

But over the next three days no one – Rex, Hildred or Tibor – had a chance to do anything other than work on the *Indagator*. With the swiftly maturing moon and the completion of the vessel ('My wonderful *Indagator*!' as Tibor kept saying, to Rex's intense irritation, almost as if he truly believed that he'd invented it) in sight, Dr Velhildegildus was fired up with unfettered enthusiasm. 'Keep at it,' he urged over and over. 'We cannot let up now!'

So from dawn until dusk the trio put the final pieces of the vessel together. At night Rex and Hildred dragged their weary bodies up the tunnel and fell on to their beds, drained and exhausted. There was no thought of solving mysteries. 'Tomorrow,' said Rex. 'Tomorrow.' And no matter how she urged, Hildred could not persuade him otherwise. He too seemed wholly consumed by the bewitching vessel.

By late afternoon of the third day, while Hildred and Tibor polished *Indagator* and checked and rechecked the seals and hatch, the levers and mechanism, Rex sat at a separate table putting the final touches to the Re-breather. Tibor had asked more than once whether it would be ready, and Rex had assured him each time, monosyllabically, that it would. Hildred was keeping a close eye on Rex. He seemed distant, preoccupied, and she was more and more fearful of where his thoughts might lead him.

In a rare moment of respite, Tibor emerged from the interior of the machine, Rex downed his tools and Hildred straightened her aching back and stretched.

'Did you enjoy your supper the other night, Dr Velhil-degildus?' asked Hildred innocently.

'Very much.' He turned to Rex. 'In fact your stepmother was at the table.'

'Oh.' Rex feigned ignorance. 'We wondered who the guests were.'

'I didn't tell you,' said Tibor plausibly, 'because I know that you and she aren't the best of friends. But I can reassure you that she has returned to Opum Oppidulum and that I kept to our agreement. I told her you were making good progress but that you might need to stay a few more weeks at the very least.'

'Thank you,' said Rex without emotion. You are a liar, he thought, but your voice makes everything you say seem like the truth, a rare gift indeed! He nodded to the Re-breather which sat before him, a simple-looking rectangular metal box. 'I too am keeping my side of the bargain.'

'The Re-breather,' said Tibor excitedly. 'The linchpin of the whole design. I cannot make head nor tail of it myself.'

'I know,' said Rex evenly. 'But I can. It's just the magnets now. It will be ready tonight.'

'Only a matter of hours,' said Tibor dreamily. 'What a sight she will be.' He noticed how Hildred kept glancing over at the lake.

'You look worried,' he said. She didn't respond but Tibor was used to that. It was an irritating habit but what did it matter? The end was in sight. The reward would be well worth the wait.

As if sensing his eyes on her, Hildred remarked, 'The water's rising very quickly.' And it was, all the time creeping surreptitiously towards the *Indagator*; it had already covered the narrow shore on the other side of the lake.

'All the better for the launch!' said Tibor. He stood up. 'Back to work, we cannot let up now!'

At exactly nine o'clock that evening, elated and exhausted, all three were finally able to stand back and gaze at their creation in its glorious entirety: *Indagator Gurgitis*. And what a magnificent machine she was. There she sat, an enormous gleaming oval-shaped mass of brass and iron and copper. Rex walked around the vessel slowly, as if seeing it for the first time, though a thousand times in his head he had imagined it, taking in every bolt, every rivet, every welded seam.

Hildred ran her fingers over the gold lettering on the side and placed her hand on the shining surface, delighting in her distorted reflection. At the front and back there was a pair of jointed legs which slotted neatly into the side of the vessel. Two extendable arms were neatly folded under the front observation glass. It resembled, from certain angles, a giant metal spider or perhaps a crab. At the summit of the machine, accessed by a small recessed curved ladder, was the entry hatch. The craft had four windows, a large round one at the front, a smaller one on either side, and a fourth at the back. Each window was rimmed with metal and the glass was eight inches thick.

'Because of the pressure,' Rex explained to Hildred. 'Tibor doesn't know how deep he will go.'

'Can we try it out, start the engine at the very least?' asked Hildred.

Tibor was in a fever of delight. 'Why not!'

They climbed in, all three, Tibor first and then Rex and Hildred. Tibor sat at the control panel and the other two had just enough room to stand behind him. Over his shoulder they could see a gleaming array of levers and dials and switches. Tibor pressed buttons and flicked switches in a precise sequence and suddenly the vessel shuddered and from somewhere inside it began to hum. Hildred placed her hands on the walls and could feel the throbbing.

'Look out of the window,' said Tibor, and Rex and Hildred watched in amazement as, by means of a couple of levers, he brought about the extension and retraction of the multi-fingered arms.

'I added them to the design,' said Rex proudly.

'They will be useful for picking up, er . . . rocks and things from the lake floor,' said Tibor.

Rocks? wondered Hildred but said nothing.

Then the humming subsided and the vessel became peaceful again. Tibor turned and his face was a picture of triumphant joy. 'It will be an adventure beyond compare,' he declared.

'You will be famous,' said Rex slowly. 'Your name will be on everyone's lips. There is nothing in the world like this machine.'

Tibor was almost beyond words. 'Yes, yes,' he stuttered. 'It is hard to believe, is it not, that a man such as I could create something so . . . incredible. And the Re-breather, it is working?'

'Oh yes,' said Rex, pointing to where he had installed the box into the wall. 'See, the green light is on. It's working perfectly.'

Outside the machine once again Rex and Hildred were both struck by the silence in the chamber. For days now it had been echoing with the sounds of hammering and clanging.

As Hildred watched Rex enter the tunnel back to the study she was distinctly uneasy. It wasn't anything he had said, it was more the way the muscles in his jaw tightened and loosened, the way his fists clenched and unclenched, and she suddenly felt very frightened.

And she in turn was being watched by an unseen figure on the far side of the lake where the water was now lapping at the entrance to the catacombs.

41

The Beginning of the End

Rex was transfixed by the pale round moon hanging in the night sky. Hildred, at his side, could almost feel his trembling rage but his voice was barely audible.

'Did you hear him?' said Rex. 'Did you hear how he congratulated himself on his design? Not a word of thanks to us. You were right. He is going to take all the credit for an idea that he stole.'

'You don't know that he stole it,' said Hildred quietly.

'However he got it,' said Rex, 'it's not his.'

'You said this wasn't about money or fame,' she countered. 'We have other things to think about now. You've been distracted by the *Indagator* for long enough. Have you forgotten why you came? Your father left something here for you, about Acantha. We must find it. We have so little time left.'

Rex exhaled heavily. 'Very well,' he said.

'Tell me again everything that you know. Everything.'

So, one more time, Rex went through the events of the night of his father's return and Hildred listened, all the time fixing him with a gaze of such intensity he felt as if he would start to smoulder. And when he finished he was as confused as ever. Hildred's face was a picture of pure concentration.

'Andrew Faye aside, I think the book is the clue,' she concluded. 'Your father warned you not to fly too close to the sun, but maybe that was just to lead you to the book. Maybe the actual answer is in another story. We need to see the book.'

Rex took the book out from under his pillow.

'You say you know all of these stories,' said Hildred. 'What are they about?'

Rex ran a finger down the contents. 'Daedalus and Icarus, The Persian Wars, The Trusted Slave, The Trojan Horse—'

Hildred stopped him. 'The Trusted Slave? The slave owned by Histaeus?'

'Yes. Do you know it?'

'Mr Ephcott told it to me once. Don't you remember it?'

'Of course. I had to try to translate it into Latin. His-taeus tattooed a secret message on his slave's head. When the hair grew back he sent him to his allies. They shaved his head, read the message and joined Histaeus in the war against his enemies.'

'Eureka!' shouted Hildred, and immediately ran out of the room to return moments later brandishing a pair of scissors. She advanced towards Rex. He looked at her in amazement. 'What are you doing? Have you gone mad too?'

'Don't you see, you fool,' she said, and her voice was at fever pitch. 'It wasn't your father who got a tattoo that night, *it was you*.'

'Me?' said Rex, and immediately put his hand to his head. 'Of course! How stupid I am! That's why I had the headache after going to Mr Sarpalius. Father said I'd fallen and cut myself but it must have been the tattoo. He kept saying the less I knew the better, so he didn't tell me about it. And he was right. If I'd known I would have told Tibor when I underwent the Lodestone Procedure.'

'The message must be on your head,' said Hildred simply, and she took a clump of his hair in one hand and began to cut. 'Mr Sarpalius must have tattooed you through the hair,' she said. 'It can't have been easy.'

'I should have guessed ages ago,' said Rex. 'That word, "compunctions", it's from *compungere*: to "prick" or "sting". Oh, I wish I'd paid more attention to Robert's lessons!'

Hildred continued to snip away. 'Oh my goodness,' she said. 'There *is* something here. I can't believe it.'

'What is it?'

'It looks like a skull with letters inside it.'

Rex could barely contain himself. 'Do you remember when Mr Sarpalius asked about my skull? I thought he meant the wound from the stones, but he couldn't have, that's what I was trying to say to you, and then that cart came by. He must have meant this.'

'I'll draw it for you.' Hildred took the book and began to

sketch on the endpaper. Rex watched as she drew a rough skull shape with letters inside.

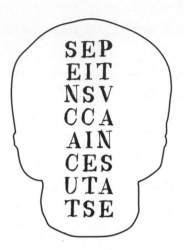

'What on earth does that mean?' asked Rex.

Hildred was poring over the tattoo and talking to herself. 'It's not just random letters, they must be words, but it's not English.'

Rex shook his head. 'Latin I bet. Even Father told me how important it was.'

'I think it's written *boustrophedon*,' said Hildred. 'I remember Mr Ephcott saying something about this.'

'*Bous* what?'

'It's when you write from left to right and then right to left all the way down the page.'

'I remember,' shouted Rex excitedly. 'It's from the Greek for cow, the way they used to plough fields up and down. So what does it say?'

Hildred took the pencil and rewrote the letters in one

line, added three strokes of the pencil and then presented
it to Rex.

SEPTIENS / VACCA / INSECUTA / EST

'Surely you know enough to translate that?' asked Hildred.
'Your father wouldn't have done it if he didn't think you
could work it out.'

Rex looked again. '*Seven times the cow must be followed.*
What cow?'

Hildred couldn't help looking very pleased with herself.
'It's directions,' she said.

'To what?'

'Presumably whatever your father has hidden.'

'But it could be anywhere,' said Rex, and his face fell at
the thought.

'No,' said Hildred slowly. 'There's only one place it's
going to be.'

Rex looked at her and then they both said simultaneously, 'The maze, he's hidden something in the maze!'

'And we find it by walking *boustrophedon,* alternating
right and left seven times,' said Hildred, ecstatic that finally
they had solved the puzzle.

'Hold on a minute,' said Rex. 'There are two ways to the
maze, through Tibor's study or through the torture chamber.'

Hildred was already at the door. She turned in that
odd way of hers, when it looked as if her body stayed in
one place and her head swivelled almost the whole way

around. 'Hmm,' she murmured. 'It's one or the other, and it's far more likely your father would have found the entrance down in the torture chamber, so let's start there.'

Of course, the chamber was locked (with a new padlock) but this was no obstacle to Rex. Soon he and Hildred saw once again the torturer's arsenal: the branding irons, the pokers, the poisons and the leeches. Hildred showed Rex the secret keyhole.

'This explains how Gerulphus was in here that day,' said Rex. 'He must have been coming back up from the labyrinth.'

'Yes, from feeding dead people to that monster,' said Hildred with a grimace, and she looked as if she had a bad taste in her mouth. She held up the lantern and they stepped through the hole into the catacombs and the panel closed behind them.

'So,' said Hildred, her face ghostly in the yellow light. 'We'll go right and left seven times until we find something.'

Inevitably they reached an intersection but Hildred confidently took a right. At the next intersection they took a left, followed by a right, and at the fourth intersection a left. They were both acutely aware of the empty cavities on either side, where once bodies had rested.

'You know, I think Gerulphus has been feeding that monster for a while,' said Hildred. 'Surely there should be more bodies down here.'

'And who exactly was that fellow in the other cell?' asked Rex.

'I found this caught on the door,' said Hildred, and she showed him the piece of red cloth.

'That looks like part of a warder's uniform,' said Rex, but Hildred didn't answer. She took one final right turn and they found themselves in a small chamber where the tunnel had widened. On the floor propped against the opposite wall was a bleached skull.

They looked at each other with mounting excitement. 'My tattoo is in the shape of a skull,' said Rex quietly.

Hildred picked it up and examined it. 'It's just a skull,' she said.

'Maybe it's some sort of marker,' suggested Rex. 'Maybe there's something buried here.'

Feverishly they both began to dig. The earth came up easily, damp as it was, and before too long Hildred's broken nails scratched across something that wasn't sand or grit or dirt.

It was the front of a large brown book.

'It's one of those record books,' said Rex. 'Like the ones they burned and you found. But why would my father hide a record book?'

42

Too Much Information...

Rex sat beside Hildred with the lantern while she dusted off the cover.

'Hold the light closer,' she said, and began to turn the pages. 'It's just like the others,' she said, 'with lists of the patients and their cures . . .'

'Look for Ambrose Grammaticus,' said Rex, and he watched as Hildred ran her fingers up and down the columns on each page. Then her face visibly paled.

'What is it?' asked Rex anxiously. 'Have you found my father? What does it say?'

'It's not your father, Rex,' she said slowly. She pointed halfway down the column and there, written in black ink, with their dates of admission, as clear as day, were three names: *Ida Runcible*, *Walter Freakley* and *Gerulphus Godsacre*.

'Fingerknots!' exclaimed Hildred. 'They were admitted over a decade ago!'

Rex sat in stunned silence. 'I don't understand,' he said eventually. 'How can they be patients?'

'There can only be one explanation,' said Hildred. Rex could see fear in her eyes. 'All three of them are lunatics.'

'Lunatics? But they can't be. They work here.'

'Who says? We've only ever had their word for it. Listen to this.' Hildred had flicked over the page and began to read aloud. '*Ida Runcible: Ida worked as a cook for a wealthy Opum Oppidulum family. After some months she took against her employers for reasons unknown, and poisoned the whole family with toxic fish,* Salpa salpa, *a type of noxious bream found in Lake Beluarum. In small amounts it induces temporary insanity, in larger amounts certain death. When questioned she said the tea leaves told her to do it. Prognosis: Not expected to be cured.*'

'Toxic fish?' said Rex, thinking of the fish she had been cooking the other day. 'What about Walter Freakley?'

Further down the page Hildred came to his entry. '*Walter Freakley: after being rejected for a job on the river Foedus in Urbs Umida, Walter attacked and killed a boatman and commandeered his boat. He posed as a ferryman for nearly two weeks, robbing his passengers and turning them into the water. When questioned he said that he was the reincarnation of Charon, ferryman of the dead, and that he believed the Foedus to be the river Styx, the mythical river between the real world and that of the dead. Prognosis: Not expected to be cured.*'

'And here's Gerulphus. He was admitted before the other two.'

Rex listened incredulously. 'Oh my, this is truly dreadful! I can't believe it! They're all mad.'

'It must have been when the lunatics escaped recently,' said Hildred, thinking quickly. 'For some reason the three of them stayed behind.'

'Well, Freakley likes boats, so he became the ferryman. But what happened to the real ferryman?' Hildred and Rex exchanged glances. Knowing what they now knew about Walter, they had a good idea. 'That explains why he couldn't row straight!' said Rex grimly.

'And Ida Runcible was a cook before she went mad,' said Hildred. 'Remember, she complained about not having any tea. It was because she was under lock and key that Chapelizod didn't allow them to have tea. It was bread and water. As for Gerulphus . . .'

'We're lucky to be alive,' said Rex, shaking his head. 'We've been living side by side with crazed murderers!'

Hildred frowned. 'But this still doesn't explain why your father hid the book.'

'Let me see,' said Rex, and he took the book and flicked on through the pages. 'It only covers the first six months of that year,' he said. 'There wouldn't be anything about my father.'

'There's something at the end,' said Hildred, and she pulled a piece of newspaper out from between the last two pages. 'It's an old article from the *Hebdomadal*. It's about another breakout. Hold up the light.'

She began to read.

BREAKOUT AT DROPROCK ASYLUM

It is now a week since three dangerous lunatics escaped from Droprock Asylum. The superintendent and the head warder are missing, presumed dead, and still there is no trace of the escapees. By now they have probably changed their names and tried to alter their appearances but each has a distinctive feature which the mayor and the constables hope will aid in their capture. We at the *Hebdoma-* *dal* have been asked to warn the public not to approach these people as they are a danger both to themselves and to others and will stop at nothing in their bid for freedom.

The descriptions of the three are as follows:

Gerulphus Godsacre:

A huge man, grossly overweight, sent to the asylum by his parents who claimed that he was

'Gerulphus?' interrupted Rex. 'If he escaped then why is he still here?'

Hildred shook her head. 'I don't know. And he's not fat!' She read on.

Meredith Whipspittle:
Ms Whipspittle is described as an uncommonly pretty young woman, but do not be fooled: she is a devil in disguise. Her mind is incurably disturbed. She was incarcerated in the asylum after the suspicious deaths of her two husbands. She claims to be at least ten years younger than she is. Although she has

the social skills to pass as a normal member of society, indeed she has the ability to mix in all circles, she can be identified by one distinctive feature: the little finger on her right hand is permanently rigid and cannot be bent.

Claude Boughton:

Thought to be the ringleader, and an extremely persuasive character, Mr Boughton is afflicted by a number of conditions. He is certainly delusional: he likes to refer to himself as Doctor although he has no medical qualifications at all. He also claims to be able to control minds. He suffers from *Tetragonocephalitis* and exhibits the classic head shape of the disease, namely an overtly square jaw and skull, caused when the brain swells in all directions and distorts the cranium.

'Stop!' said Rex. 'This is even worse than I thought.'

Hildred stopped reading.

'Meredith and Claude, they're Acantha and Tibor, it has to be. The square head, the stiff finger. They've changed their names but they were in here too!'

'There's more,' said Hildred. '*Far from being a healer, Claude Boughton is actually a convicted murderer. He was committed to the asylum after the remains of his parents were found buried under the floorboards of his house. Both he and Meredith Whipspittle were also accused (but not convicted) of being active An-dro-phagues.*'

Hildred stumbled slightly over the last word.

'An-dro-phagues?' repeated Rex. 'Now why does that word seem familiar?'

'Say it again,' said Hildred. 'Slowly.'

Rex repeated it twice. 'Androphague, Andrew Phague——'

'Andrew Faye,' finished Hildred.

Rex was stunned into silence.

'It's not the Society of Andrew Faye,' said Hildred. 'It's the *Society of Androphagues.'*

'But what is an Androphague?'

Hildred looked thoughtful. 'When I was with the Panopticon——'

'Don't tell me,' said Rex, 'did you have an *Androphague*? What did he do?'

Hildred didn't seem to hear, or else she ignored his interruption, and continued. 'Mr Ephcott taught me many things. A little Latin, a little Greek, philosophy, logic –' that explains so much, thought Rex – 'I believe that this word could have its origins in Greek. *Andros* means "man" and *phagein* is the verb "to eat".'

'Oh,' said Rex. 'Then it means "a man who eats?"'

'No,' said Hildred softly. 'It means "man-eater".'

'Man-eater?'

'Yes.'

Rex saw that the book was shaking in Hildred's hands. He looked into her eyes. Time seemed to slow. He finally understood.

'Rex,' said Hildred softly. 'Tibor and Acantha were accused of being cannibals. They thought he ate his parents.'

Rex staggered backwards. He felt as if his heart had stopped, as if he had been punched in the stomach, as if something had been torn out of him. Wordlessly he dug deep into his pocket. 'I think it was these trousers,' he muttered. He pulled out his hand and held up a small gold object.

'What is it?' asked Hildred.

'It's a gold tooth,' said Rex. 'But not from a fish. I think it's Chapelizod's.'

'How do you know?'

'It's initialled.' And indeed it was, quite clearly: 'C.C.'

Hildred examined the small object carefully. 'But where did you get it?'

'I found it in the bottom of the cooking pot at Acantha's.'

'Now *I* don't understand,' said Hildred.

Rex's eye welled up with tears. 'Oh, Hildred,' he said, 'I think those monsters ate Cadmus Chapelizod.'

Hildred started shaking her head. 'But, Rex, if Acantha was a cannibal, what does that mean about—'

'My father? You tell me,' he said, and he began to laugh hysterically.

'Calm down,' said Hildred firmly, trying to hide her own fear. 'This can't be true. Your father was a good man taken in by a very wicked woman.'

Rex stopped laughing but he was far from calm. 'I can see it now,' he said with an odd smile. 'Cecil Notwithstanding warned Father about Chapelizod, that's why he told Acantha not to see him any more, but Acantha refused. And then she fed him the poisonous fish – she said it was bream – just enough to send him mad. She might even have got the idea from Mrs Runcible. They were in the asylum at the same time. I remember now, she didn't eat hers. It was perfect. Chapelizod, the superintendent of the asylum, declares him insane; Stradigund, the helpful solicitor, does the legal paperwork. And of course, they're both cannibals too. As for that pest controller, it wasn't meat he was delivering, it was *people*.'

'Well, that is meat, I suppose,' said Hildred, in such a state of shock she was hardly aware of what she was saying. 'Oh Lord, do you suppose he's the one taking the beggars?'

'Yes,' said Rex grimly. 'That's exactly it. Acantha laughed about it, she called them pests, but *that's who they were eating*. And then somehow the pest controller must have caught Chapelizod and he ended up in the pot.'

They were both silent as the deeply disturbing revelations sank in.

'But your father,' said Hildred carefully. 'When he came back that night, to warn you, to get you away from her. He can't have been a can— one.'

Rex was increasingly agitated. 'Acantha said that he liked her cooking.'

'That doesn't prove anything,' said Hildred hesitantly. 'He saved you. Surely that's what's important?'

'But he couldn't save himself,' said Rex. He turned to Hildred. His face was as stone, his voice hoarse, like gravel.

'Do you want to know what really happened to his hand? Do you?'

'Rex, you're scaring me,' said Hildred as she looked into his burning eyes.

'He didn't lose it in an engineering accident.'

'Then what?' she asked in a shaky voice.

Rex looked directly at her and with his shorn head and his wild eyes he looked more like a madman than anyone else in the asylum. He opened his mouth and hissed through gritted teeth, 'He ate it, Hildred. My father ate his own hand!'

And then he collapsed in a quivering heap on the floor.

43

Bad Timing

Rex was beyond consolation for a long time. All the while Hildred sat beside him, her arms around his shoulders. She could feel his chest heaving and hiccupping. She stroked his head, the stubble from the shorn part rough against her palm, and murmured softly to calm him. After a while his sobbing subsided and he managed to speak.

'It was dreadful,' he whispered. The lantern was burning low by now and Hildred stared hard at his lips to make out what he was saying.

'You don't have to tell me if you don't want to,' she said. 'I can see that it is upsetting.' But the truth was she wasn't sure she wanted to know.

'No, I have to. It's been a burden to me, a terrible weight. You see, when Father went mad he took a sword from the suit of armour and . . . and he chopped off his hand. It was utterly ghastly . . . the noise, the blood. Then he screamed at Acantha, "Is this what you want?" and before we could stop him he took his hand and he began to tear at it with his teeth. He was like an animal. But she just sat and laughed. The housekeeper and the bootboy and the butler came in and they grabbed him. Later, when I told him I didn't believe he was insane, he said that his hook was proof of his madness.'

'Poor, poor man,' said Hildred. 'It must have been the toxic fish. Oh, Acantha is pure evil!'

'That's why he wouldn't take me with him. Acantha had already fed him that . . . meat. He used to go to the dinners with Chapelizod and Stradigund. He said it was a disease. I think he was afraid he might eat me too,' said Rex. He wiped his face and stood up. 'Hildred,' he said grimly, 'what if I am one too? A cannibal?'

Hildred got to her feet, shaking her head. 'How can you be, Rex? You've never eaten a . . . person . . . have you?'

He looked down at the gold tooth. 'I ate some of Chapelizod, just a smidgeon, I swear.'

Hildred hoped that Rex couldn't see on her face the revulsion that was churning her up inside. 'Is that all?' She laughed lightly, to comfort him, to comfort herself. 'It's no worse than chewing your fingernail.' Then her logical nature took over. 'Look,' she said, pointing at the book, 'you've got the proof we need now, about Acantha and the others, Chapelizod and Stradigund. Let's just get out of here. We'll take the boat.'

Wordlessly and heartsore the solemn pair hurried back through the maze, taking great care to reverse exactly the right and left turns they had taken on the way, until at last they reached the panel that led into the torture chamber.

'We'll just sneak away,' said Hildred. 'In less than an hour we'll be in Opum Oppidulum and we can take the book to Cecil Notwithstanding. He'll know what to do.'

She pushed on the panel and it opened noiselessly. They stepped into the torture chamber . . . and walked straight into Gerulphus and Tibor.

Now it has to be said that it was very bad luck indeed that Rex and Hildred bumped into Tibor and Gerulphus at that moment. A few minutes later and they would have been gone.

You see, Gerulphus, by habit, had come down to the torture chamber earlier and, seeing the padlock on the ground, he had resolved to find out exactly who was responsible. He went straight to Tibor who denied everything but suspected immediately that Rex and Hildred were involved. With the launch of the *Indagator* so close he could not ignore the fact that they might be up to something

'I don't quite trust that girl,' he confided to Gerulphus. 'There's something distinctly odd about her.'

'I believe it might be in your interest to find out what they are doing,' suggested Gerulphus cryptically.

So in a rare moment of collaboration Tibor and Gerulphus went to the torture chamber. As a previous inmate of the asylum, Tibor was well aware of both the torture chamber and the second entrance to the catacombs.

'The boy's father was an engineer, you know,' said Tibor

thoughtfully. 'It would not surprise me if he can break a padlock.' He frowned and looked at Gerulphus. 'You really do remind me very much of the Gerulphus I used to know,' he said. 'But he was a much larger fellow.'

'People change, Dr Velhildegildus,' replied Gerulphus. And it was at that exact moment, just as a flicker of understanding began to cross Tibor's face, that Rex and Hildred chose to appear. All four stood in surprised silence.

Gerulphus spoke first. 'That's one of the asylum record books,' he said slowly, looking at the volume Rex was clutching tightly.

Tibor frowned. Certain things were suddenly beginning to become crystal clear. He looked at Gerulphus, a thin, etiolated man, and began to wonder, to imagine how he might be with a little more flesh on his bones. He remembered the piles of ash around the place. 'I thought you said the lunatics burned things like that.'

'It looks like one got away,' said Gerulphus.

Rex watched with mounting fear as Tibor closed the cell door and locked it from the inside. He nodded to Gerulphus and in one swift simultaneous movement each man grabbed a child. Tibor took Rex and Gerulphus took Hildred and it was merely a matter of moments before they found themselves immobilized on the tables, strapped down tightly at their ankles and cuffed at the wrists.

Gerulphus had the book and Tibor stood at the end of the table with his arms folded across his chest.

'Dear, dear,' he chided. 'What a shame it has come to this. And everything was going so well. Didn't I tell you not to pry, Rex? Why did you not heed my warning? Have you read the book? No need to answer, I can find out. After all, I have my Lodestone.' He pulled it from his waistcoat pocket and swung it over Rex's face teasingly. Rex gritted his teeth but his heart sank. He knew his weaknesses. He could not fight this. Gerulphus grinned – an odd sight.

'You, young Rex, you're no fun,' said Tibor. 'I know you can't hold your tongue, but, Hildred, let's try it on you.'

'No!' shouted Rex. 'Leave her alone.'

Rex watched helplessly as Tibor stood over Hildred and began to swing the Lodestone back and forth. He tried not to listen to his caressing, silky tones but how could he not? The shadow of the Lodestone was immense and filled the room as it swung back and forth, back and forth across her. Rex had to look away.

'Now, my dear Hildred,' crooned Tibor leaning right over her. 'Tell me the truth, have you read that book?'

'No,' she replied evenly.

Rex was surprised at her cool-headed response. He recalled she had boasted that she was immune to his charms but he doubted her resolve would last much longer.

'What do you know about me?'

'Merely that you are a doctor of the mind,' replied Hildred dully. 'A renowned one.' Tibor bristled visibly with pride.

'And my companions?'

'Gerulphus is the caretaker and Walter rows the boat. Mrs Runcible is the cook.'

'Do you know where we came from?'

'I believe you are from Urbs Umida. I do not know about the others.'

While Hildred so expertly avoided the questions, Rex was battling the urge to blurt out the answers. He began to repeat over and over in his head the poem he knew –

Oh, how I love to wander, wander, wander
Wander, wander along.
And as I go, a-ho-ho-ho,
I always sing this song.

– but he couldn't get past the first verse. He just couldn't block out the torment of that mellifluous voice of exquisite temptation. Oh please don't let him ask me, he begged inwardly.

'What about Andrew Faye?'

'I do not know that name,' said Hildred in a monotone.

Rex marvelled at her self-control.

'Hmm,' said Tibor, staring down at Hildred. 'She's a tough one. But a few hours down here will loosen you both up. And, if need be, I have plenty of tools here to aid in your confession.' He looked at his pocket watch. 'Well, Rex,' he said, 'as you know, I have to go for a while. There's a full moon tonight and I must take advantage of it. Shame you won't be there to see it. But do not worry; I will be back, after my voyage.' He looked at Gerulphus. 'Leave them here,' he said. 'They're not going anywhere. But you and I, we need to talk.'

And with that Gerulphus and Tibor left. Above the

thundering of his heart Rex heard the door being locked and then the rattle of the padlock. He glanced over at Hildred. She was squirming about, a look of intense concentration on her face.

'Hildred,' he hissed, afraid that Gerulphus might be listening at the door.

She didn't answer, just wriggled some more, and for one terrible moment he thought she might be in some sort of trance.

'Hildred,' he hissed again, louder this time, and he saw his spittle fly across the gap between them and land on her face. She started – as much as she could, being so tightly tied down – and turned to face him.

'What is it?' she said. 'I'm concentrating.'

'How did you do that, not answer his questions? He even had me going under. His voice is just so hypnotic.'

Hildred smiled at him. 'It was easy,' she said. 'Didn't you know, Rex? I'm deaf. I can't hear a thing.'

44

The Maiden Voyage of *Indagator Gurgitis*

'That will be all, Mrs Runcible,' said Dr Velhildegildus curtly, half pushing her out of the study. 'I do not wish to be disturbed again tonight. Please make sure that I am not.'

'Very well, Dr Velhildegildus,' she said, backing out reluctantly, waving the cup. 'But I wouldn't feel right if I didn't warn you. You can't argue with the leaves. It's been every day this week.'

Tibor tutted with intense irritation as he locked the door.

Gerulphus was waiting by the bookcase. 'That woman and her damned tea leaves!' he laughed. 'A monster, she says, in the dregs! I can't see it.'

'In my experience people see what they want to see,' said Tibor. He went to the window and looked out at the full moon. Perfect timing. He would sort out those meddling children later, when it was all over. Actually, maybe he would just leave them in the torture chamber for Gerulphus to sort out. He had no more use for them.

'I must say, Gerulphus, you've been very reasonable about the whole business.'

'Forgive and forget, I say,' said Gerulphus.

'Very noble,' replied Tibor. I suppose the promise of a bag of diamonds always helps, he thought, then said out loud, 'Shall we go?'

Without further delay Tibor pulled on Gibbon and slipped through the secret entrance, followed wordlessly by Gerulphus, to meet his glorious destiny.

Gerulphus was suitably, if monosyllabically, impressed by the machine, all for Tibor's benefit of course – after all, he had secretly watched it being built. Tibor, however, was barely able to contain his excitement as he stood by *Indagator Gurgitis*. The water was now only a few feet away from the machine.

'Take my Lodestone,' said Tibor, handing it to Gerulphus. 'There are magnets in the Re-breather; Rex said it might affect it.' And, he thought, I won't be needing it again.

Taking a deep breath Tibor put his hand firmly on the ladder. This was it, the moment he had been waiting for. With this machine he was to discover the secrets of the lake and harvest its treasure for himself and himself alone. Well, a few for Gerulphus, for his silence, and perhaps he would send something back to Melvyn Halibutte.

It had not been easy for him to return to Droprock

Island. It held painful memories. But it was worth it: with *Indagator* and the diamonds, and Acantha, he would be richer than he could ever have imagined.

Tibor climbed quickly to the top of the craft and dropped lightly into the gleaming metal ovaloid. Once inside he pulled down the hatch, spinning the lock until it was tight. He took his seat at the controls with gleeful anticipation. The panel in front of him was simple enough: white buttons, shiny brass toggle switches, four small levers and a large central lever on a ball. That was the beauty of a lever-and-cogwheel-based engine, clean and simple. None of that steam and choking smoke he had heard about. He switched on the Re-breather, waited for the green light, and then for the second time he pushed buttons and flicked switches to bring about the satisfying thrum of the engine. He flexed his fingers and closed his hands around the main lever. Slowly he pulled it towards him and in a matter of seconds the whole machine rose smoothly upward, supported by its four long legs.

Indagator Gurgitis was alive!

Effortlessly and smoothly, on account of the hydrolastic suspension, the deceptively strong legs carried *Indagator*'s weight towards the lake's edge. Tibor's heart was racing as first one leg and then a second stepped into the dark water. 'Calm yourself, calm yourself,' he said gently – indeed, was he not the best person to advise himself in those matters!

In the rear window he could see Gerulphus standing on the promontory holding a stick. He gave him a parting wave as forward he went, watching the water rise higher and higher on the glass, until finally he and

Indagator were completely submerged.

Tibor was more than a little relieved when the exterior lights (Rex's idea – what a clever use of the luminous lichen!) lit up the way ahead, albeit in blue.

Give the boy credit, he thought. Grammaticus knows his stuff.

And Tibor Velhildegildus knew that he was on a journey that no other living person had undertaken. In some ways that was more important even than jewels.

After a short distance, the lake floor began to drop. Tibor was concerned that the ovaloid might not be able to cope with the slope but he was soon reassured as to her stability and together, man and machine, they made their steady progress into the depths. He looked out in wonder at the alien world through which he was now travelling. He marvelled to think that his eyes were the only eyes ever to behold the creatures down here, creatures that none above even knew existed.

'And they say nothing lives in the lake!' he murmured.

How wrong they were, for it veritably teemed with life.

All manner of oddities swam past his windows: transparent fish, of sorts, with huge eyes and each possessed of an alien beauty. And the colours! Vibrant blues and greens and mauves (he was reminded of his foulard which he had burned) and other hues he could not even name. For a second he actually believed there might be Paradise on earth.

The slope gradually levelled out so he tilted the blue beams downwards to scan the lake floor and then his heart somersaulted. The entire floor of the lake was covered in thousands, millions perhaps, of glittering jewels of every colour and size: rubies, sapphires, emeralds and, yes, diamonds.

'Oh my,' he said over and over again. 'Hooper was right. I am to be wealthy beyond my wildest dreams.'

The two arms at the front of his elegant craft reached out and began to gather in the jewels. As they raked through the sandy bottom, little sparkling clouds rose into the water, like stars in the sky, then fell back down to the lake floor. The mechanical fingers scooped them up and dropped them into a net which allowed the sand to filter through, along with the smallest of the jewels, but not the larger ones.

Tibor was aquiver with excitement. As he gathered the shimmering harvest, he was planning a glittering future. He would travel the world; he would never have to work again, never have to listen to another idle wealthy woman's trivial complaints (by all accounts a spell in the care of Chapelizod would sort most of *them* out. Whatever did happen to that fellow anyway?). And then there was Acantha – or perhaps he should call her Meredith. What a wonderful woman. Introducing him again to the delights of the Society of Andrew Faye. He had not had enough of that over the years! When they escaped all those years ago they had decided, despite their blossoming love, that for safety's sake they should go their separate ways. And now, so much to catch up on.

He mused on. He would have no obligations, no ties. For that's what money bought you: not material goods, but freedom. He thought back ten years to the night of his escape. Over a number of weeks, using both his voice and his Lodestone, he had persuaded the then superintendent that he was perfectly sane. Unbelievably the foolish fellow had not only released Tibor (then Claude, of course) but had taken him to his study where, still under the influence of the Lodestone, he had proudly shown him the entrance to the catacombs. His last words were, 'I had it built as a precaution in case the lunatics ever broke out.'

Free and in possession of the keys, Tibor had released Meredith and his cellmate Gerulphus, and they had made good their escape down to the rocky pier. It was only then that they realized that there was no way the boat would hold the three of them. In those days Gerulphus really was immensely overweight.

Of course, I could probably have cured his appetites with the Lodestone Procedure if I'd had the time, thought Tibor, but it was not to be.

So he and Acantha had pushed off and left Gerulphus on the shore.

What a surprise it had been when he had met him again! He hadn't recognized him at first, he was so thin, but then tonight in the torture chamber, when it really mattered, Gerulphus didn't let him down. *They both knew what was in that book.* But the diamonds would be reward enough. His debt was paid.

One more netful, Tibor decided, and then he would ascend. Tomorrow when the water subsided he would be off. I wonder if *Indagator* could cross the entire lake, he mused, but of course the Re-breather wouldn't last that long. Well, now that I know *Indagator* works, my future is secure.

He had it all planned. He was going to dismantle the machine and have it transported to Urbs Umida. In fact really he only needed the Re-breather, that was the most important part. He still had the plans, he knew it could be built, and he had his haul of jewels. Either way, he was a winner.

And he had Acantha too. Just his sort of woman.

We share the same tastes, he thought, and laughed.

The atmosphere in the ovaloid was becoming a little stuffy, a sign, Rex had warned him, that the Re-breather was reaching its limit, but he knew he had another hour or so left, plenty of time to get back to the surface. At that moment a large fish passed by the window and Tibor watched in amusement as it rubbed itself violently in the bejewelled sand on the lake floor. To his surprise he saw that some of the jewels lodged in its scales.

'Now wouldn't you want to be the fisherman who hauled that in!' he said to himself. On an impulse he extended the arms again and caught the fish. But the fish was not going to give up without a fight and it struggled and flapped about so much that it managed to free itself. Then to Tibor's amazement it started to charge at the window, hitting it repeatedly. 'Bad-tempered little fellow,' said Tibor. He withdrew the arms, swivelled his chair to face the other direction and readied himself to return to dry land.

It was only then that he saw the large dark shape moving through the water. At first he thought he had imagined it. It was just out of range of the lights. He leaned forward and peered into the gloom. There was definitely something out there. It passed across the window again, nearer this time, and Tibor could see that it too had scaly glittering skin.

His heart stuttered when he saw the smaller fish swim towards it. The similarity was immediately obvious. There was no doubt in Tibor's mind that these two were related. He began to feel uneasy. The larger fish – much, *much* larger, he realized – was now only feet away from the craft and filled the entire window as it passed. It was not in any way attractive, with its jutting-out jaw sporting long, furled tentacles, its grotesque jelly-like eyes, its ugly six-toed flippers, its black fins and the powerful tail. Even the jewels caught in its scales could not make it any less repulsive.

'It's merely curious,' said Tibor, trying to convince himself as it swam past again. And then, to his great relief, it changed direction and swam away into the darkness. Quickly he initiated the walking sequence and *Indagator* took one step forward, but before it could make any more progress something hit the side of the craft with such force that he was thrown violently sideways and cracked his head on the main lever.

Tibor swore softly, reeling from the shock. The vessel righted itself but there was another tremendous blow and he was thrown forward to hit his head on the window.

'What on earth!' he exclaimed.

He turned in his chair, his head throbbing and his vision blurred. He looked out of the window and saw to his utter horror the cause of the blows. 'God's blood and bones!' he shouted, and braced himself for the impact.

The monstrous fish, that grotesque manifestation, was attacking him.

Then everything began to happen at once. An alarm sounded. Tibor looked around wildly. 'What now?' he shouted. He saw a flashing red light. The Re-breather! It couldn't be – it should have an hour to go. His chest tightened. He was running out of air. In desperation he banged on the Re-breather. The front panel dislodged and something dropped out into his hand.

It was a little brazen egg. On the side of it was scratched:

INDAGATOR GURGITIS

Tibor gasped for breath and in horror. This egg was his craft, his *Indagator* in miniature, complete with the ladder and the legs, the hatch and the windows. There was something tucked under the hatch. Tibor pulled out a piece of paper, unfolded it and read:

I invented the Re-breather.
Rex

'He knew all along,' whispered Tibor. 'He *knew*.'

He saw the fish coming straight at him, its gaping maw as wide as a cave, and he saw its jagged teeth as the jaws closed around him and he was propelled down its throat into its belly. And before the lights went out he saw in its bilious gut even more diamonds. He laughed like the maniac he was. He should have known.

It was all in the tea leaves.

45

Loose Ends

Gerulphus sat in Tibor's study with his feet on the desk and examined his polished boots. They were Tibor's but he didn't think he would be needing them now. The Lodestone swung gently back and forth from his right hand. In front of him was the record book and beside that a large pile of gems: his own collection; a few from the underground shore, but mainly prised from the creature's scales.

Gerulphus thought about the last few weeks. He had enjoyed playing at caretaker. And what pleasure he'd got from feeding those vile warders to the big fish. He laughed softly. Patience is a virtue, they say. Well no one could deny that he had been patient. Ten years he had lived down in that maze, since the night Dr Velhildegildus (or Claude Boughton as he was known then) and that vile woman had rowed away, leaving him on the shore. He was too fat, they said; he would have sunk the boat. He was captured soon after, blindfolded and taken deep into the maze by the head warder, a punishment for unruly lunatics. But Gerulphus had tasted freedom and he wasn't going to give it up so easily. Turning on the warder he used his bulk to flatten the life out of him and took his keys.

For the first time in his life, Gerulphus was thankful that he was fat. For it was on that very fat and flesh that he lived as he crawled systematically in the dark like a mole searching for the way out. There was plenty to drink; if you dug in the sand you reached water very quickly. He always crawled downward, marking his pathways with piles of bones, certain that one day he would find his way back to the door in the torture chamber. And he did.

By then he had grown used to underground life, enjoyed it even, so he took to popping in and out of the asylum for food, usually at night, when no one was looking. It amused him to think that he was the cause of all the speculation about the ghost in the maze. They came looking for him sometimes but they never found him. He was well aware of the new superintendent, Cadmus Chapelizod, and heard the screams from the torture chamber as he and his warders carried out their 'cures'.

And then one day he found the blue chamber and the underground lake. He had seen the monstrous fish many times; it visited the underground lake almost every day. It was only recently it had begun showing up with diamonds in its scales. To get near it he began to feed it: dead lunatics from the walls, then, when there was the breakout, he took great delight in throwing the cruel warders into its jaws. They had come down to the maze to hide and he had caught them easily in the dark. He kept them in the cell near the lake. They deserved it, the way they had ill-treated the lunatics.

The breakout changed everything, of course. When he realized that the asylum was empty, Gerulphus emerged and found only two people left: Freakley and Mrs Runcible. They didn't want to leave either. It was their home and for now they had the chance to do what they'd always wanted to do.

But he had never forgotten Claude's betrayal.

And then, incredibly, Claude himself in the guise of Dr Velhildegildus came to the island and Gerulphus saw at last his chance for revenge. But he bided his time. What was a few more days after ten years! Dr Velhildegildus didn't recognize him he was so thin, but Gerulphus knew exactly who this 'doctor' was; how could you forget that square jaw?

He'd watched them down in the underground chamber, building that thing. He'd heard Tibor and Acantha plotting, and heard the screams of Cecil Notwithstanding as they tortured him. They had left his body in the maze near the torture chamber. Gerulphus felt sorry for him but ultimately saw no reason not to feed him to the fish. Gerulphus picked up the book and turned it over in his hands. The fact that Rex and Hildred had found it was only a minor setback. Yes, the lunatics had burned the books to keep themselves warm, and he had encouraged it, but it would appear that Ambrose had found the most incriminating. Obviously he had read it and then hidden it for Rex.

That's what comes of doing people favours, thought Gerulphus. He'd invited them both, Hooper and Ambrose, to stay in the maze for a few days but they were determined to leave. Now he knew why. To think, he'd even given them a couple of diamonds each to help them on their way! 'No good deed goes unpunished,' he murmured philosophically.

He thought of Rex and Hildred in the torture chamber. Should he go down and release them? No. There would be someone over soon enough from Opum Oppidulum, and besides he wanted as much time as possible to get away.

As for Tibor, what did that man take him for? Did he think that he, Gerulphus Godsacre, was just another feeble-minded fool? He was badly mistaken. Gerulphus was not like those knuckleheads who had tried to swim across the lake. 'But he needed me tonight, when those children found the book,' he said softly. 'Oh yes, I was useful to him then. But did he really think he could pay me off with his diamonds? Did he think that would make up for his betrayal?'

Gerulphus wondered how far the self-styled doctor had managed to get before the monstrous fish caught up with him; for naturally as soon as *Indagator* had submerged he had summoned it with his stick.

Satisfied that everything had worked out as he wished, Gerulphus gathered up his jewels and put them in a dark leather drawstring bag. He looked one last time at the book and then threw it on the fire and watched it burn.

46

A Girl of Many Talents

'If I could just reach these manacles I could use my pick-lock,' groaned Rex. He looked over at Hildred. 'Sorry,' he said. 'I don't suppose you heard any of that.'

He was still reeling from the revelation that she was deaf. He thought back to all the times she seemed in a world of her own, the times she had ignored him, the way she stared at him so intensely, and now it was all crystal clear. He couldn't believe he hadn't guessed. She *was* in her own world: a world of silence. And that was why she stared; *she was lip-reading.* That's how she knew what was in the letter from Acantha. She didn't read it through the paper, she was lip-reading Tibor. And that was how she knew Acantha was coming down to the *Indagator*. She could feel her heavy tread. And, of course, she was completely immune to Tibor's mesmerizing voice.

'It happened over many years,' she explained. 'I can hear some things, high-pitched noises.'

'Like Walter's whistling?'

'Yes,' she laughed. 'And the creature's singing. They are very similar.'

'The creature's singing?'

'That monstrous fish, it sings as it approaches. I could feel it when we were on the lake. I think it echoes Walter's whistling. And I feel things too, with my hands.'

'So that's why you always felt the walls. That's how you "heard" the moaning.'

'Yes,' said Hildred, squirming around on the table in a very odd manner. 'But now stop talking and let me concentrate.'

Before Rex realized what was happening she threw off her manacles and sat up.

'That's better,' she said, and shook herself quite violently. With a series of clicks and pops she seemed to reassemble her joints. She looked over at Rex with a big smile. 'I'm a contortionist, remember?'

Rex laughed softly. 'You are full of surprises,' he said. 'Now, take my picklock, it's in my pocket, and open these cuffs.'

When they were both free again Rex went to the door. 'It's no use,' he said. 'It's padlocked from the outside.'

Hildred was unworried. 'We'll have to go down into the maze. If we can get to the underground chamber then we can come back through Tibor's study.'

'But how can we do that?'

'Easy,' said Hildred. 'When I followed Gerulphus, I left a trail of bones!'

'You really do think of everything,' he laughed.

Then Hildred frowned. 'Where's the book?'

Rex shook his head. 'Gerulphus has it.'

47

Article from

𝔗𝔥𝔢 𝔒𝔭𝔲𝔪 𝔒𝔭𝔭𝔦𝔡𝔲𝔩𝔲𝔪 𝔥𝔢𝔟𝔡𝔬𝔪𝔞𝔡𝔞𝔩

GRAMMATICUS DOUBLE TRAGEDY
by
Alf Hack

The ill-fated Grammaticus family have been struck yet again by misfortune. It was reported last night that Mrs Acantha Grammaticus (widow of Ambrose Grammaticus) and Mr Alvar Stradigund, the family solicitor, were both found dead at the dinner table in Mrs Grammaticus's town house. The local physician has said that it looks like a straightforward case of food poisoning. Diseased meat was found in the kitchen. Constables are searching for the butcher but so far he has not been traced.

High water levels continue to present problems for Opum Oppidulum, with reports of flooding near the lake shore. The latest Madman's Tide has exceeded all previous records and there are fears that the lower parts of the asylum on Droprock Island, where Mrs Grammaticus's stepson, Rex, was residing under the care of Dr Tibor Velhildegildus, has been flooded. It is unclear whether there are any casualties. As soon as the water subsides a boat will be sent over. At present it is not possible to land.

The search continues for Cecil Notwithstanding, a dedicated journalist on this very newspaper.

'I think we chose a good time to leave town,' said Gerulphus, tossing the *Hebdomadal* behind his seat. He turned to the driver. 'I see from your cart that you are in the business of pest control.'

48

A Letter to Robert

My dear Robert,

I believe this will be my last letter to you. Shame will no longer allow me to keep up our friendship, but let me say now that it has meant a great deal to me these last few weeks.

I have experienced horrors that are a great burden to me and until such a time as I can forgive myself I cannot live as others in the world of men. I want you to remember me as I was; I pray God that you will never know me as I now am.

I am in good health, I suppose, and I have a purpose, which is a comfort for I believe it is the only thing that keeps me going. I seek a man called Arthur Buttonquail, for I have news of his daughter, but much more than that I cannot say.

I have found that words are not enough any more. Goodbye, Robert.

Rex

SIX YEARS LATER

IN THE MOUNTAIN VILLAGE OF PAGUS PARVUS

49

The Confession of Rex Grammaticus

'I have been told, Mr Zabbidou, that you pay for secrets,' said the young man.

Mr Zabbidou nodded and handed the youth a glass of golden liquid. 'I do,' he said. 'And I can tell that yours is a great burden. Take a seat. Have a drink. My assistant here, Ludlow, will write it all down . . .'

My name is Rex Grammaticus and it is with great relief that I confess on this page to a secret of the greatest magnitude. It is true that many a child finds just cause for his misbehaviour in his parents' treatment of him in his formative years, but although I might blame my father for what has taken over my body I cannot say that it was his fault.

I have lived for years denying what I am, resisting daily the terrible urges that rack my body without warning; but I am not strong and I have given in too many times to mention, when it has become too hard to bear. My father was right — it is a curse.

I beg you neither to pass judgement on me nor to condemn me, just to listen while I unburden myself.

Six years ago, still a boy, I was placed in a predicament that was brought about by circumstances wholly beyond my control. After a series of unfortunate occurrences my companion Hildred and I found ourselves in a rocky tortuous maze beneath the old asylum on Droprock Island in the centre of Lake Beluarum. Although we were initially confident of our way to the safety of an underground chamber, by means of strategically placed finger bones, we hadn't bargained on the rising waters of the lake.

We made good progress at first but we had only one lantern and the oil was burning rapidly. When we reached the next interchange of tunnels we were distressed to find that the rising water had washed away the markers. The tragedy that unfolded is as fresh in my mind today as it was then . . .

'We must go back,' urged Hildred. 'If we stay here, we will either drown or succumb to the cold.'

We attempted to retrace our steps but then disaster struck: the lantern died.

'We will have to feel our way,' said Hildred, and she took my hand.

We had barely gone more than ten yards when Hildred stumbled and let go. I heard her scream, and then the most dreadful crunch, and I could not tell whether she was ten feet or a hundred feet below me.

'Hildred!' I called to her uselessly in the dark, knowing that she could not hear me — she was deaf. I knew what had happened: she had fallen into a hole in the middle of the pathway, a hole we had passed earlier when we had light. I could hear her moaning softly

below and I could tell that she was in terrible pain. I went on to my stomach and felt my way in the dark to the edge of the treacherous hole. I reached down and against all hope I touched her hand. Freezing water was seeping up through the rock.

'I'm coming to get you,' I said, and slipped down into the water. It was knee deep and my breath was taken away by the shock of the coldness. I was feeling all around as best I could in the pitch blackness and then I touched her head and raised it out of the water. She coughed and took a deep breath. She was shivering violently.

'I don't think I can put my bones back together this time,' she whispered.

She couldn't stand, and every time I moved her she screamed. It took all my strength to drag her back up over the edge of the hole. Exhausted I sank down on to the rocky floor, her head on my lap.

'I'm sorry,' she murmured. 'For doing this to you, for leading you into danger. I wanted so badly to help you with your father . . . I suppose because I never found out about my own.'

'You're bleeding,' I said. I couldn't help myself. The smell of blood was powerful to me.

'It's not your fault,' she whispered, and she brought my hand down to her face and I could feel that she was smiling. 'If I die,' she whispered, 'I will be gone. What is left is no more than a shell. Save yourself.'

I thought she was rambling, from the knock on the head. 'What are you saying? What do you mean?' And then I understood and I was enraged. 'I cannot, I would not!' I protested.

'Let me feel your heart,' she said. 'It is a good heart. It's not your fault.'

She didn't speak again.

I found out later that I sat with Hildred in the dark for nigh on fourteen days and nights. The waters crept higher and higher and I moved further back up the tunnel to avoid them.

I slaked my thirst easily enough but the hunger was almost unbearable.

On the fifteenth day I woke from an uneasy sleep. Something was different. The water was retreating and there was a strange blue glow just under the surface. I waded in and to my utter astonishment I scooped up one of the blue lights from Indagator. *Now I could see again! Then something brushed against my leg and when I looked down I saw bobbing on the surface my brazen egg. I reached for it but it began to move away, as if of its own accord.*

'Could it be?' I dared to wonder.

I laid poor Hildred's remains in one of the cavities in the wall and vowed to come back and afford her a proper burial. Then, holding up the blue light, I followed the egg on its purposeful journey.

The waters were subsiding quickly but the egg was following its own course, pulled by a force stronger than the water. My body was cold to the core but my heart was hopeful. I followed it through the icy water until, mirabile visu, *I saw up ahead the familiar blueness that heralded the underground chamber where I had built* Indagator. *No man can possibly imagine the depths of my relief at the sight, for now I could make my way out of the maze.*

I stepped into the chamber, only ankle deep in water, and watched the egg float across to a half-submerged metal box near the tunnel entrance and clang up against it. I knew now that the Perambulating Submersible was destroyed — the wreckage was all around me. I recalled the many hours I had spent down here with Dr Velhildegildus, the thieving, murderous lunatic, constructing

Indagator. *I never did find out how the lunatic impostor got his hands on the plan, and I confess by the end I didn't care. I was so utterly consumed by vengeful rage as I built it, at his betrayal of me and my father's work, that I can only think that I too lost my mind. It is the only way I can reconcile myself to the crime; it sickens me to think that I am no better than Acantha.*

And in my madness I used the brazen egg to sabotage the Re-breather, knowing that it would kill Tibor. How ironic then that ultimately my murderous act saved me; for it was the magnetic Re-breather that attracted the egg back to it and led me out of the maze.

So I am alive and Dr Velhildegildus is dead. He sleeps now eternally but I – I have not slept a full night since . . .

A Note from F. E. Higgins

Poor, poor Rex. Would it have been any comfort to him to know that it was not the Re-breather that killed Dr Velhildegildus, but the monstrous creature? But is intention murder, or only the act itself? Rex's burden was heavy enough without thinking that he was a murderer too.

And what a burden. Throughout history various cultures have believed that you can gain a man's strength from eating his body, and that once tasted it is irresistible, but down the years the practice has become a taboo. Rex knew what fate awaited him, the curse his father had talked of, for he had tasted Acantha's stew. The stew wherein he found Chapelizod's gold tooth.

I have tried to find out more about 'Andrew Faye' and I have concluded that the name itself was a secret code between cannibals, a way for them to identify each other. Acantha recognized Tibor Velhildegildus as soon as she met

him, and he recognized her. He commented on her smell —
a secret sign between androphagues, perhaps?

The fish, *Salpa salpa*, does exist and is a member of the
bream family. Highly toxic, it causes terrible fevers and hal-
lucinations if eaten. Even the monstrous creature was not
wholly immune. I do wonder if Mrs Runcible was feeding
this very same bream to the warders Gerulphus had jailed
down in the secret cell in the maze. That would explain
the smell in the tunnels. I also wonder if Rex ever did find
Arthur Buttonquail. Perhaps it would have been better if
he had not, for he said himself that he had nothing else to
live for.

Let us hope that he got some relief when he finally made
his confession to Joe Zabbidou. How interesting, too, that
once again we arrive back at the village of Pagus Parvus and
Joe Zabbidou and Ludlow Fitch. If you wish to know more
about Joe and his young assistant, you will find their story
in *The Black Book of Secrets*. Gerulphus, of course, went off
and met Lady Lysandra Mandible. For his story read *The
Eyeball Collector*. And if you wish to know more of Urbs
Umida, the Sinister City, then you will find out just how
vile a place it is in *The Bone Magician*.

As for myself, the ever stranger world of Ubigentium,
where all these tragic tales have taken place, is calling out
once more and try as I might I cannot resist its call.

What further mysteries await I can hardly imagine, but
rest assured, whatever they are, I will tell all . . .

F. E. Higgins
Opum Oppidulum

Appendix I

Rex's Re-breather
Re-breathers have been around since the 1600s. Rex seems to have invented a fairly sophisticated machine and there is no doubt that if it had worked, along with the Perambulating Submersible, it would have been much sought after.

Chapelizod's Gold Tooth
It was not uncommon in the past for people to have their initials engraved on gold teeth, a sort of primitive tracker system, I suppose, in case they lost them.

Steganography and Histaeus
Steganography (Greek for 'concealed writing') is the art of hiding a message in such a way that only the sender and the recipient are aware of its existence. Herodotus, an ancient Greek historian, tells the story of Histaeus and his tattooed

slave in his Histories. This story would have been familiar to any educated child in Opum Oppidulum.

The Dunnets

And finally, I cannot finish without mentioning the Dunnet family (remember the quirt-wielding quadruplets from Rudy Idolice's Peregrinating Panopticon of Wonders?). Descendants of Billy and Rosalyn are alive and well in Kent. So pleased were they to find out about their talented ancestors that they made a very generous donation to The Starlight Foundation as a mark of their gratitude.

TALES FROM THE SINISTER CITY

THE BLACK BOOK OF SECRETS

F. E. HIGGINS

When Ludlow Fitch suffers an unspeakable betrayal he runs from
the rotten, stinking City. On the night he enters Pagus Parvus a
second newcomer arrives at the remote village. Joe Zabbidou,
a mysterious pawnbroker who buys people's deepest, darkest
secrets, is searching for new customers – and for an apprentice.
Shadowy Ludlow seems perfect for the job.

But as he begins his new life recording the villagers'
fiendish confessions, Ludlow's own murky past threatens
to come to light . . .

Shortlisted for the Waterstone's Children's Book Award

TALES FROM THE SINISTER CITY

THE BONE MAGICIAN

F. E. HIGGINS

FOR YOUR *DELIGHT*
AND *DELECTATION*:

THE BONE MAGICIAN

SEE HIM BREATHE LIFE INTO DEAD BONES DAILY.

*YOU WILL NOT
BE DISAPPOINTED!*

Since his father disappeared, Pin Carpue has lived alone
in the dismal city of Urbs Umida. Then he meets the
Bone Magician – a man who can make the dead speak – and
Pin is drawn into a mysterious world of illusion and deceit . . .

TALES FROM THE SINISTER CITY

THE EYEBALL COLLECTOR

F. E. HIGGINS

A foul tale of **DEATH** and **REVENGE!**

THE PLACE: Grim and gruesome Withypitts Hall.
THE HERO: Hector Fitzbaudly – a boy
with revenge on his mind.
THE VILLAIN: A story FULL of villainous rogues . . .
but pay attention to the GHASTLY glass-eyed fiend
known only as the Eyeball Collector.

*Another poisonously brilliant adventure from the
dark imagination of F. E. Higgins.*

A selected list of titles available from Macmillan Children's Books

The prices shown below are correct at the time of going to press. However, Macmillan Publishers reserves the right to show new retail prices on covers, which may differ from those previously advertised.

All Pan Macmillan titles can be ordered from our website, www.panmacmillan.com, or from your local bookshop and are also available by post from:

Bookpost, PO Box 29, Douglas, Isle of Man IM99 1BQ

Credit cards accepted. For details:
Telephone: 01624 677237
Fax: 01624 670923
Email: bookshop@enterprise.net
www.bookpost.co.uk

Free postage and packing in the United Kingdom